Exterminator 69

Books by John Tanner

Exterminator 69
An uncharted Journey into the Abyss

Exterminator 69

John Tanner

SPEAKING VOLUMES, LLC
NAPLES, FLORIDA
2023

Exterminator 69

ISBN 978-1-64540-766-9

To my loving wife Maria Cecilia
who saved me from myself on too many occasions to mention.
My one and only—Mayday Lima Foxtrot—

Acknowledgments

I want to thank my wife for being there for me as I endeavored to write my first novel. She was instrumental to the work as she painstakingly proofread for me on many an occasion and helped to round out the rough edges. I also want to thank my publisher for their hard work and dedication they have shown in bringing this book to fruition. Words are not enough to show my appreciation for the help I have received from the both of them on this journey.

Chapter One

Regular Friday Night?

"Well, if that ain't the shit," he said aloud to himself, while thinking about the girl that had just recently snubbed him. It was yet another failed relationship. Mick Tanner, also known as exterminator 69, was on the job, bored out of his mind, and had started talking to himself again. Unfortunately, talking to himself was beginning to become something of a habit. Being an exterminator on call to kill bugs was like waiting for Santa Claus. It seemed like a year's worth of waiting until you got the call, and then you were expected to be there yesterday, since it was almost always an emergency. Well, at least I enjoy killing those little bug bastards, as a small almost imperceptible grin spread across his face.

Slowing down for the exit, he pulled off the interstate and looped onto Mulberry drive, all the while watching for Roy the policeman, who usually worked that corner. On this muggy, hot afternoon he didn't see him. Curious, he thought, Roy was always around at this time of day. Oh well, maybe he was getting an early lunch, like he did on many an occasion. He had one call to go to that afternoon, and it was to get some wasp nests that ran up along the eves of a house; and according to the homeowner were becoming aggressive. It seemed like a piece of cake job to end the day and then shoot off to the local bar. In his mind, he was already imagining the chicken wings, beers, and how he would smile and laugh with the pretty waitresses, hopefully meet up with his latest attraction, and finally relax after a long weeks' worth of hard miserable work. The temperature outside was unbearable. It was over ninety degrees with ninety percent humidity and working out in the blistering sun had its distinct disadvantages in Texas on days like this. He didn't mind so much the heat; but when you are trying to kill bugs in this type of heat, they become a lot more aggressive and nastier when the temperatures are soaring and poison is being sprayed in their direction. Even bugs have short tempers when it is hot outside. Arriving at the woman's house, he proceeded to angle his truck in the driveway so he could easily get at his equipment, situated as it was in the bed of the truck. Next, he decided to check in with dispatch and let them know what he was doing.

"Hello dispatch, this is exterminator 69, come in beautiful."

"Exterminator 69, I can read you loud and clear, and I have a boyfriend."

"That is fantastic Sally, but I am still here, and just want to let you know where you can find a real man, once you get tired of that guy."

He always liked to give her a hard time about how much he wanted her, even though he really didn't, just because he knew it made her feel better. Not to mention, she also liked the foreplay as her boyfriend was a boring jerk.

"What can I do for you Mick?" she said with obvious disdain over the phone.

"Just letting you know I am at the wasp job. This should be my last gig for the day. I won't be coming back to the office after I'm done."

"Hey Mick, the boss wants to speak with you about something. Hold on for a second, will you?"

She said this in such a way that he had an ominous feeling about what the boss wanted to speak to him about. Apprehensively he waited on hold for his boss to come on the line, somehow knowing deep down inside, that his dreams of chicken wings and beer were about to go up in smoke.

"Mick, there seems to be a little problem over in Bishop, Texas. Twenty-Nine Myrtle Street, to be exact. Exterminator nineteen failed to show up, um . . . well, really, he did show up but decided not to complete the job, if you can believe it. I am going to need you to go over to the woman's house this evening and finish up a job over in Bishop. It seems like an easy job getting rid of some German cockroaches. It shouldn't take you too long. Do you think you can handle it?"

The silence that elapsed before Mick replied to his boss spoke volumes.

"Sure, boss. What is the address, again?"

He switched the off button on his dispatch radio and went into a full-on tirade.

"What the hell does this asshole think I am, his pet pig? Goddamn it if I don't have to drive another half an hour to kill bugs on a Friday afternoon, just because some other exterminator has a problem with his friggin brain. I can't wait till this jerk face retires. This is un-fucking believable . . ." he swore out at the old CB style radio dispatch gear.

"Hey Mick, this is Sally, you forgot to hit the mute button. The boss would like a word with you when you return to work on Monday, he says. He heard the whole thing. Sorry . . . and, oh by the way the address is Twenty-Two Myrtle Street."

Beads of perspiration slowly began rolling down the sides of his face, as he realized what a hole he had just dug himself. Not only had his life just turned into some comical soap opera at work, but he had to complete the job at hand, turn around and drive to Bishop, all the while thinking about what his boss was going to say to him on Monday. This was definitely going to ruin his weekend.

"Thanks a lot Sally. Have a great evening with that boring jerk of a boyfriend of yours."

He hung up. He knew it wasn't nice and he shouldn't have said it, but he felt she needed to hear it. Besides, he was in no mood to massage her ego any longer, especially not after the present fiasco that he felt she was partly responsible for. With an extended sigh, he began pulling out the paperwork for the present job. Two hours later, and three wasp stings along his left arm, he managed to reach his final job for the day. He was surprised to see Roy the policeman's car parked outside the adjacent house. His disposition brightened. He hadn't spoken to him for a few weeks and felt the need to hear what he thought about their team's chances for the upcoming football season. He pulled over to the side of the road and decided to chat for a while before his final job of the day.

He looked over at the large Victorian country house. It had one of those immense porches, the ones that wrap around a house. It was a perfect venue for sitting around and talking on slow evenings. A simple old country house in the middle of nowhere, he reckoned. Probably built by some German immigrants at the turn of the century looking for a new start on life, and now handed down to another generation probably looking to get away from working the land. One man's dream is another man's nightmare even between generations he mused. He caught his mind wandering again and snapped himself out of it.

Dead ahead in his sights and not much to look at was the house across the road at the end of the street. There were probably thousands of German cockroaches slithering through the walls. Fucking pig people, he thought. He was not in the best of moods. Not only would he have to cancel his upcoming date for the night, but also had to work overtime. He had pissed his boss off and was forced to work late into the early evening, and said hurtful words to Sally. What else can go wrong? The answer to that question, he was going to have to kill some cockroaches.

He moved his hand over the middle console, opened his glove compartment and fished out a small bottle of whiskey. Crown Velvet with some ice-cold Coca Cola he kept in a cooler under the passenger seat made everything better, or at least more tolerable. I am going to kill those bugs and make their mama pay for them being so ugly, he said to himself. Unsealing the new whiskey bottle, he poured it over the ice cubes, listening to it crackle as the hot alcohol mixed and melted with the ice. The blissful mixture of intoxicating sounds that emanated from his glass had him virtually panting like a Pavlovian dog waiting to be fed. He relaxed back into the upholstered seat of his truck. Next, he added some Coke to the mixture and took a long hard swig from the glass. He could immediately feel the warmth inside of him. He took another drink. Then he refilled his glass and gulped that one down as well. The glass was empty and, even though he was feeling morally jerked around and a bit agitated, at least his head felt clear. It was time to do some business, he thought. Exiting the truck, he walked up the driveway. He felt a tingling jerk up his spine like something was wrong, but he shrugged it off as nothing but the effects of the whisky, although in the back of his mind he knew it not to be true.

Thoughts and words pervaded his mind, and he sang a few ditties to himself, as an abstraction from the boredom of his job.

"Orange, green, blue, and yellow, I guess I am not your fucken fellow (that girl was not going to be around him, especially if he had to call and pull a stupid no show like this he thought). "Red light, green light, stick it in your ass, I just keep on working and following the boass," he drawled in his southern accent.

He stopped and just stared at the house, for what reason he didn't know. He felt a cold wave of anxiety flow over him, even though it was the middle of summer in the late afternoon Texas sun, and nearly one hundred degrees! He looked up at the house again trying to figure out what he was feeling, why he had an unsettled feeling in the back of his mind? Glancing again at the structure, he noted that it was an old, probably turn of the century, three story farmhouse that dated back to the late nineteen hundreds. Even so, everything seemed in order. So why was he having this feeling of dread? A voice in the back of his mind was screaming at him to be wary of this place. He looked around. The yard was recently mowed and the paint on the house was in fine shape, but still he felt this ominous and black foreboding presence around him. A coldness seemed to surround him and seep into his veins, just the opposite of how the crown royal had warmed him. Why should he feel like this, he thought? Something was wrong with this house his inner spirit screamed. Thoughts were racing through his head. Don't go in that house. The devil lurks in the corner of those rooms, and you will never come out alive. Run now, and run away fast, while you still can. Again, he looked up at the house, this time with a feeling like he was being watched, but he didn't see any movement in the windows. His intuition was screaming at him to leave. How could this be and what was the matter with him, he thought? Why had the other exterminator failed to do the job?

Shielding his eyes from the sun's late afternoon glare, he thought he saw someone peep behind a window shade, but he wasn't sure. He looked at the front door and saw that it was wide open. Good, he thought, at least he knew someone was at home and, besides, he rationalized to himself, Roy, the policeman was inside as well. Then again, why was Roy the policeman at the house? What could possibly be wrong? Shrugging his shoulders while fighting back his intuition, and falsely strengthened by his pick-me-up concoction, he saddled his way up to the door and looked around for anyone who might live in the residence. There was no movement as he walked toward the front door. He could see it was a huge house with at least a few acres of farmland behind it. They always made these old houses big for farming families, he thought. His sense of duty to fulfill his work brought him to the front door without much thought of his previous feelings. He tried to brush them aside. He was the licensed killer, of course, and bugs be damned and everybody else watch out, he mused to himself. I am the master of my destiny.

What he did not realize was why his brain had switched into a highly alert status and was warning him not to approach the house. There was no noise around him, not a cricket chirping, a bee buzzing or a bird singing. The house and its surroundings were deathly quiet. The air did not seem to rustle the leaves, while the heat of the sun did not seem to burn as intense as at the other houses he had visited during the day. The house and yard seemed to be suspended in some sort of ether which shut out all sound and movement. It was like it was trapped in some sort of cold storage, which would not allow the house or property to gather heat from the sun's rays. The dark green house stood in a cold defiant anger, seemingly detached from all the world around it.

As he entered the home, he called out hello a few times, to see if anyone would answer. His greetings went unanswered. He tried again, only louder this time. His voice seemingly echoed and reverberating back at him like he was between the walls of a slot canyon in New Mexico. Where is Roy and the homeowner he thought? He decided to check his phone. He tried calling the office, but he wasn't getting a signal any longer. That is strange, he thought. He moved back outside of the house to the front lawn to see if his phone could get a signal. He could see the bars begin to show a signal on his phone. The phone must be being blocked by something in that house, he thought.

He decided to call his latest attraction he had been daydreaming about all day. He got her voice mail and left a message.

"Hey Francine, this is Mick, unfortunately something came up and my boss wants me to work late. Can you give me a call so we can reschedule our night out or maybe just move it back a few hours? Thanks, talk to you later."

He had tried to sound suave and cool when leaving the message, but he knew no matter how he spoke it, it wasn't going to turn out in his favor. She was out of his league. She was a sexy, long-legged brunette with a professional job as a paralegal. He didn't like leaving the message, but had no choice, seeing as how the afternoon was beginning to start its push in to the early evening.

As he approached the house for a second time, that was when he realized how quiet it was in the yard. He was used to hearing the sounds of insects this time of the year, and he strained his ears to hear any sound at all, but he heard nothing. At the front step, he poked his head inside the door for a second time and called out if anybody was home. Still, he got no answer. He crossed over the threshold with a determination to find Roy, and, if he was lucky, use the facilities which appeared to be located down the hallway off the front entrance. In the background, an almost imperceptible sound, like that of a chainsaw blade cutting though a tree, began to creep into his ears. Nearing the bathroom door, the sound grew audibly louder. Peeking his head around the corner, he dropped the work papers and clipboard in his hand. In front of him, the remains of Roy were swarming with ants! He was propped up in the bathtub submerged halfway up to his waist in water, while the remains of his shoulders and head were slumped up against the wall. What was left of the top upper portion of him, above the waterline, was a mass of red muscle, enormous reddish black ants, and globs of yellow fat atop rib bones. The skin from his body was almost completely gone, as well as his nose, as the ants crawled easily amongst his appendages and organs. The whole bathroom was covered with swarming black, maroon fire ants! And that wasn't the worst part of it. Just as incredible was the reaction when he poked his head inside the bathroom. The ants actually appeared to turn with a simultaneous motion and look at him as though they were one organism! Some of Roy's ribs were sticking out from where the ants had eaten down to his entrails, and his skeletal face was missing one eye.

He stood staring at Roy, with his jaw wide open in disbelief, absorbed in horror looking at the ghastly spectacle. What brought him to

8

his senses was a jarringly painful fiery burning sensation across his whole lower leg, much like a hot poker had been shoved into him.

"Goddamn it," he roared.

He knew exactly what fire ant stings felt like, having been stung and bitten thousands of times before, but on this occasion, he actually yelled out in pain as the burning sensation was excruciating. Smacking them off of his leg, while running back down the hallway, he could see them converging on him from different areas of the walls and ceiling, like they knew where he was and were trying to stop him! They were attacking as though they were one sentient beast! Blowing right past them and getting out onto the front porch was the only thing on his mind. He stumbled on the door jamb and fell face forward on to the porch stairs leading down into the front yard. The fire ants were enmeshed within his pants legs immediately.

In the vanishing confines of his mind, he was being bitten and stung thousands of times over and over again. Along both legs he could feel the searing miniature pin pricks and the flashing pain that went along with it. It was like getting stung by fifty ground bees at once but a thousand times greater. Screaming in pain, he jumped up off of the stairs. Undressing while running toward his truck, he had his pants and shirt stripped off within seconds, while at the same time attempting to smack off the ants still clinging and stinging him. Seconds later, he found himself in his underwear, at the handle of his truck door. Jumping into the front seat shaking and enraged with pain, he was involuntarily gasping for breath. Fumbling inside his glove box he found what he was looking for. He drove the epi-pen into his leg, which he always carried with him in case of emergencies like this one and looked at himself in his rear-view mirror. His face was bloated, beet red and scraped up. A guttural sound like that of a bear getting ready to charge emanated from his abdomen and came out of his mouth. "Aarghh . . ." This cowboy was one pissed off and hurt mother fucker, like a bull that just got his nuts yanked on before a rodeo. He looked down at his legs above where the boot line had been, he was a flaming red conflagration of bright red pin pricks, pulsating on every square centimeter of his body all the way up to and in certain instances above the line of his underwear. There were still a couple of the little bastards on him, he killed them with a few karate chops that even Bruce Lee would have been proud of. Then he found one last fire ant wandering on his stick shift. Very carefully he opened the empty bottle of whiskey, which he retrieved from under the passenger seat, and flicked him inside for future examination. These were no ordinary fire ants and at this point it was personal.

Slathering himself down with aloe-vera lotion over his swollen legs, he very carefully pulled on his waders. They were a snug fit because of the size of his swollen legs. Although irritated and raw, he drew them closely along the upper half of his chest and cinched them tightly. Next, he brought out a shirt that scuba divers normally wear and strapped on two tanks of poisonous death along his back. This was war and he was going to do battle. Within the metal tanks, there was a potent combination of industrial strength bug killer, mixed with boric acid, moonshine and bleach. He had concocted this solution over the past four years and was going to try and market it some day. To say it stopped bugs dead in their tracks was an understatement. He even had a small lighter switch which when pushed, lit the poisonous spray into a fine line of fire.

Strapping on a pair of goggles over a beekeeper mask he kept in the back of his truck, he was one hell of a sight for any Halloween party, but frankly, there was almost no part of his body unprotected or vulnerable. Finally, he slipped on a pair of rubber industrial gloves and snapped rubber bands around his wrists. He didn't care that the temperature was ninety-five degrees outside and about one-hundred-twenty-five degrees with his suit on; vengeance may be left to the lord on Sundays, but today was Friday and he had been wounded and the vengeance would be all his today. This was especially true after he had seen what they had done to his friend Roy. There is nothing more dangerous than a wounded boar, a stuck pig, or a bull in heat, and he felt like all three of them combined. Exterminator 69 was ready for battle.

Getting out of his truck, he could see the swarming ants all over the front porch, as well as all over the balcony. Some even had the audacity to approach his truck. He could feel them looking at him! He ran at the front stairs spraying with a vengeance. As the spray hit them, they began crumpling into squirming masses, soon to be fetal positioned corpses. It only took him a minute to clean off the front porch and make his way into the house. Peering inside the doorway, he could see they were in separate groups bunched on the ceiling, the entrance to the bathroom hallway, and emerging from the fireplace. He was about to start spraying the hallway when he felt a painful sting on his neck. They were dropping from the ceiling and biting his neck through his protective beekeeper mask! In that rage and excited adrenaline filled moment, he switched on the firing mechanism, which brought poison and fire together at the same instant. He was a flame throwing madman and began torching and annihilating everything in his path. He directed the line of poison directly at the ants on the ceiling as the fire spread upward in a thin long spraying motion. Working his way through the living room, he must have left at least ten thousand burnt ants in his pathway before he got to the bathroom hallway. Peering down the long hallway he could see them retreating from him, as if they knew he had something that could kill them? Very curious, he thought. Within minutes the whole house was ablaze, and he found himself running out of the house escaping the flames. Back at the truck, he pulled off the beekeeper mask and gloves, gasping for air. He took a few moments catching his breath, and then called Sally to report what was happening.

"Sally you are not going to believe this, but fire ants killed Roy Flint and are attacking people as if they were one connected sentient being. I need you to call the police and the fire department, get them over to 29 Myrtle Street, quick. The house is on fire and Roy is in the bathtub half eaten. Hello! Are you there?"

"I'm here, but I'm having a hard time believing what you just said. What did you just say?" the apprehensive and incredulous reply came over the phone.

"Did you hear me? I am bitten all to hell and the homeowner is nowhere to be found."

"Are you serious, because really I am not in the mood for your practical jokes tonight?" she sarcastically responded.

"Listen I am not fooling around this time. I think I may need an ambulance for the ant stings I have all over my body. Now call the fire department and the police, will you!" he screamed into the phone.

"The boss is not going to like this at all. That woman with the German cockroaches has been calling from Twenty-Two Myrtle Street for the past hour. Did you forget and go to the wrong house?"

"Oh shit," was all he could mutter into the phone, because of course he had gone to the house across from 22 Myrtle Street. He had gotten confused when he saw the police car in front of the house and reacted when he saw what the ants had done to Roy. He was sweating profusely in his waders and scuba suit, while the fire kept getting bigger in front of his eyes. Early on in his childhood he had been diagnosed with ADD, attention deficit disorder, but he had found the right job to keep his mind active and on track to complete his assignments, which of course meant killing bugs until they were exterminated. This time, though, it seemed he had really messed up and targeted the wrong bugs and the wrong house. Unfortunately, he also had a mild case of turrets syndrome and when he was excited and or agitated, it ballooned into a serious case, as it did in this instance.

"Goddamn it fuck, fuck, fuck, fuck'en greasy bastard boss with the shit, shit, shitty ass work on a fuck, fuck, fucken Friday night . . . Oh fuck, fuck, fuck it all to hell," he began yelling and moaning at the same time into the phone receiver.

Sally, on the other end of the phone, couldn't help but start to giggle.

"I will let the boss know what you think, Mick, about your performance review of your most recent job," as she laughed into the phone.

"Fuck, fuck, fuck you Sally . . . and tell the woman with the cock cock cock cock cockroaches, whatever you want. I am du du done for the night."

With this he hung up the phone and looked out at the house engulfed in flames. Sally didn't even have time to tell him that their boss Joe was gone for the evening, but she guessed that wouldn't matter to him at this point, anyway. The house was sinking into itself, its beams crumbling together and sagging inward, in a slow-motion melt. The air, scented with the aroma of old pine wood, continued to burn furiously inside of the old house. There was nothing more to see. Mick started the car, mostly for the air conditioning, and began changing into his regular clothes, as painful as it was.

Chapter Two

Mick Turns the Tables

With red eyes flaring into the deepest black of the night, he walked farther into the forest away from the burning farmhouse. He had been the shadow in the window. He was alone as he always was. He never had any company, ever, or any date, or friend or acquaintance, and this was by choice. Not any extra word was ever spoken to anyone. He never spoke a word that required anything but efficiency. He was not concerned with people, since he was ultimately going to enslave or kill anyone that opposed him! He meant to do this very soon. That is, if his plan worked. But something had gone horribly wrong, and he had begun to have his first doubts. Something had gone awry, and he could not understand how, since initially everything had gone according to plan. He had instructed his ants to kill the policeman, simply because he had shown up and investigated the premises after a dropped 911 call by the homeowner.

Earlier in the day, he urged on his best feeders to get a hold of the helpless victim while she prepared biscuits in her kitchen. The caretaker of the old home was Miss Louise Weatherby, an old farmers' widow, who was his first sacrificial lamb. He had selected her particular farm as the beginning of his rise to power based upon the proximity of some of his larger ant colonies. He had established thousands of these colonies over the past decade. Her demise was the starting point for the ultimate downfall of the human race. To drive a species by force is one thing, but to sing to it and control it was quite another type of accomplishment, he thought. He sang to the ants with the hum of the antichrist. The hum stopped people in their tracks. And the louder the hum became, the more agitated and frenzied the fire ants became. Motionless victims almost to the end, that is until they crumpled and screamed in pain from poisonous stings and bites. Louise, bewildered and powerless to stop them, had struggled in her kitchen against them with a frying pan in her hand. A final attempt to call for help was why Roy had showed up. The ants had fried her nerve passages, injecting their stings in a thousand places across her body. She had cried out for help when she saw the ants coming toward her, but she was powerless to stop them. They had swarmed her, stung her to death, and then cleaned her carcass. She was the very first person on the planet to succumb to the billions of ants which lay just below the surface of the ground.

After years of research and genetic modifications, he had created his secret army which he alone knew how to manipulate, control, and do his bidding. Unbeknownst to all, this satanic beast had a day job, lurking in the shadows of the military for whom he transplanted nuclear waste into underground caverns beneath the western mountains that formed the spine of the Rocky Mountains. That was his day job. By night he had amassed specialized knowledge in the fields of genetic mutation and experimented with fire ants for over two decades. He never forgot anything or anyone, and all the knowledge available on earth was at his disposal in order to fulfill his prime directive, to kill and enslave humanity.

He had succeeded on almost all accounts, but he felt ill at ease. Somehow that dumb bastard, an exterminator of all things, had outwitted him and killed a multitude of his precious minions. The exterminator had been bitten and stung, scared out of his mind and ill equipped once he saw the half-eaten policeman Roy, but somehow that nonsensical human had come back with a liquid fire unbeknownst to him. This one imbecilic man had taken a hold of his dominion and rendered them momentarily powerless. It was impossible! He had perfected these ants for years, and no compound known to man could stop them, that is up until now. He had tested everything available to mankind and nothing available on the market had been able to stop them or him, but for this one man. Humanity was ripe for the taking except for this damn exterminator, exterminator 69. It was quite improbable, illogical and preposterous.

Mick gazed up at the ice white clouds, like stationary icebergs, set against the backdrop of a sky beginning to darken. Staring into the heavens, from his vantage point inside the truck, he realized he was daydreaming once again. This was a common occurrence for him. In front of him stood the old nineteenth century house, a blazing mass of ponderosa pine wood. It sure did smell good, he thought, as it crumbled in front of his eyes like a Victorian drama with the plot gone awry. He had performed this massacre. Once again, he was the anti-hero, he thought. Stoically he viewed his handy work as burning wood embers swirled upwards into the sky. Listening closely, he felt he could actually hear the individual ant bodies popping in the inferno that lay in front of his eyes. The pop, pop, popping sounds reminded him of when his mother used to make popcorn on the open stove.

He decided to rethink his past actions. He had gone to the wrong house and at a most inopportune time. If he had kept his mind on his work rather than trying to talk to Roy about the upcoming football season, he would never be in this predicament. He had discovered Roy half-eaten by ants and had burned the house down in a rage of pain and revenge. The reality of what had just transpired over the past hour made him sick to his stomach. It was all wrong. He knew he was in big trouble, not only with his employer, but also presumably with the police. There was going to be a lot of explaining to do. He found himself paralyzed with everything that had just transpired. He turned his attention back to the fire and away from his thoughts of the impending trouble he was up to his neck in. He decided he could daydream for a little while longer.

Pirouetting orange and yellow plumes of flame raised themselves in a dance of destruction that filled the sky. He could feel his mind wandering. He was embroiled in some hot Spanish salsa dance which was playing out before his eyes as the roof of the house began to collapse. The poison he had spread along the old dry beams and floors of the house worked the same as if he had poured gasoline over them. The blaze hypnotized him into a trance, and along with the shock he had just experienced, calmed him as he stared at the raging fire. In the back of his mind, he kept mulling over the fact that his career, life and freedom were probably coming to an end on a Friday night, when he shouldn't have even been working. He was physically hurt and mentally distraught. On the other hand, he was immensely enjoying the spectacle laid before him, knowing the ants who had just attacked him were frying and popping to death. In a perverse way, he was pleased with himself, knowing that the fire was directly due to his intervention, since nobody else was prepared with the special poison he invented. He was caught between a sense of sickening remorse and a feeling of immense personal satisfaction.

He put his hand on his dick, and pulled at it a bit, as his cock had shrunken to the point that it was uncomfortable. He felt the need for some strength and began to massage himself between his fingers and soon his penis had grown to a manageable length. He immediately felt less constrained. He was seeking some normalcy in the off-balance situation he currently found himself ensnared within. He thought of how incredibly sexy she had looked at the hotel room when she had taken off her bra and panties after a night of drinking and carousing. He started stroking himself, thinking of the lost piece of ass he had been pining for just a few hours earlier, as the flames shot upward into the sky. By the time the fire had ebbed a bit, so had he, by ejaculating, and the luxurious moment was preserved in his mind like a prehistoric ant in amber. Wiping his hands and himself off on a towel, he threw it on the passenger floor and fumbled around in his car for his camera. He snapped off a few pictures of the burning house, although he wasn't sure why, and then decided to relax for a few more moments prior to leaving. He loved fires.

Mesmerized by the crackling flames and the heat which emanated from the house, his daydreaming took on a whole new twist while watching the house burn down. He found himself hypnotized, enmeshed within one of the strangest dreams and or vision he had ever experienced. The skies crackled, hissed and boomed with anger as dark banks of clouds formed to cover the daylight with menacing speed and fright. In a daze of confusion and foreboding, he looked upward as the sky went grey blotting out any remaining spots of white light. Lightning flashes, far above the clouds, and thundering booms from across the sky, immensely louder than any thunder he had ever heard, created a cacophony of sound in his ears. Fear was palpable among the wandering confused crowds, that only moments before had felt some respite from the demons that had unleashed themselves in an orgy of killing. Somehow, he knew the battle between good and evil was not over but had really only just begun. And then it happened.

From the sky came a booming shot, like a meteor falling to earth, flaming earthbound at an incredible speed. Something massive was being hurtled to the earth, launched at such an incredible speed that it only took seconds for it to reach the ground and tumble to a stop. It did not make any sense, but neither did the demons who guarded the underworld and occasionally crept above its surface to ply their wicked ways. It was a piece of a temple, a Corinthian column, half smashed and broken, thrown out of the heavens as though dismantled and discarded to a junkyard. The sky began flashing all across its dome, with pieces of marble statues and temples from the Gods, crashing down to earth. In a grand spectacle, the flaming pieces came to shatter the buildings and lives of those below and rest among the masses. In size, some were enormous, some as big as houses, and others the size of playground balls; but either way, they were killers as they indiscriminately began smashing and cutting into people with frightening speed and deadliness. Screaming and running in all directions the populous, terrified and confused, were looking for anywhere safe to hide as the sky rained down death upon them.

The remnants of our past gods relegated to a bygone era were crazy insane with their thoughts, which pulsated between dark and light, mind and meaning, sentient an inanimate, reality and myth. They felt ultimate betrayal. The underworld was responsible for the destruction of their temples, their powers and kingdom forever dismantled. The Gods were losing their powers. They had been relegated to mere figments of our imaginations, former masters, while the demons, haunting below the ground, howled with delight at their destruction. The landscape of the planet, decimated beyond reason or hope for any continuity of life, burned and kept burning. Desperately a few survivors, huddled in fear, grasping for answers to questions beyond their capabilities. Death lay out on the horizon. They could see it. It was moving ever so much closer, imperceptibly, like a mass of snakes beginning to wake from their long winter's hibernation, crawling amongst each other in a dance of life and death. It was then that they realized the sun was going to explode, into a Supernova the size of a hundred Jupiter sized planets, with the Gods fighting the demons for hegemony and control of a burned-out planet.

Mick awoke in a cold sweat. It was the most vivid, surreal and scariest daydream he had ever experienced in his whole life. He could see his visions so clearly, he felt he could almost reach out and touch them. This time, though, he was glad to be able to refocus on the fiery nightmare in front of him. Sighing, he knew he had to call Sally again. They would eventually find Roy's body, but for now he slowly began to drive away from the burning house. He heard his phone ring and he could tell by the number it was Sally. That was convenient, he thought.

"Mick, the woman from up the street has seen her neighbor's house on fire, and she has decided she doesn't mind the bugs so much now, so she said you should just forget about visiting her. She cancelled the appointment. She sounded very frightened and also said to please not come by her house, nor that man you were working with wearing the black trench coat. I really have no idea what she is talking about and honestly, she sounds positively scared out of her mind. You have definitely frightened the bejeebers out of her. Do you copy on this Mick?"

Mick's mind raced, and he thought back to the shadow in the window. Of course, he thought, there was someone else who was hidden, directing the whole goddamn nightmare he found himself embroiled in! He slammed on the brakes and made a U–turn for the neighbor's house. He was going to have a talk with that woman.

"Sally, I hear you loud and clear, but I am going over there right now to find out what she saw, Capiche?"

"Oh . . . Jesus. Mick, you are certifiably insane! I knew you were going to visit her once I told you. Could you try not to burn her house down or end up on America's Most Wanted before the day is over?"

"Sure Sally. I will get us another star with the Better Business Bureau this time and by the way, could you . . . please not call the cops, if you haven't already? I really need some time to try and figure this out."

"I got to go Mick. You may think what you want of me, but I am never a snitch. If I read about you in the papers tomorrow, it will be your own doing, honey."

He smiled as he hung up the phone and pulled into the long narrow driveway. For a platinum blonde office manager in her mid-thirties, she was alright sometimes.

Chapter Three

Edith Baxter's Last Entry

The woman with the German cockroach problem had been watching through her kitchen window the whole day. In fact, she had been eavesdropping on her neighbor's house previous to this, like she always did, when she had seen a tall man with raven colored hair enter the house earlier that day. She had contacted the police and had alerted Roy to a suspicious man at Louise's house. She let him know that someone was at Louise Weatherby's house, and that she had suspected a burglar. Roy let her know he would check on it as soon as he could. For his part, he was a bit annoyed about another call from the town snoop, Edith Baxter. He was in the middle of another chicken sandwich moment, and it was not to be denied, especially by biddy Baxter the town snoop. It was around midday when she called. Forty-seven minutes later, to be exact, Roy had showed up, which she marked down on her daily log. She knew he had been eating somewhere by the way he looked so satiated, and by the way he touched his belly as he got out of the car, readjusting his holster belt and gun. She was disgusted by the behavior, and although she generally liked Roy, she was going to let somebody know about this latest transgression of his. She would find out, oh so casually, where he had lunch and at what time. She was a professional busybody if ever there was one.

Edith Baxter was approaching her seventieth birthday. She had lost her husband five years ago to cancer and, ever since his death, could not help herself from spying on everyone in town. The town's business became her personal business. Otherwise, she contented herself with gardening and her two pussy cats, Teddy and Bear. Teddy was a four-year old Maine coon cat that she got from a shelter with seven toes on his front paws, while Bear was a fluffy mixed brown Himalayan that loved to curl up in the sun on her back porch. It was only just recently that she noticed some carpenter bumblebees which had decided to make the highest eve on her house their home, and she had sighted a few dead cockroaches in her garage. That was when she had decided to call the exterminator. She was puzzled that Roy had never left the house, and annoyed that Dinkin's exterminator service had promised to have someone show up before the end of the day. She marked all of this down in her daily log and then decided to go to her back yard for a few hours and prune her azaleas.

Later that afternoon, she saw Mick pull up to her neighbor's house, even though she had placed the service call. He took a drink of something and proceeded to enter the house. She suspected it might be alcohol and made a mental note to smell his breath when he finally showed up at her house. Roy's truck was still parked outside of the neighbor's house, and she began wondering why the exterminator was there, and not at her house. Well, maybe they knew each other, she thought, and that he had just stopped by to chat. It was very likely since it was such a small town, and everybody knew Roy. Still, this was getting marked down. What happened next kept her glued to her window with her mouth open wide enough to fit in a peach. The exterminator came screaming out of the house and fell down on the porch. He was smacking himself all over, obviously fending off some sort of stinging or biting insect. He looked utterly bewildered and in a state of terror. Her mind was racing as to what sort of insect was attacking him. It must be ground bees or wasps she thought. He stumbled to his pickup truck and slammed the door. She watched him take another drink. She was very suspicious as to what he was drinking and snapped out of her trance long enough for her to write down the last few minutes of what she had just seen in her log. She was almost finished writing when she noticed the upstairs curtains move back and the man with the long nose and the raven hair peering down at the exterminator's truck. She picked up her Canon 400X zoom camera and snapped a few pictures. Nobody could ever say she was not thorough when it came to telling a story or gathering the evidence. Suddenly the man turned her way and looked directly at her. Immediately a shiver ran down her spine, one like she had never felt before. She felt like she wanted to run and hide. Did he see me, she thought? How did he know I was taking his picture, or did he? Was it just a coincidence that he had looked her way? She felt her heart skip a few beats, and she ducked out of his view and steadied herself by the refrigerator and got a glass of water to calm herself. She was very frightened of this man, and not sure why, but she was not going to the window for fear of being seen again. Instead, she went to her front door and began peering out the peep hole at the scene across the street.

By this time the upstairs curtains were closed, and the exterminator was getting out of his truck. Her mouth opened again in disbelief. He was dressed up like a combination deep-sea diver and sport fisherman and proceeded to grab a tank out of the back of his truck, which he subsequently strapped on his back. His whole body was completely covered from head to toe and was walking with authority like he was going into battle. She checked her watch. Sixteen minutes had passed since the Dinkin's exterminator service man had shown up. As he entered the house, she heard him scream from all the way across the street and that was when she saw what appeared to be flames being directed all over the neighbor's living room! Soon the whole house was on fire, and she couldn't seem to get her eye close enough to the peep hole. Then, out of the corner of her eye she recognized the tall raven-haired man walking briskly away from the burning house, all while keeping to the edge of the property. She could tell he was skirting the property's perimeter, trying to stay unnoticed. She saw his vehicle, a black town car hidden behind some brush and tall weeds. Racing swiftly to the window, she had just enough time to snap a few photographs of the car as it peeled out onto the highway and was gone. She marked all this down in her log. She felt powerful knowing that she had witnessed a burglary, called the police, witnessed some nitwit exterminator commit arson and had plenty of pictures to back up her story. At the same time, the man who had looked at her scared her to death, and she felt weak just thinking about him.

She turned her attention back to the exterminator and noticed he was back in his truck watching the house burn down in front of him. He seemingly didn't care or was in a state of shock. She watched him closely and thought she saw his arm moving up and down, but he wasn't drinking anything anymore. She was puzzled as to what he was doing. Then it hit her like a bolt of lightning. He was jacking himself off in the truck while in the front yard, watching a roaring fire, which used to be Louise's house! It only took him a short time, thirty-eight seconds to be exact, to finish what he started, and then he just sat and watched the house burn down. Immediately, she ran to her phone and tried calling Dinkin's exterminator service, but it went to voice mail. She most certainly did not want this crazy man at her house, and she assumed he must be calling his workplace. After seven frantic minutes and twenty-eight dials she got in touch with Sally who promised to relay the message to Mitch.

She watched him drive off past her house and felt relieved. This was the most excitement she had felt, well, since her husband had passed away and she had gotten a humongous life insurance check. She hated to admit this to herself. She sat down on the couch and tried to pet the cats, but they were nowhere to be found. Then she heard the pounding at her door. She froze on the couch thinking it might be the man in the window, but then again, it might be Roy. She did not know what to do. For an instant, she thought of just not answering the door, but her curiosity was piqued, as the person continued to pound on her door. She heard herself cry out, "who is it?" in a barely audible voice?

"It is Mick Tanner, from Dinkin's exterminator service, you called about some cockroaches, and I really need to talk to you for a second."

Her terror turned to rage as she realized who was at her door.

"You, why you filthy pervert! I saw what you did over at that house. You burned it down and then jacked yourself off while watching my neighbor's house burn down. I saw it all and I am telling the police everything."

"Huh, please listen to me ma'am. I need to talk to you. I apologize for my indiscretion, but I didn't know anybody was watching when I did that. And uh, the situation is a lot more serious than you think. I found Roy, the policeman, in the bathtub dead, half eaten and by some god-damn ants, of all things. I talked to my dispatcher, Sally, and she said you might have seen someone leave the house. Here look at this if you don't believe me."

He held up the enormous ant, contained within the Crown Velvet bottle, which was still struggling to survive up to the peephole. It was desperately trying to gnaw its way through the crown velvet bottle. Even though it should have been dead, with two of its back legs gone and being charred, the ant was still showing extremely aggressive tendencies and a prolonged fight for survival. She could recognize that this was no ordinary fire ant. Curiosity got the better of her again as she peered at the ant struggling to not only survive but to free itself. No wonder he had screamed in such agony when he had stumbled out of the house, she thought. Also, the news about Roy was shocking. Her curiosity was overcoming her fear. Still though, she did not want to let him into her house. He might just have killed Roy and he was most certainly a pervert! She had several deadbolts on her front door and decided it was best if she met him while someone else was around, especially after what had just happened. Something was amiss, she surmised, since she had been the one to call for the exterminator service and Roy as well. She heard him speak again.

"Ma'am if there was someone else at that house across the street I have to know. Roy is dead and there is a killer on the loose presumably. If you want, I can ask Sally, the office manager you spoke to, to meet us here at your house if you feel more comfortable with her here. Please?"

She accepted, but only on the condition that she call Sally and let her know of the situation, and that he should stay in his vehicle until she showed up. Forty-six minutes later Sally showed up. Sally slowly drove by the farm house, that was still burning, before she pulled into Edith Baxter's driveway. She could not keep herself from smiling at Mick who looked like he had just been through hell and back. She parked behind his truck and exited her car. Mick was sitting in his pickup truck looking at what appeared to be a liquor bottle with a bug in it.

"You really dug yourself a hole this time, huh cowboy? For your sake, the boss knows nothing about this, and I canceled my date with my boyfriend just for you, so we could talk to the town gossip." With a slight pause she grinned, "Were you really whacking off in front of the house while it was burning to the ground?"

Mick snorted and grunted a few times, and then under his breath mumbled in a low voice, "Ah fuck her, that nosy sonofabitch. She watched the whole thing go down without lifting a finger to help me or call anyone else for help, and then won't talk to me without you around. Fuck her. After I find out what she knows I am going to stuff that legal pad she carries around up her ass."

Sally burst out laughing. None of this was funny but the whole situation was so absurd she couldn't help herself. For a good long while she could not control herself even though she could feel the eyes of Edith looking through the kitchen window at her and Mick. After she pulled herself together, she began to look at Mick in earnest. He really was in bad shape she thought. His face was puffed up from the numerous ant stings, as well as he had some facial cuts and bruises to go along with his overall look of having just lost a bar fight. With her hand, she parted some of his hair to the side so that it looked a little better.

"Now honey, I know you don't like what just happened, but let's not shoot the messenger who just might be able to save your fat boy country ass. Seeing as how you just burned down someone's house, with a dead policeman inside, you may just want to protect that legal pad she carries around with her and not think about getting any stains on it. Do you Capiche?"

If nothing else, Sally was usually right and had a nice way of telling him to cool off and direct his anger somewhere else. He nodded and smiled at her in such a way she knew he was going to watch what he said. The meeting with Edith actually went quite well all things considered, especially after what she had observed over the past few hours. Mick knew it was only because Sally was present that they had been allowed into the house. Edith had been able to tell her whole story to not only a woman, which made her feel safer, but also to a third party who had been thirty miles away. When she came to describing the man in the window she had seen, Mick could feel goose bumps along his neck seeing her shiver with fright. She was shook up about the whole episode and definitely scared of the black-haired man. He remembered how he had felt before first entering the house, and the deep foreboding feeling that he had shrugged off, assigning the feeling as the effects of the heat and the liquor.

As they were preparing to leave her house, she let them know she had taken some pictures of the man in the window and of the man's car as he was driving away. Mick swiveled around on his heels of his cowboy boots with his eyes bursting wide open. Before he could say anything, Sally asked to take the camera to the local film developer in town and get the pictures developed and return as soon as they could. Edith, in her excited state, and knowing she needed to calm down a bit, readily agreed. She knew she would need to show the evidence to the police since this was now a murder investigation. Damn, that girl is quick and smart, he thought as he got into his truck. If he had said anything to Edith Baxter, it would have been wrong or come out the wrong way. Sally knew just the way to say things, like it was a favor to her, and of course she didn't mind, and she would have the pictures back as soon as they were processed. The two of them left, agreeing to meet back at Mick's house once she got the film developed.

Edith felt exhilarated to have told Sally the whole story and was imagining herself as the town hero. She felt invigorated and alive for the first time in years. She could barely contain herself. She could already envision her picture in the newspaper for solving such an important crime. She felt like the heroine, Miss Marple, in an Agatha Christie book. She laughed to herself about how that country jackass was going to be fed to the media like the buffoon and pervert that he was. Inwardly, she had not felt this good in years. What a day she thought to herself and then remembered that she had not seen her pussycats all day and it was time to feed them. Perhaps they had gone outside, she thought. Grabbing a few aspirins and a glass of water, she made her way into the living room. Her brain hurt and was throbbing for some reason, almost as though she was experiencing some sort of vertigo or tinnitus. The excitement must be overwhelming her, she thought.

As she approached her sliding door to the backyard, she stopped short. She could not believe what she was seeing. There, directly in front of her, stood the man she had seen across the street in the window. With his black hair, long crooked nose, and beastly smile set widely across his face, he began laughing. As she screamed, she could hear his laughter from outside, as a humming in her ears grew stronger. He was looking straight at her, and she did not know for how long they both stood there looking at each other, with her screaming and him laughing. She turned and ran for her bedroom and the phone. Entering her bedroom, through her peripheral vision she could see that Teddy and Bear were there, which should have been reassuring, but she was in a rush to call the police.

Who was she going to call, since the only policeman they had in town was dead, and that was when she realized that something was wrong with the cats. Her cats were looking at her in a most peculiar and frightening way. Their eyes shone brighter than she believed possible, the hair on their backs rising at an alarming rate. They appeared extremely agitated and hostile, as if they were getting ready to attack something. But why? The humming in her ears would not stop! Both of her cats were as big and as scared as she had ever seen them in her life. She knew something was wrong, and she tried to talk cat language and calm them down, while dialing 911. They attacked her at the same time, clawing and biting her face, hands and eyes. She had barely enough time to dial the three digits, before she was busy attempting unsuccessfully to fend off her cats and protect her face. Teddy and Bear were merciless as they clawed, ripped and bit into her. She could feel one of them ripping into her neck as she continued to scream for help. She was rolling around on the ground furiously trying to fend them off of her. The painful biting and scratching continued endlessly, and she could hear herself screaming, although she knew nobody was around to help her. Her face was being ripped apart as well as her hands as she tried to keep them off of her. They were acting like wild beasts from the jungle who meant to kill her, and no amount of her screams or cries of pain stopped them. In fact, the more she screamed, it seemed to spur them on to even greater violence. One of them had latched on to her throat puncturing her larynx, while the blood that covered her face had blinded her to the point that she could not see them anymore. Meanwhile, in the background she could hear the humming noise as loud as ever, interspersed with that man's incessant evil laughter.

Edith Baxter was killed by her house cats in exactly three minutes and twenty-nine seconds due to a tremendous loss of blood from a punctured aortic artery. She suffocated on her own blood within her throat. Unfortunately, nobody was there to put that down in her log. The shock was pronounced on her face, as she lay still with her eyes wide open looking up at her bedroom ceiling. She didn't have much of a face left. A final bite to her windpipe had proceeded to shut up her cries for help. Her sweet pussy cats, whom she had catered to for years, had turned into absolute abominable monsters and for no apparent reason. But she knew in her mind, even as she was being ripped apart and dying, that the man in her backyard was responsible for causing her cats to turn against her. In her last moments before she succumbed to the savagery of her two cats, she even felt a ping of remorse for the dumb exterminator who had faced him earlier that day, and now regretted her self-righteous thoughts about his imminent demise. And then it was over.

The operator on the other end of the police line had heard a tremendous amount of screaming and pleading, while she was being bitten to death, but she had never been able to say anything prior to her cats attacking her. Eventually the humming sound stopped. The cats subsequently stopped their attack, sniffed their kill, and then nonchalantly went out to the living room to get some sun and clean themselves off from all of the blood that was smeared into their fur and dripping from their jaws. They both hoped that Edith would wake up soon and feed them since it was past their dinner time, and they were getting hungry.

Chapter Four

Mick: The Enigma

Sally agreed to help Mick by getting the pictures developed, and then meet him at his small bungalow where he lived on the outskirts of town. For Mick, it was the perfect residence. He could sit out on his porch after work, while the sun was setting off to the west, smoke some weed he grew in the backyard, and relax with some tunes from Johnny Cash or Merle Haggard. He drank light beer, although it really didn't help him keep the weight off. He weighed about 220 pounds and stood just over six feet tall. He was not fat, but he certainly wasn't skinny. He had begun to get that middle-aged pot belly that most men get if they stop exercising, but he really wasn't worried about his looks as he got older, he was comfortable with who he was. As he drove up to his house, he thought of how much he loved the area. His nearest neighbor Billy was over a quarter of a mile away and was one of the coolest if not quirkiest guy he had ever met. Billy was the kid that everyone picked on in school and a bit of a loner to boot, but really was a likable guy, if you just gave him a chance. Unfortunately, most kids never did. His dogs, a border collie and a German Shepard, he could hear barking as he turned into the driveway. The dogs, or boys as he called them, knew he was home. Their barking never stopped until he got out of the truck, and they continued to jump up on him and give him kisses until he let them inside and fed them. It was a daily ritual he lived for.

After feeding them some beef ribs he had saved from lunch, and letting them chew on the bones, he set down to business and tried to get organized. Sally would be at his house, and he needed to examine that little beast which was still struggling to get out of his liquor bottle.

Making his way to the bathroom, he put the ant on the kitchen counter, after uncapping and then capping him back in the bottle to get the little bugger some fresh air. He didn't want him dying prematurely.

The shower was the best thing that happened to him all day and he hated to leave its hot sauna like comfort. Toweling off, he tried to fit the pieces of the day together and make sense of what had happened to him. Everything was fine until his boss asked him to do that extra job, which was not even in his territory. He now understood that something had spooked that other exterminator, and that was why he had refused the job. He was going to have a talk with that man before this was all said and done, he said to himself. Evidently that other exterminator had seen something, he thought. Looking into the bottle and seeing the ant still struggling for its life, he believed he knew what it was. He now regretted not telling his boss no as well. Goddamn it he swore to himself. Why do I always have to say yes to whatever someone asks me to do? Can't I ever say no to anyone, he thought? Why am I always that guy who helps out when someone calls to help them move their stuff across town, or get rid of some bugs for free, or clear a cesspool blockage, or even to put in new windows? He was checking off a mental list of jobs that people had asked his help with and he had agreed to in the past. It began to dawn on him that people took advantage of him because he was a good-natured guy with a soft heart. And now look at the fix he was in because of it! He was angry at himself for letting his boss push him around again this afternoon. Taking a dart from his collection he flung it halfway across the room, hitting a voodoo doll of his boss in the neck.

"That's from the cupcake to you, bitch!"

Mick was an excellent dart player. Nobody could beat Mick in the county, maybe not even in the state in dart throwing, and he had tournament wins to prove it. And when it came to Vodun or voodoo, as the commoner called it, he also believed he knew what he was doing. He wondered how his boss felt at this instant, if he was experiencing a sore throat?

Sally drove up while he was pondering the lousy fix he had gotten himself mixed up in. Meanwhile, Sally had gotten the photographs developed at a local pharmacy but had yet to be able to look at them. Even though she had known him for four years, she had never been to Mick's house and was immediately intrigued and impressed by the landscaping around the front yard. She expected his house to be some rundown cottage with peeling paint, and for him to be in an overgrown yard with knee high weeds, in a white t-shirt with a beer in his hand. She pulled into the driveway looking at an immaculate front yard, with two elegant Japanese red maples on either side of the driveway. A fountain, with a little boy that looked like cupid, was peeing into a Koi pond filled with fat orange, brown and white fishes. Bordering the yard were various plants and shrubs of all types, properly spaced out around the front yard, with trellised vines, an intricate sculpture garden and deep green grass that appeared to be of the Kentucky bluegrass variety. The house looked as though a gingerbread man was about to waltz out of the front door. The house had been freshly painted a bright white satin color, meticulously bordered along the eves and windows with a deep maroon red, along with a pine green front door, which made the house stick out against the freshly cropped lush green grass in the front yard. She was delighted and astounded by how nice his residence looked. It was so nice that she began to think she was at the wrong house.

Mick walked out onto the porch, strung with red glowing Japanese lanterns, and greeted her with a warm smile. Together they went inside as the rich coolness of the night began to descend upon the prairie land of west Texas. He was drinking a cup of coffee and offered her one. He noticed the puzzled look in her eyes as she looked around, and inwardly he was amused by her initial shock concerning his personal abode. It always did with people who visited him. She was in for a bigger shock than this, he thought, as he escorted her into his house. Besides having some mild disorders including attention deficit disorder, turrets, and borderline alcoholism, he also was a bit neurotic when it came to the cleanliness of his personal self, house and yard. She was amazed to see that there was not a smidgeon of dust to be found in the house, a dirty dish lying about, a leaky faucet, or even a piece of chipped paint or tool out of place evident anywhere in the house. It was like she was entering a fancy bed and breakfast. She walked around and came to the conclusion that another one of his many disorders included being obsessive compulsive. She was correct in that assumption. He saw the look on her face and let her know that he was a bit neurotic about keeping the house clean and organized. The only time the house got messy was when the dogs came inside, prior to getting them bathed, which he did on a nightly basis. She felt a little bit uneasy, almost as if she did not know the man she had taken for granted for the past four years.

They sat down in his living room and began looking at the pictures. There were plenty of pictures of her cats, her yard, and numerous different pictures of people from the community, albeit sometimes in awkward situations, and finally those of the burning house. The pictures of the man's getaway car were excellent, and a partial license plate was obtained. In fact, all of the pictures were high quality. Edith Baxter was a fantastic photographer with an expensive top of the line camera. The problem was that on some of the last pictures taken the images were blurry. The man with dark hair, she had spoken of, could not be clearly identified in the pictures. It was apparent he was there, standing up against the window, but he was shrouded in a hazy fog that was covering his face. It was maddening. The harder they looked at the pictures the less they could ascertain what he looked like. Distinctly though, his eyes shone like two little pinpricks of red through the haze. They decided he most likely had blue eyes because the way photographs sometimes changed the color blue into red. That was until they examined a few of the other pictures and clearly noticed the blue eyes of her Himalayan pussycat Bear. Both of them were puzzled by this seemingly contradictory finding. As Mick continued to examine the pictures for more clues with a magnifying glass, he noticed Sally was beginning to wander around his house examining his personal effects. He could not help but realize that she was very curious about what his house contained and its appearance. A house spoke volumes to the mental state of the person living inside of it and he felt she was sizing him up. He was right.

Upon entering his study, to the left of the kitchen, she noticed a college degree hanging on the wall. It was from Louisiana State University, a Bachelor of Science degree conferred upon him in the study of biology with a minor in geology. That was an odd choice of two very different fields, she thought. Then she looked to the right of the picture and saw that he had a master's degree in evolutionary theology from the Order of the Rosicrucian Church of Science and God based in Halifax Nova Scotia! She looked at the degree on the wall a second time because she could hardly believe what she was reading. She walked back into the kitchen with a look of bemusement on her face and confronted him. She never had any idea he even graduated from high school. That's funny she thought, their conversations had never been real up until the last two hours, after four years of knowing him. She realized that he had always been superficial with her. They each had a shallow understanding of each other and the misconceptions that followed. It was like knowing the doorman you see every day and never really knowing him.

"I had no idea you had degrees from LSU in such varying topics as biology and geology. But to have a master's degree, in evolutionary theology from the prestigious Order of the Rose of Cretans, I am truly humbled to be here. What do they teach in evolutionary theology, how to create gods?"

She had a broad smile across her face and felt rather smug and witty about changing the Order of the Rosicrucian to the Rose of Cretans. Without looking up from pictures he was examining, Mick replied to her question that was flecked with the intent of goading him.

"Actually, those two years I spent in Canada were extremely thought provoking with intensive study in the fields of biology and natural selection, parapsychology, world religions, natural science and zoology. We delved into how different organisms, plants and animals mostly, affect each other when they first come into contact with one another in this continuously changing planet, and also how some of them evolve symbiotically or in some instances parasitically. Conversely, other creatures are diametrically opposed and attempt to exterminate each other and shape each other's natural universe. The reason why it is called 'evolutionary theology' is because of the belief that evolution and the struggle for existence is in fact the overriding determinant of life on this planet, although it is really yet to be determined how in fact the genesis of man came to be so highly specialized versus the other creatures that exist among us. Don't you find it amazing that we have harnessed the power of animals around the world, like the horse, dog, cat, water buffalo, goat, sheep and many other creatures to do our bidding, and to help us to make our lives better and more sustainable? The credo of the organization is that knowledge and the continued study of our natural living and breathing planet will provide us the answers eventually to understand how mankind, religion, science and the animal planet have been transformed to mold our general way of thinking. Unlike other religions that profess to know everything from books written thousands of years ago, we pride ourselves on trying to make sense of the past and of the knowledge we now know of today. If Jesus were around today, and his spirit is by the way, I think he certainly would be in our camp, that we must try and inculcate the lessons from the past with the advanced technologies that mankind has at its fingertips today. Really the belief in the natural and the supernatural should be viewed as on the same continuum, but just on different levels of the spectrum. It is simply looking at the world through different lenses, so to speak, like through the looking glass."

He went back to studying the pictures, while she stood there, feeling like a speck on the ground. How could this ignoramus she had known for over four years, and thought of as a hillbilly fuckwit exterminator, have just spoken to her so eloquently and with such common sense, be the same man? She decided she had been wrong about who he really was and that she had better start to take him a little more seriously. This man was quite the paradox. She took some of the pictures from the kitchen table and began to scrutinize them for anything she might have missed, all the while feeling quite embarrassed and a bit unsettled with her previous notions of her coworker and his mental capabilities.

She looked at one picture after another and finally found herself staring at the pictures of the burning house. The house fire had started on the lower level where Mick had begun confronting the ants with his specially modified poison. Two of the pictures appeared as though they were taken within a second or two from each other since she could see the very gradual spread of the fire. And then she noticed it! In one of the pictures, the latter one, there was no shadow in the window. In the earlier picture, there was definitely someone peeking out from behind the curtains in the upstairs bedroom. She pushed the picture over and pointed at the window. Mick scooped up the picture and tried examining it with the magnifying glass. There was certainly someone present they both agreed, but it was difficult to get a good look at the person's face. They decided that this particular picture they needed to get enlarged.

Then they would go back to Edith and see if they could get her to recognize the man before they went to the police. It would be good to have her on his side before the police began questioning him. They did not have any inkling that Edith Baxter was lying in a pool of blood, while they continued examining the photographs.

Chapter Five

Pussy Problems

The phone calls had inundated the fire department and police station. Neighbors from miles around could see the smoke and flames that were coming from the direction of the farmhouse. When they could not get in touch with Roy, the local sheriff, they had alerted the next town's officer who resided in Kingsville, Texas. Unfortunately, the local sheriff was on a fishing trip in Boise Idaho for the week, but they were able to alert the lieutenant in charge, Stan McCormick. Stan immediately attempted to get in touch with Roy but without any luck. Next, he called the fire chief from the next town over, but he didn't need to worry, as he had already dispatched two fire trucks and an ambulance to the scene. It took them almost an hour to arrive at the burning house. Stan was waiting for them. What they found was a burnt down house and an empty police car belonging to Roy. Upon examination, the firefighters soon came to the conclusion that a combustible accelerant had been used to start the fire.

With that evidence, Stan McCormick knew he was at the scene of a crime involving arson, and he would be needing answers. He decided to get some immediate answers and find out what the locals had seen, if anything. Starting at the nearest house, actually the only house in the immediate area, he knocked on the door of Twenty-Two Myrtle Street. Getting no answer, he rang the doorbell two more times before looking in the window. What he saw made him do a double take, jump back a step or two, and make him almost fall off of the porch. Two cat's faces completely covered in blood peered out from behind the kitchen window. He immediately ordered the door kicked down. Two officers, guns drawn, kicked in the front door. The two cats ran like hell away from the officers, and after a quick search of the premises, proceeded to find Edith's lifeless body in the bedroom. What they found inside the house baffled them. Edith Baxter had been savagely killed, with a tremendous loss of blood and a fatal wound to her neck, which were seemingly inflicted by her house cats! There was no evidence of any forced entry into the house, either from the front or back doors. It was an utterly outrageous and unmistakable conclusion from the facts at the scene of the crime. Teddy and Bear were official suspects according to the coroner's report that was being written!

Stan McCormick had been a police officer for over twenty years and was truly baffled. He found himself scratching his head on Edith Baxter's front porch. He had just asked the medical examiner for a third time if any human marks were found on Edith's body and had been told not yet once again. There were no fingerprints anywhere in Edith's bedroom, but the whole house was being dusted for prints anyway. Sitting on the front porch, he kept pondering the murder he had just stumbled upon. He knew this was not going to go over well with the newspapers and the media once they got wind of this story. It was certainly going to put Bishop, Texas on the map for police incompetence as well as probably get some attention from the news starved national media. Perhaps, the most ridiculous part of the evening had been when they rounded up the two cats into a dog cage and taken their pictures, as proof of the blood lust they had inflicted upon their owner. Visions of newspaper headlines that read, "Crazed cats insist on wet food" or "Two crazed Texas pussies lay down the law in Bishop," danced through his head. Needless to say, he was a bit perturbed and uneasy when he heard himself being summoned from across the street.

"Hey Lieutenant, I think you had better come over here and take a look at this."

The fire chief stood within the smoldering remnants of the house and was flanked by a few other firefighters who were all staring at what appeared to be a bathtub. As he got closer, he could see the bewildered looks on their faces. That was when he saw the body. There in the bathtub he saw the half-eaten skeletal remains of what appeared to be a man. The upper part of the body was completely charred and smoking from the fire, while two fat hairy legs lay beneath a dirty water line within the tub. It appeared that the man had died prior to the fire taking place and had initially tried to find refuge within the tub, from whatever had attacked him. The smell was overpoweringly awful. Not so much from the skeletal part of the body since it was picked clean, but the lower half of the body had been virtually boiled in the tub and a sickening smell of hot fecal matter, death and chicken pervaded the air. Stan stood back from the scene and threw up his lunch. The vomit spewed across the bathroom tile floor. That was when he saw the steaming badge which he had vomited upon. As he attempted to compose himself, next to the firefighters, he looked them in the eyes and pointed to the badge lying on the ground and motioned for the forensics expert. He continued to try to contain his stomach from any further upheaval. He summoned over the forensics expert of the fire team, who carefully put on a glove, and retrieved Roy's puke covered badge from the debris. An hour later the medical examiner, Desmond Beauregard, began giving his unofficial report to Stan McCormick while he sat on Edith Baxter's porch in a mild state of shock.

"Roy was alive less than five hours ago. In fact, he had eaten a chicken sandwich at the local diner. I found some wrappers in his squad car and a receipt for his purchase. In my opinion, he drawled in his southern Louisiana accent, he entered that house very much alive and had decided to use the restroom. At that point it is anyone's guess, but I figure soon thereafter he was attacked while he was taking a number two by some type of voracious insect and had attempted to fend them off by getting in the bathtub and filling it with water. On his legs, bloated and boiled as they were, I found stinging marks which look very similar to those of fire ants, which are local to the area around here, although the stings do seem to be much more severe in nature. He succumbed to the poisonous stings while at the same time being eaten by whatever it was that attacked him. After he was already dead and eaten, it was just bad luck that the upper part of his skeleton had been charred to a burnt crispy, kind of like what you find when you cook sausage with onions and there is something at the side of the pan."

Stan looked up at the examiner in disbelief with the latest analogy the old man had just thrown his old friend Roy into, as though he was part of a potluck. The anger inside of him rose up.

"Goddamn it. You are telling me that I have two homicides and an arson case on my hands, and the prime suspects are two pussy cats and a pile of fucken ants! Who the fuck is going to believe this! I have worked over twenty years in this business and, if anybody told me this story, I would be calling up the special squad car with the men in the white suits, to come take that man away. I need more answers than what you are giving me."

"Stan, I think what you have here is quite a mystery, indeed. But, the facts is the facts at this point. The bodies and the marks on them don't lie. Nobody can say anything different from the evidence we currently have at our disposal. I got to say this though, this is the most puzzling case I have ever had in my forty years as a medical examiner. Not since those 1998 New Orleans witchcraft murder cases have I been as stumped. Oh, and by the way, we might have another murder victim. My guys believe they may have stumbled upon the remains of the owner, Louise Weatherby, in the kitchen. My guys are checking on it as we speak."

Stan, his anger having subsided listening to the cold logic of the old southern gentleman next to him, let out a deep sigh.

"I know what you are saying, but I just can't wrap my head around this right now. Not one iota of this is making any sense, and the only two witnesses I have are licking their assholes with their tongues at present," as he glanced over at the dog cage with the cats locked up inside. "What I do know is that someone used an accelerant to try and get rid of the evidence and no ants or cats can do that, because if they can, I am going to call the funny farm on myself."

A few hours later some good news finally came to Stan McCormick. Two different sets of fingerprints were found within the house which did not belong to Edith Baxter. An immense sense of relief swept over him, knowing that he now had two solid leads into the murders of not only Edith Baxter, but more than likely Roy and Louise as well. He and his investigators cordoned off the area for future further examination and police work and decided to get the fingerprints back to the local station. At that point they could put them into a national database and start making sense of this mystery. He supposed everything was going to work like clockwork now. He was still troubled by the obvious wounds to Edith, ostensibly from her cats, but maybe there was a logical explanation, he thought, although he was beginning to have his doubts. And Roy, although half eaten, maybe was killed prior to that and then was scavenged by the ants, like a cast aside carcass. It was not probable but at least it was possible, he thought. The facts really did not add up so far in this investigation, but at least he had some solid leads besides pussy cats and fire ants.

Chapter Six

Alea Iacta Est
(The die is cast)

As the horseman of death, the spawn of the devil was ultimately prepared for the inevitable battle between good and evil. Just as Julius Caesar led his army across the Rubicon, in defiance of the wishes of the Senate, knowing full well that the course of history would forever be altered, the man in the window also understood the importance of his actions over the past twenty-four hours. For him and everyone else on the planet, the die had been cast, and there was no turning back. Throughout his whole life he had been planning for this day. He had successfully learned everything there was to know about the creatures of the planet and how he could control them through various methods such as mutation, inbreeding, cross breeding and ultimately mind control, by utilizing differing pitches and wavelengths of sound combined with genetically altered nuclear waste.

His most important accomplishment had been the cross breeding of the genus Solenopsis, of which there were over 201 species worldwide. More commonly known as the fire ant for their painful stings, their bodies are divided into three sections, the head, thorax and abdomen. With a set of antennae and three pairs of legs they also have a formidable set of mandibles, for biting and tearing. Some of the genus are known as Formicine ants, which cause irritation to the skin by spraying formic acid, while others are known as Myrmicine ants, which have a dedicated venom-injecting sting of alkaloid venom. His special cross bred fire ants sprayed formic acid as well as injected the alkaloid venom and were officially unknown to anyone in the world, one of 202 worldwide species to be exact. Furthermore, he had cross bred them multiple times to be resistant to any manmade poisons available on the planet through his access to the nuclear waste at his job. His experiments over the past decade with differing poisons and chemical compound solutions had made his specially constructed species, a super strong cohesive army that until today, he thought to be unstoppable. Billions upon billions of his hybrid fire ants were at his disposal. What he needed to find out was what had killed his soldiers today, and more importantly who was this rogue exterminator who had access to this flaming poison that he didn't know anything about.

He had studied fire ants for decades. As far as the typical behavior of a fire ant, therefore not species 202, they usually constructed large mounds in open areas that fed mostly on young plants and seeds, and when the opportunity presented itself, would occasionally attack small animals and kill them. Normal fire ants will bite their prey, only to get a grip initially, and then sting from the abdomen a toxic alkaloid venom called Solenopsin, a compound from the class of piperidines. A painful sting then ensues and hence the name of the fire ant. More aggressive than most species of ants in North America, they have pushed many of the local species away from their local habitats. With an ability to survive extreme conditions, they are actually one of the few species that do not hibernate. They can make nests in trees, although they usually choose to be underground and next to water for obvious reasons. Their dome shaped mounds can reach a meter to two meters in height and typically only have a small group of queens or one single queen.

The queen, much larger than either worker ant, soldier ant or the male drone, has one primary function and that is to reproduce. A typical fire ant colony queen lives up to seven years and can produce up to sixteen hundred eggs per day. After the queen mates, she then proceeds to rip off her own wings. The male drone ants have only one function and that is to mate with the queen and then thereafter die. The worker ants take care of the colony and the young eggs, while the soldier ants, with noticeably larger mandibles for fighting, provide the offense and defense for the self-contained community.

The venom of the fire ants is composed of multiple alkaloids derived from piperdine, and as with many allergies can cause severe reactions, such as anaphylaxis. The stings develop into bumps which cause an intense amount of pain and irritation, since many of them happen at the same place on the body. If infected, due to scratching after being bitten, scars are inevitable. Many local treatments involve aloe-vera gel and even the use of urine on the part of the body that is stung. In some people severe allergic reactions to fire ant stings cause serious swelling, chest pain, severe sweating, and a loss of breath. Along with a slurred speech and a tremendous amount of discomfort, the actual attack can be ultimately fatal if not treated quickly.

The only known natural predator of the typical fire ant is the Phorid fly. Slightly smaller than vinegar flies, they were imported to Texas on purpose after the accidental importation of the fire ant to the Alabama dockyards years earlier in the 1930's. With fire ants rapidly spreading throughout the south of the United States, the flies were introduced to halt the spread. Known as Pseudacteon tricuspis, or Pseudacteon curvatus, which means ant-decapitating flies, they search out the fire ants and lay their eggs on the thorax of the ant. The larvae will migrate to the head and begin feeding on the muscle tissue and nervous tissue of the ant, in a parasitic relationship. Within two weeks the ant's head falls off as the larvae release an enzyme, thereby dissolving the membrane which had previously kept it attached to the ant's body. Two weeks later, the fly pupates from the empty shell of the ant's head as a new Phorid fly soldier and begins anew the search for another fire ant to attack.

Species 202 is unique to all the other species of fire ants that populate the planet. More aggressive than any other species previously known to man, they attack large animals as well as small and with eyes more powerful than their counterparts are able to direct themselves directly at their intended victim. With a venom comprised of both formic and alkaloid poisons they are twice as lethal as their contemporary cousins as well as twice as big. Housed in colonies underground, deep beneath the earth sometimes in excess of one hundred feet, the queens reproduce at an extraordinary rate. Typically, sixteen hundred eggs a day were at maximum produced by any average fire ant queen. Within species 202, fire ant queens produced over ten thousand eggs a day and up to a dozen queens populated the lower chambers of the colony's mounds. Millions upon millions of these deadly fire ants were now clustered within each colony. Surrounding Bishop, Texas and its outlying areas thousands of these colonies pervaded the local landscape, unknown to the populous.

Also, unique to species 202 was a mind control genetic mutation, introduced to their DNA and triggered by noise. Nuclear waste had been implanted within their genomic sequence, thereby mutating their development. Furthermore, installed deep below the ground adjacent to the ant colony nests were humming devices that served as speakers which mimicked the overall buzz sound of the colony when in normal action. When a certain amplified signal was sent, the ants would, for instance, increase their sexual activity or know when to rest. Also, if everything was normal and going well, a low hum would soothe them and keep them working, but if this noise was turned up and they became agitated, they instinctively knew to commence attacking whatever threatened the colony. This could just happen to be anything within their sight of vision as they streamed out of their burrows. The raven-haired man was most proud of this particular development he had instituted, after all of the inbreeding and crossbreeding that he had undertaken for the better part of a quarter of a century. He was ultimately prepared for the inevitable battle between good and evil, as the horseman of death.

Placing his hand on his government identity card, which allowed him access into military bases across the country, he slipped it into his pocket and contemplated making a house call on Dinkin's exterminator service. He needed to find out who it was at Louise Weatherbys house on Friday, and more importantly what type of poison was used to kill his fire ants. This shouldn't be hard to find out from these ignorant foolish humans, he thought. From his earliest memories, he could recall of his childhood, he knew he was different. He did not care to play with other children, nor did he care to listen to anything adults had to say, and he certainly did not want to participate in any games or social activities. He liked to be alone and scorned the human race as ignorant conceited fools. By far and away, he hated the nuns at the orphanage where he was raised, surrounded by their sanctimonious beliefs that they were righteous, and in some way conquering evil with their daily penances to God.

His conception, if he ever knew about it, would have made him laugh. A young prostitute, strung out on heroin and needing a fix, was alone and walking the streets of downtown Lubbock, Texas. With the wind howling and rain steadily pouring down upon the young woman, she kept looking back at the cars to see if any of the male drivers were interested in her services, as she walked the frigid streets in the dark while the midnight hour approached. Soon a black car pulled up and rolled its passenger side window down and motioned her to get inside. Feeling relieved to get out of the rain and finally make some money, she opened the passenger car door and got inside quickly. Typically, she would have scoped the man out prior to entering the car, but with the rain coming down in sheets she made the decision to enter the car first. Maybe now she could get some work and buy some drugs, she thought to herself. It was a fateful decision.

"Hey thanks buddy. Are you interested in some action, tonight? You have no idea how cold it is out there."

As she said this, looking over at him, she noticed her car window being rolled up and the man's face still had not turned toward her. He wore a hood of some sort and then the doors on the car locked. She felt frightened. He grabbed her by the hair, shoving her head into the dash of the car with enough force to daze her. Seconds later, he injected a needle into her arm, emptying a sedative into her blood system.

"You're welcome, miss. I thought you might need a lift so to speak and decided to give you some help with your current predicament. It is awfully nasty weather out there tonight, and I want to make sure that the filthy animal that you are, gets taken care of really well. Now I know you are not going to remember most of this after tonight, but you will fulfill the wishes of my master just fine."

Clawing at the handle of the door, screaming at the top of her lungs, she instantly regretted getting into the car. With the rain making it hard to see even a few feet in front of the car, they headed for a seedy motel along old route 66. On the ride over, the man kept continually hitting her with his fist, as he drove the car with his left hand. The continued punching, combined with the injection he had given her, were already showing the effects upon her.

"You bastard. Let me go," she sobbed.

"Certainly, I will let you go, but not until you have had a night of pleasure you will never forget, she-bitch."

He stopped the car in front of the motel and jerked her out of the car, dragging her by her arm and hair into the filthy room, which he had earlier procured for the evening. He threw her onto the bed in the middle of the room. She was helpless to say anything or stop him from controlling her. Whatever he had injected her with was pushing her into an almost catatonic state. She was barely awake, in a daze, aware of her surroundings but unable to do anything to defend herself. In her drugged state, she knew she needed help but somehow knew she would not find any. The room was spinning. The man talked quite calmly to her, but she knew he was as cold as ice. When they had first entered the squalid motel room she could feel the presence of others, or things within the room. There was just enough light in the room to make out the outline of the bed and a television stand. In the corners shadows stood. She felt lonely and afraid, regretting she had ever gotten hooked on drugs, but she knew it was too late to feel sorry for herself.

Once inside the room, with the door closed, the man hit her across the jaw with such force he caused her to lose a tooth as he began ripping off her clothes. Spitting out one of her lower teeth along with copious amounts of blood, she found herself being tied to the bed and began feebly whimpering. There was no hope for her now. The man was a deranged sadist. As she lay naked and trembling, spread across the bed, the man went to the back of the room and unlocked some sort of cage, an animal cage! Jumping out of the cage a large furry animal, the size of a large dog or wolf, proceeded to jump on top of the bed, and with red snarling eyes looking straight into hers, penetrated her vagina with its cock with such a hard vengeance that she gasped and screamed. The animal, which resembled some sort of hyena like wolf, was driving into her so hard she knew that she was beginning to bleed internally. Clamping down on her neck, he drew more blood, this time from her neck and continued to lay waste to her, all the while cutting into her insides. Finally, she knew he had put his semen into her as the animal howled with delight, momentarily letting go of her neck. Afterward, half in and out of consciousness, she felt the rest of the half dozen men or spirit demons in the room finish her off, one by one, until she was unconscious from the tranquilizer and loss of blood.

In the morning, the caretaker of the hotel found her amidst the horrid scene, half alive, and immediately called an ambulance and the police. She barely survived. Nine months later under the care of a state psychiatric ward, she gave birth to a boy, who was immediately given up to a local orphanage administered by nuns. She died during childbirth complications, having never regained her sanity after that dreadful night. The spawn of the devil was alive. It was the sixth day of June in the year 1966.

Calling Dinkin's, the raven-haired man got an answering machine instructing him to leave a message, but he received some valuable information from the office's weekend recording. The office would be open at eight in the morning on Monday. He began to formulate a plan. He would show up at least an hour before they opened, in order to scout out the area, the entry and exit doors, and surrounding businesses. He was going to be well prepared to find out all he could about this special poison, procure it, and then exterminate the exterminator. What he didn't know was that Exterminator 69 had a good hunch he would be there as well.

Chapter Seven

Skunk Diddly-Doo

Later that evening, Sally and Mick traveled back to Edith Baxter's house. He needed another ant specimen, a healthy one, if possible, from the other house and also wanted to talk to her about the man in the pictures. They were met by a maze of police tape across both yards and houses. Mick ducked under the tape at Edith Baxter's house and went straight to where the front door used to stand. Sally went to say something and lost her voice. She realized he was running his own investigation and was going to do whatever he wanted. Besides, she reasoned, he was so deeply enmeshed it wasn't going to hurt anything at this point anyway.

From the police tape that surrounded Edith Baxter's house Mick had a bad feeling she had been murdered while they were gone. But just how, was what he wondered? He was fairly certain that if she was dead, then it was because of the man in the window, with either the red or black eyes who was behind it. He surmised that the man had returned right after they left her house, since the police were already gone and both structures were taped off. This meant he was a very bold and deliberate killer. Just what were his intentions, he wondered?

He found copious amounts of blood on the carpet in the bedroom where she had died, although there seemed to be no evidence of any forced entry, that is, except for the front door having been kicked down by the police. That meant they had probable cause to enter the home. What was strange was that there were no signs of any struggle with any intruder. The bedroom where she had been killed was a puzzle. The perfume bottles and figurines sat untouched upon the bureaus and the white bedspread lay undisturbed, but the carpet next to the nightstand was drenched in blood. There was cat fur all over the place, especially the carpet, where most of the blood was located. The phone was covered in blood, still dangling downward from the nightstand. He could almost see an outline of a body on the floor.

"Oh my God!" he spoke aloud and whistled. The evidence was pointing to the fact that her own cats had killed her.

Did the man who controlled the ants, also have the ability to somehow control the cats? How could he do it? He thought of the humming sound and wondered what it was all about. Could he be some sort of demon with telepathic mind control powers? And where did he gain the scientific knowledge on how to mutate ants? It was an extraordinary development; and, if true, was an extremely disturbing development. His mind was racing, realizing that he needed to accomplish a multitude of tasks prior to facing him. How was he going to beat the devil he wondered? He had to work out a plan and desperately needed more time to conduct some investigative work. It would start with those ants in the burnt down house. Necessity dictated he find out just how these particular ants were so different than other species of fire ants. Meanwhile, he was quite aware that he was probably being hunted. He thought about how to best combat this devil bastard that confronted him. His inner spirit was frightened by the power this man wielded.

Mick's senses had been warning him, as to the lack of soul in the man, and furthermore he had been alerted by the lack of sound, like when he was in the yard just before he was attacked by the ants. Everything that had transpired had deeper connotations, and he sensed this was not just a run of the mill normal occurrence. If he had any chance to survive, he would have to use common sense, faith, his intuition, and develop some offensive and defensive traps within the next few hours and days in order to prevail for what he believed was coming his way. In his mind's eye, he believed he was in combat with Satan. This realization dawned upon him when he thought back to the image of the man. He had felt the blackness and dark waves of hate from the demonic spirit of the man who stood behind the window. He fully realized it now. He remembered just how taken aback he was, by the negative energy and the anger emanating from within the man, just by being near him.

He needed a good plan of attack. He didn't figure on being in the office Monday morning waiting to be his prey, but rather in the surrounding woods next to his office, which extended for miles in either direction. Filled with mature poplar and spruce trees and high sawgrass it would make the perfect concealed observatory. He would watch and wait. Plus, he could concoct a few traps that could be useful in the event the psycho man beast showed his true side. Mick was a superb hunter and could lie as still as a titmouse when lying in ambush. He made a decision to approach him as though he were dangerous prey. Deep in his heart he knew what a precarious situation he currently found himself a part of. The devil wanted him dead . . .

Waiting for Mick while he examined Edith Baxter's house, Sally began to wonder if he realized the precariousness of his situation. She did not feel the immediate need to run, but her mind was telling her to think this thing out. None of much of nothing was making sense, she told herself. She knew that two people were dead, perhaps three. Furthermore, her co-worker for four years was probably the prime suspect of the murders, even though just a few hours ago she thought him to be a half-wit incapable of getting to the bottom of anything but maybe a chicken bone.

But things had changed. She realized that he was secretly brilliant, perhaps autistic, perverse, and obviously eccentric as well! He was a biologist, geologist and theologian with secreted college degrees and kept his true personality to himself, all while living in an immaculate home. He definitely showed a tendency to having a few obsessive-compulsive disorders. He was acting in a completely opposite manner from the man she knew at work. He was a Heyoka perhaps. An American Indian spirit man, who was the opposite of what he appeared to be. She began mulling this over in her mind. If this was true, this meant he had been putting on a disguised personality for years. But for what reason? Why act like a stupid hillbilly? That is, of course, unless he needed to hide something that he was doing, or maybe he was a wanted man . . . and then nobody would suspect him of anything since he was acting like a dipshit. Her mind was racing with possibilities.

In a weird way, she found herself strangely attracted to him. This was the most excitement she had ever experienced in her life, and the adrenaline was stimulating her. He was acting courageous, direct, astute, polite, and most of all as mysterious as anyone she had ever encountered. He was acting like a gentleman with a firm grasp of the situation. He was a total enigma. No longer was he stupidly toying with her about his want of her. She noticed that he had not mentioned a thing, or done anything suggestive, ever since this whole situation had gotten serious. He was being extremely professional, and she found herself for the first time being second in command in their relationship. He was acting differently, a more aloof man, from what she had ever seen before and had not paid her any attention for these past few hours. She loved it. She was aroused by his actions or lack thereof, and surprised by her sudden change of heart, as she found herself thinking of him. One day ago, he would have been the last person on the planet to get a shot at being with her. This was utterly stupid and crazy, she thought, as she gazed out the car window waiting for him to return.

Mick returned from the house and let her know what he thought as they rode back to his house. Edith Baxter had been murdered by her cats. The man in the window was responsible for their actions, but the police were probably going to try and pin the murders on him. After he spoke for a bit, without much reaction from her, he realized she had been strangely silent.

"Everything all right over there?" he asked quizzically.

"Sure, just thinking about that poor old lady." She lied while dropping her head to examine a picture, so he could not see her eyes. She needed some time to compose herself and her thoughts.

The next morning Sally awoke to the sounds of Mick talking on the phone. The only problem was she didn't know what the hell he was saying. He appeared to be speaking in a combined Spanish and English dialect, Spanglish. For at least ten minutes she listened to Mick and tried to understand what he was saying, and then she heard him hang up the phone. Within his spare bedroom, she lay in bed thinking about the previous day's events while taking in the ambiance of the room. The bedroom was decorated with fishing poles, a large marlin mounted on the wall above a small fireplace, a cross with Jesus on it, and pictures of him and numerous other people on fishing excursions.

She realized she must have been dog tired from the day before, since she was still wearing her clothing from the previous day. In truth, she didn't even remember going to the room she had awoken in. She wanted a shower, but decided to find Mick first and see what he was doing. She found him in a well-lit basement which, with the amount of scientific equipment set up, resembled a laboratory. He was peering into a large magnifier examining an ant. Without moving his head from what he was examining he spoke.

"Well, good morning, Sally. How are you feeling? There is coffee ready in the kitchen, if you like."

He was in an awful chipper mood considering the current state of things, she thought.

"Yeah, I'm fine. I think I just need a shower to clear my head. How did I get to the bedroom? I don't remember even falling asleep."

"That's right. You fell asleep on the couch. I picked you up and moved you to the guest bedroom. Did you get a good sleep?"

Sally let out a sigh. She was still groggy from waking up.

"Thanks. I did. I'm going to take you up on that offer for a cup of coffee and go take a shower. Learn anything yet?"

Mick cocked his head sideways, his eyes burning bright with excitement from gathering data on this previously unknown species and bobbed his head up and down.

"They are an interesting species is all I can say at this point. They are extremely resilient and as tough as the crud at the base of your shower. They are resistant to a multitude of things most fire ants aren't. Whomever developed them put a lot of time and effort into altering their genetic makeup. I will get you caught up once you're done with your shower."

And with that Mick swiveled back on his chair and continued his study of the little beast.

Mick arrived at his workplace the following day and prepared for what he surely thought would be the devil's appearance on Monday. He had a wild hunch that Lucifer would begin his search for answers to who the exterminator was by showing up at his workplace first thing in the morning. He began by smearing citronella plant juices along the walls of the office as a clearing agent to throw off the devil's sense of smell. Then he proceeded to burn sage throughout the office and score black marks of the dead plant under the casements of the windows and on the undersides of the chairs. This would hinder the devil's senses, by weakening his ability to think clearly, based upon the sage's cleansing effect. Next, he hung crosses in all of the closets in order to make him feel uncomfortable, as he would be able to sense them, but would not be able to see them. He then turned off the buildings air conditioning system so that it would be stifling hot when anyone entered the office. Finally, he bathed the plant in the receptionist area in holy water and dumped copious amounts of salt in the water cooler next to the receptionist desk. He knew that the devil, if he had taken on the form of a human body, would still need plenty of water to keep his body cool. Finally, he was ready to set his coup de resistance. Working above the ceiling tiles, right next to the employee files, he began to rig a paint bucket to fall downward upon the opening of the file cabinet drawer. His master stroke of genius was going to be implanted within the file cabinet where his employee records were located. He assumed that the devil would need to find out where he lived, in order to kill him. So, he set up a trap to spring when the top drawer was opened. When it did pop open, it would be under an extreme amount of pressure from an animal tranquilizer gun, which he would rig. Once the drawer popped, it would shoot a tranquilizer dart into the person that opened the drawer, as well as embed a microscopic chip that would allow him to track that person's movements through the use of a GPS system. At that point, fire engine red paint was set to dump over the person who had opened the file cabinet. And inside of the specially made paint can he had a special surprise. Just before going to bed, while Sally was passed out asleep on the couch, he had trapped a skunk and removed its glands. After cutting them out very carefully, he put them in the can of paint and mixed vigorously. The awful smell would further keep the demon disoriented. He was not going to let this man forget this day, or let this evil spirit get the jump on him, he thought. The animal tranquilizer was enough to take down an elephant and he surmised that this would be the most effective way in knocking out the devil. He already had multiple victims to his credit, and he knew it was either him or the devil that was losing this fight. The ensuing battle was going to entail using every bit of theological knowledge he owned, his intuition, and a blistering amount of internal strength, as well as a bit of faith in good karma and the uses of Christian dogma.

Outside of the office, behind the tree line just outside of the parking lot, he set up a blind in the trees about ten feet off the ground to observe what was happening. After hours of preparations, he knew it was time to get ready for guerrilla warfare, exterminator 69 style. In the blind behind the office, he began applying green and tan paint to his face and then made sure his binoculars were attached to a tripod, which was placed on the blind's stand. He slept the night on the stand behind the blind within a sleeping bag.

When the first rays of sunshine arrived, Mick downed a few cans of premade coffee and began the stakeout. He thought about how this might be his last day alive, and he tried to muster some inner courage for the battle that lay ahead. Hidden by the blind, he looked out at the office and scanned the areas behind him, just in case. He was nervous. He had fully rigged the office and also had a certain number of traps set in the woods just in case of what he called a FUBAR (Fucked up beyond all reality) event. For hours, he waited patiently. What made him so nervous was that he knew that this demonic man was also looking for him. Earlier in the morning, the garbage men had come to pick up the trash from around the office park. He saw his boss Joe arrive and go into the office just after daybreak. He looked tired and agitated. Probably because of him he thought. He wondered how his throat felt. Bastard deserved it.

Thirty minutes later, a black sedan entered the parking lot and circled around the building, before stopping at the front entrance in the visitor parking spot. It was his car. As he exited the car, Mick felt a surge of adrenaline rush through his body. This man was evil beyond comprehension, and he somehow could sense it. He could see the man sizing up the situation, as he closed his car door and began a slow walk toward the entrance of the building. After buzzing the intercom, the man pulled something out of his pocket and showed it to his boss who had answered the front door. It was some sort of identification. His boss Joe allowed him into the building, and he could see through the glass windows that they went to the boss's private office. Obviously, this man had some sort of police or authoritative credential which persuaded his boss to let him into the premises before working hours had even started.

Entering the premises, the raven-haired man's senses immediately picked up interference from the tart citrusy Citronella smell mixed with the burnt sage fragrance in the air. The heat inside of the building was well over ninety degrees, and he saw Joe fumbling with the thermostat on the wall. The plant at the receptionist desk was basking in the heavenly waters of his holiness. The demon man came to the obvious conclusion that the exterminator had visited the office and the anger became visible in his face. Thinking the two, Mick and Joe, were in cahoots with each other, his anger exploded. Through the plate glass windows, he saw his boss being thrown to the floor. Then, he was picked up from the ground and flung like a rag doll into the wall slamming his head against the door frame. He watched through the binoculars as the man yelled at him in anger, pointing his index finger straight at his face. Joe, bewildered and utterly in shock from the instantaneous confrontation, got up and swung wildly at him with his burly arms. That was a big mistake. With lightening quick speed, he grabbed Joe by the shirt with one hand and with his other hand quickly moved to the pants area and grabbed his crotch yanking him forward. With Joe's cock held in a vise-like grip, plus one of his balls, he squeezed as hard as he could and spoke.

"Show me your employee files or I will castrate you in the next few seconds and with extreme pleasure."

He grinned as he spoke the words and Mick, out in the blind, saw a pitiful looking man writhing in pain in his grasp. Joe was screaming in pain, and even though he was nearly a quarter mile way, he could clearly hear his cries. He pointed to the file cabinet where the employee records were held. Joe was instantly dropped by the man and left writhing on the floor. The man stood in front of the file cabinet and attempted to open the drawer, but it seemed to be jammed or stuck, seemingly wedged shut. Frustrated and irritated by the underlying thought that some imbecile human was attempting to foil his plans, he yanked on the drawer as hard as he could. The effect was immediate, instantaneous, and absolute. As he fell backwards from the pressure of the drawer opening, he was shot in the chest, right next to his heart with an animal tranquilizer, searing his body with white hot pain. Never, had he ever felt pain like this in his human existence. He had never been humanly wounded before. The sound from his throat was an unearthly howl that resembled that of a wounded wolf. As he stumbled backward, he was immediately and completely bathed in a shower of liquid red paint which covered him from head to toe. Gagging and unable to breathe or speak, or momentarily move, he found himself dumbfounded by what had just happened to him. And then the smell enveloped everything, that of the skunk glands which had been mixed within the can of paint.

Joe was having a hard time fathoming what was happening in the room. The vicious intruder, who only just a few moments ago had threatened to castrate him, was covered in red paint and struggling to see while howling in a bellowing rage. He was gagging, half puking over the smell of a skunk in the office, and in awe about the paint that had miraculously dropped from the ceiling. He was immobilized before he came to his senses gagging. The intruder, covered in red paint, went into whip-like action. Furious at the trap that had been laid for him, with his face and body drowned in fire engine red paint, his spinal column literally arched with the power of the dark side. With beastly howls of rage and pain emanating from him, smelling like a dead skunk, he attempted to wipe his eyes. He found the water cooler and began dumping the entire container upon his face and head. At first the water felt good and then the burning from the salt placed in the cooler came upon him, and, like a wounded boar stuck with a lethal spear, he screamed even louder at the burning pain he felt in his eyes. Flinging the water cooler across the room, he grabbed a towel and stalked out of the building, getting into his car. Proceeding to slam his foot down on the accelerator while in reverse, he crashed into the only car in the parking lot, Joes, and then sped off. With his eyes burning red and inflamed like the fires from hell, he could just barely make out that another car was coming toward him in the opposite direction. It was a police car, and in his rage, he directed his car directly into the path of the policeman's and accelerated so that they were barely fifty feet apart. They were going to collide head on! At the last second, the police car swerved into a ditch that ran along the side of the road, crashing into a fence that ran adjacent to the road. Looking in his rearview mirror, the devil roared with laughter while driving away. He would be back.

Stan McCormick could hardly believe what had just happened to him. On route to talk with the owner of Dinkin's exterminator service, he had just been run off the road, by what appeared to be a man covered in red paint deliberately attempting to crash head-on into his police car!

He got out of his car and inspected the damage. The front of his car was buckled inward from the crash, spewing radiator fluid through the grille with steam pouring out from the hood. Stan McCormick shook his head. What else was going to happen to him? He got on the police radio, let dispatch know that he would need a tow truck, and that he would be at Dinkin's Exterminators when they arrived. It was a half a mile farther up the road. Shaking his head from side to side, he began the walk up the dirt road. After a short walk, he got to the parking lot and found a car with a smashed in driver's side door while the front door to the office was wide open with red paint visible everywhere. He had a pretty good hunch that the same man that had just run him off the road was also responsible for this mayhem. A path of red paint drops and splotches led him to the front door of the office. Cautiously he began to make his way to the open door. Approaching the office, he heard what sounded like a man moaning in pain. Pulling out his revolver, he found Joe in one of the back offices holding his crotch in a fetal position, lying on the floor in the middle of a completely smashed office that reeked of skunk. For once this day, he thought, he wasn't the unluckiest son of a bitch on the planet.

Dropping down from his blind hidden in the trees, Mick hurried to his car and drove over to the front of the office. It was time to see his boss and meet the police. When he arrived, his boss Joe was sitting up in his chair and drinking some water he had gotten from the bathroom faucet. He had a dazed, hurt, and confused look on his face. The policeman had a note pad out and was questioning him, as far as he could tell. Joe appeared lost and a bit bewildered, but had stopped sweating as profusely as opposed to a few minutes prior when he was in a state of panic after having been attacked by the unknown assailant. Mick walked into the office and announced himself with a bellowing loud "Morning Joe..." The police officer, already tense, jumped up from the chair where he was sitting, while Joe having heard his employee Mick's voice thousands of times, merely shook his head and exhaled out a long breath. Stan had drawn his gun from his holster looking about as twitchy as a rattlesnake facing a mongoose. Mick, playing the good old boy, and knowing he needed an edge to get on the policeman's good side played the fool, and yowled like a hurt dog and hit the ground as though he had already been shot and covered his head with his hands. He wanted him to believe that he hadn't seen anything and just happened to come into the office.

"It's OK officer he works for me," Joe said.

Realizing it was merely an employee of Dinkin's, he put his gun back in his holster and wiped the sweat away from his brow with his handkerchief, sighing heavily. It had been a long few days.

"What in tarnation is going on Joe? I came to talk to you about my last assignment and . . ." then pausing and curiously looking at his boss, "what the hell happened to you?"

"Listen Mick we got big problems. Somebody just came in here, asking for YOUR personnel files, and nearly castrated me when I didn't give him what he wanted fast enough. As you can see, he tore through this office, and then I don't know what happened. Honestly, other than getting my dick nearly yanked off and being thrown across the room, I am not sure what or who that guy was. He had some government credentials and asked to speak with me. You know anything about this?"

"Well, actually, that is what I came here to talk to you about as I have had a mighty strange time of it ever since you assigned me to that case of the woman with the cockroaches last Friday."

At this point Stan's ears perked up like a dog listening to a whistle. Here was the break in the case he was looking for.

"So, I go over to that house you tell me to go to, but only I see Roy's police car at the house next door and got confused on what house to go to. I mean you know how I am. So, I go there to see what Roy is up to. I call out if anybody is home, get no answer, and start feeling kind of funny about the place. Well, anyways, I get into the house and call out again but don't hear anything. But just prior to that I think I see somebody peering out from behind a window curtain in the upstairs bedroom. So, I got my work order on my clip board and walk down the hallway and see a bathroom, and decide to relieve myself, and I'll be goddamn if

Roy isn't sitting in the bathtub half eaten and covered in fucken ants! I'm speechless, drop my clipboard and I actually see the little bastards turn towards me and come after me. That is when I got stung up and down my legs and ran out of the house."

Pulling up his pants legs and showing off all of the white pustules that covered his legs from the stings he continued with his story.

"I got to my car, suited up for battle, and after a few minutes decided I had to go back in to see if I could save what was left of Roy. When I got back inside the house, they dropped on me like white on rice, and somehow found the unprotected part of the suit around my neck. Well, that's when I proceeded to take those sons of bitches down and killed them all. But unfortunately, you see I could only kill them with the flame mechanism turned on and so ended up burning the house down as well. After I left the house, I called up Sally who let me know that I had gone to the wrong house, which was just across the street, but thankfully she let me know that Edith Baxter, the town snoop, had witnessed everything."

At this point Mick stopped and pulled out a cigarette, lit it up, and pulled on it long and hard. He offered one to his boss and the police officer. Both of their jaws were wide open in disbelief from the story he had just related and sat staring at him. Joe accepted the cigarette while Stan with an unnerving look declined it, although at that moment he really did want one.

"What are you fucking saying, Roy is dead, and ants attacked you!" his boss yelled.

"Yep, that's what I said."

"You went to the wrong house and burnt it down!"

"Yep, that's what I said."

"Ants looked at you and attacked you?"

"Yep, that's what I said."

"How the hell do you think I am going to believe this horseshit of yours! Are you on drugs?"

Mick took a long drag from his cigarette and looked his boss straight in the eyes.

"Well, that is a good question, but seeing as how you are nearly a crippled eunuch from some unknown person who was requesting my files and easily accessed the office, I am kind of wondering what you are thinking happened?"

Now, Mick knew he had their attention as both of them knew he had a valid point. Furthermore, he could see the bewildered faces of Stan and Joe and could almost literally hear their brains racing for answers. This is where he decided to enlighten them on a little bit more of the story. He knew he had to do this right and take it slow, or else his ass was going to be the one that ended up in the pokey paying for all this mayhem. So, he took a long drag on his cigarette, thought hard about how he was going to relay the story, and scratched his head, acting the country bumpkin as much as he could. He knew enough to leave out certain details about what happened the night before especially since he knew the old biddy was dead and Stan didn't know that he knew that. He surmised that the two of them were as incredulous as he was of the events of the last forty-eight hours and were hanging on his every breath for an explanation. He continued with his story.

"So, here's where it really gets kind of weird. I called Sally and asked for her help with the old woman across the street and she agreed to meet me there. We talked with her, and you are not going to believe this, but she took pictures of what happened, and saw the guy who I saw as well in the window when I first arrived! I believe it is the same man that just yanked on your dick."

Unbeknownst to Stan, but deftly realized by Mick, a grin reached across his face as the news hit him like a thunderbolt. He had someone and the first clear evidence of another suspect besides an exterminator doing his job. It was the man who had run him off the road that was covered in red paint. Mick was watching his words and working hard to make this possible.

"In any case, we thanked her and let her know we could get the prints developed and I have them right here. The only problem is that the photos with the man in the window seem to be blurry for some reason. But we got a partial license plate number."

Stan's grin tightened into a scowl. Mick produced the photographs from his hunting jacket and dropped them on the desk with as much nonchalance as he could. Stan scooped them up immediately and began going through them while Mick continued to tell his story.

"So, then I go back to my house later that evening and start examining one of the ants that attacked me, since they hurt me awful bad, and I realize the bastard is still alive even though he has been partially squashed and stuck in a crown velvet bottle for six hours! After examining it, I find it is an unknown species that has never been documented before and is actually following my eye movements! I just didn't know what to make of it, but I suspect that somehow this is a genetically modified species, that was somehow under the control of the man, and that he had them attack me and Roy. I know it sounds hard to believe but I think the devil is at work here somehow, God help us all."

Both of them were looking at him with a sense of dumbstruck awe and stupefied amazement. They could not understand if this was for real, or he was telling them the biggest cockamamie jackass story to ever be told. And just who was this backward hillbilly, with supposed stunningly insightful theological observations, and scientifically accurate entomological knowledge and observations. It was really too incredible to believe! Mick continued on with his story for the next hour going over his plan of attack against the man at the office. He told them how the red paint was designed to fall over him and how he rigged the dart connected to the tracking device which drove its way into his chest, how he had placed the crosses in the closets and the salt water in the water cooler. He talked about how he and Sally had gotten the whole story from the neighbor in depth, going back over almost every detail, except some of the more embarrassing moments, and of how he managed to find Roy and destroy the ants, and finally escape the house. They also learned about his special poison he had been working on in secret for years.

Meanwhile, Stan was attempting to corroborate with his headquarters about what phone calls had been made and preparing to get the photographs to a specialist to be examined for a closer inspection. He didn't want to believe it, but his recent experiences were as unsettling as the story he was being told. Stan didn't know whether to believe him or arrest him until Mick pulled out his global positioning monitor from his pocket and locked on to the red man's coordinates. The tracking device was working. Stan jumped up from his seat and grabbed it. His location was off the main highway in the back mountains, behind an old quarry and silver mining town which had been deserted for over forty years.

Stan wanted to believe him, but the story was just too far-fetched and interspersed with theology. After Mick had stopped talking for a while and seemed to have finished, Stan stood up and announced that he was under arrest for the suspicion of arson and murder. Stan knew that a bunch of what Mick had said corroborated with the crime scenes, but also knew that he had a legal system that was looking for an arrest, and not some crazy devil spiced story involving mutant ants. He figured this would at least give him enough time to unravel the story being told and also would allow him a more thorough questioning of him at the police station with others present.

As he began reading his Miranda rights to Mick, he felt a certain uneasiness inside of him, which continued to mount. The room was charged with a static-like electricity, that was coupled with an irritating humming noise, becoming louder every second. Stan, confused over what was happening, continued to read Mick his rights. Mick, also sensing something was amiss, looked at the tracking device, but he needn't have bothered. Five feet from them, standing outside the large window with an angry paint reddened face, was the devil man with a smug evil looking grin upon his face. Driving his hand into his coat pocket, Mick pulled out a pair of hunting earplugs and shoved them in as fast as he could. Stan, a bit bewildered by the furious activity in front of him, stopped his recitation of the law and glanced over his shoulder to where Mick was staring. As he did so, he had just enough time to see the man who had tried to run him off the road earlier that morning dodge away from the window and head back toward the front of the building. The calm in the room was shattered by Joe screaming at the top of his lungs.

Looking around the room, they knew they were in trouble. By the thousands, ants were pouring into the room. Through openings under the doors, and by way of air ducts and grates in the walls, and in places that no one even knew were openings, ants were converging upon them, coming into the room in swarms. Joe had been the first one to be stung, and was holding his leg, while attempting to knock off and kill the ants that were viciously attacking him. Mick realized that the buzzing, that had preempted the attack, had dulled their other senses. This gave the ants the advantage of the element of surprise, and coupled with poisonous stings, was a deadly combination. Stan was stamping up and down trying to kill any of them that came under the door, but it was only a matter of time before the ones emerging in rapid succession from the grates up at the top of the wall reached them.

Mick grabbed Stan's gun from his holster, swiveled on his heels toward the large window in the office, firing all six rounds through the double paned window while simultaneously trying to swat away the ants that were converging upon him as well. He could feel the stings on his back and neck as they were dropping from the ceiling onto his head, neck and shoulders. Grabbing the chair, from where he had been sitting a few seconds prior while being arrested, he ran at the window and heaved it through the bullet ridden glass. Glass shattered in every direction, striking them with its spray, but also giving them a clear way out of the ant infested room. Leaping through the large, jagged hole in the window, Mick was free, he immediately began running toward the front of the building. Joe, having completely forgotten his injured genitals, leaped through the window and tried to somersault at the end of his dive, but ended up hitting his head on the ground, and stunned himself, as he lay sprawled on the ground. Stan was the last one out of the window, screaming in pain from ants that covered his feet, legs and hands. Madly he brushed the ants off of him and helped Joe to his feet as they fled away from the building as fast as they could. With Stan supporting Joe, they partially walked and ran toward the parking lot. Arriving at the front of the building, they heard the screeching of tires, while they watched the tail end of the black car speed away into the distance. Mick had jumped into his truck and started after him. Out of his passenger window Mick hurled Stan's gun toward him. It landed in the rocks and dust of the parking lot skidding to a stop at his feet.

"No hard feelings Stan, but here's your gun back. You can read me my rights later. I'm going after that bastard."

Far off in the distance Mick could see the plumes of dust as the black car sped down the road. Within a few minutes he had lost sight of the other car. At the main road, he slowed down to a stop and made the decision to go back to his house and regroup for the coming battle. He didn't remember the drive home. His mind was a jumble of thoughts and images that jumped about in his head. Without even realizing it he had poured himself a crown velvet and coke and was trying to make sense of what had just happened. He had fully expected that the dark-haired man was going to show up at his workplace when he sprung his trap, but he really could not believe that after being wounded, no less with an animal tranquilizer that could take down an elephant, and having paint dumped all over him that he would return so quickly and try to finish off the three of them. This man beast, or whatever he really was, was extremely powerful, resilient and dangerous, almost like the ants he controlled. He was in a battle with an unknown assailant who controlled a genetically mutated species of ant that technically could be classified as a voracious stinging poisonous predator. Furthermore, he had been seconds away from being arrested by a sheriff from one county over while his boss had just gotten his proverbial ass beat. He couldn't help but smile at that comeuppance as he finished off his drink. It served the pecker head right for sending him out on a Friday evening. The more he thought about it, with his background in religious studies, he believed he knew what he was up against. The man was either the devil himself or some sort of spawn of the beast!

He breathed a sigh of relief as he pulled into the driveway. He noticed that Sally's car was parked at the side of the yard, near his low hanging apple tree. As he exited his car, he expected to hear his dogs bark, but the house was quiet. Not hearing them bark made him cautious. He approached the front door as silently as he could. Peeking in the front window, he realized why his dogs hadn't barked. Curled up on his sofa was Sally and his two dogs, Clover the Border collie and Jerry his German Shephard. He entered the house and lazily Clover stretched and jumped down from the couch to greet him. Jerry soon followed and Sally awoke as well. Rubbing her eyes, he could tell she was having a hard time waking up, but her eyes quickly adjusted as she noticed the bruises and cuts on him and the look of concern across his face.

"What happened?" Sally whispered breathlessly.

"Well, where do I start Miss Sally? I arrived at the office well before midnight and got ready for that bastard to come looking for me. I gussied up the office a bit with some holy water, crosses and some other fine things that a man such as him I knew would not like, and then I waited. I went across the street into the tree line just outside the parking lot and got into a tree stand I made and situated myself real comfortable, sat back and watched. Joe arrived early, and later so did the black-haired man that we saw in the photograph, and who I saw in the window. I was looking through my binoculars, and after Joe lets him into the building, he proceeds to just about rip off Joe's balls and dick and ask where he keeps the employee files."

By now Sally was wide awake.

"So, Joe lets him know where the file cabinet is with the records, but I have a little surprise waiting for this yahoo character. As he opens the file cabinet, which I had wedged shut so tight that he would have to pull on it real hard, which he does, a tranquilizing dart flies right into his chest pushing him back about five feet and a can of fire engine red paint is then triggered, and dumps from the ceiling covering him from head to toe. Joe is grabbing at his crotch still rolling on the ground moaning and almost damn near twitching from the pain, but I can tell is watching in amazement as all of this is happening. From within the office, I can hear the type of sound of a wounded animal makes, like a wolf or coyote being shot with an arrow. Looking for something to clean himself off with, he turns to the water cooler, which I have filled with a bunch of salt, and as he pours it on himself, he begins howling again from the salt going into his eyes. At this point I swear he turns his head in my direction and he rushes out of the building, gets into his car and takes off as fast as he can down the road."

"Oh my God I can't believe it!"

"Now just wait little sister while I tell you the best part. This bastard comes back to kill us all!"

Mick continued on with the story of the policeman getting run off the road, his imminent arrest, and then the reappearance of the man returning and the ants swarming from every possible crevice and opening that existed within Joe's office. While he relayed the phantasmagorical story, Sally felt herself ensnared within some sort of surreal dream. Finishing up the morning's hectic events, he walked over to the kitchen and started brewing a pot of his favorite Kona coffee. He had a lot of work to do.

"Sally, I am going to need your help."

"What don't you need is my question to you?" her eyes narrowing as she spoke.

With a bit of a slow grin that slowly spread across his face, he smiled at her in the knowledge that he agreed with her understanding of the situation.

"Well Sally, I agree with you, but remember this all started with you calling me on my Friday afternoon and asking me to do the company a favor, because some other exterminator would not do his job. If it weren't for you, I would not be getting charged with multiple murders, and a litany of other charges, including arson and probably resisting arrest. Let's not even mention that I am being hunted by some type of devil man that can control a genetic mutation of fire ants that kill! Furthermore, I may be a country boy, but I am pretty sure he is aware of you by now and probably you are on his hit list as well, so I think we had better work together on a plan to save ourselves. What do you think?"

Pacing back in forth in the kitchen, she was listening to what he said as well as how he said it. She was stressed out and having a hard time not showing it.

"You are such a jackass, Mick. If you hadn't gone to the wrong house in the first place and burnt it up while jacking off, I wouldn't even be here. So honestly go fuck yourself."

The amazing point of truth was told.

"Valid point Missy, and I just might later when I'm not so busy, but somebody was going to find Roy all eaten up in that bathtub and just maybe it was fate that a man with an expertise in killing bugs was there to find him. Did you ever think about that?"

The salvo had been detailed. The questions as to what the hell was going on were quite unknown. Reaching up into his cabinets, he grabbed the sugar bowl and then proceeded to pour them each a cup of coffee. Grabbing the milk from the refrigerator and the sugar he made his way into the living room.

"What are we going to do?" she almost pleadingly asked him.

"I think we need to study these ants and maybe I can find out how they are controlled. I have studied these insects for a good portion of my life and am interested about how these particular ones became so hardy and resistant.

"Jesus Christ Mick, I'm scared. I mean, now that I have had some time to think about all of what has happened in the last few days, I know now that whoever that guy is, he wants both of us dead. Why don't we just get in my car and just drive away as far we can or let the police handle it."

Mick raised an eyebrow and replied with a look that let her know he had been thinking about this already.

"Because he will be looking for us until this is finished one way or the other. Do you think that if you shoot a man with an animal tranquilizer and dump red paint all over his body, after he has already admittedly killed two people, that he will not be looking for you, and he is the goddamn devil? I think he is one angry fallen angel, devil or bastard, maybe from a one-eyed cyclops as far as I know, and he will never stop hunting us down."

Sally quickly darted her eyes away from his because she did not want him to see the uneven smile on her lips. Even with his twisted logic, and way of thinking, she somehow knew he was right. Mick was about to speak, but the loudest crash of thunder they had ever heard split across the air and made the dogs bark and howl in scared agonizing yelps. The air surged with energy and seemed to crackle with electricity. The both of them jumped up off the couch. Racing to the sliding door at the rear of the living room he could see that the afternoon, which had been clear and cloudless, had suddenly and threateningly turned dark and black with monstrous dark cumulous clouds. Seconds later humongous rain drops the size of quarters began to splatter upon the ground. The deluge of hail and rain that followed for the next few hours halted any talk of traveling or fleeing anywhere for the time being.

Chapter Eight

The Red Man Seeks Revenge

Sitting on the curb that separated the parking lot from the front steps of the building, he began examining his gun which had been thrown at his feet. He wasn't in a good mood. In fact, he felt down right pissed off and a bit ashamed. The physical bruises from jumping out the window and stings from the ants were one thing, but really it was his psyche which had taken the biggest hit. He had had his car smashed due to a scofflaw. He thought he had solved a crime and found Roy's killer, and was seconds away from arresting the perpetrator, only to find himself being attacked from all sides by some mutant variation of fire ants. He had been laughed at by a man covered in red paint who had tried to kill him twice, once by the ants he controlled and also when he ran him off the road (this lack of respect for the law was really bristling his hide). Then to top off the morning, he had his gun thrown at him, like he was some sort of dog, by the man he had assumed earlier was the killer, and ironically had ended up saving all of their lives! He shook his head and tried to make sense of the complex murder investigation he was enmeshed within. Everything had been normal just prior to when he received the call from the neighboring county to investigate a common everyday house fire. Now his life was upside down and topsy-turvy.

With a toothpick he found lying on the ground, he began wedging out the grains of sand from within the gun's chamber. He was all alone in the parking lot and kept looking around to see if there were any signs of the ants returning. He knew he wasn't going back in that building. Joe, the manager who had been complaining that he thought one of his testicles was crushed, had left in his dented car and driven himself to the hospital. Meanwhile, he had chosen to wait for police backup. Unloading the bullets, he tried pulling the trigger. It didn't work. The gun was still jammed up with dirt and sand. He tried to concentrate on cleaning his gun, but it was hard for him. No longer were his two prime suspects in cages, although the cats were still down at the station.

Mick had told him the craziest story in his twenty years in law enforcement, but he somehow believed him. With his own eyes, he had seen the ants converge upon them, attack, and try to sting and bite them to death. He had seen the evidence in action. He had seen Roy's half picked over skeletal remains and the woman killed by her pussy cats. All signs pointed to the fact that there was something more afoot with this investigation than just usual police work.

He really did not want to believe it, but deep down inside, he was frightened. Frightened because he had never felt this way with any case he had ever investigated in his life. It was a new feeling to him, and he wondered if this is how death appeared to victims, before it happened. It had always been different before this case, but now he was uneasy. It was natural to be nervous or scared before taking down a fugitive, or being involved in a gunfight, but this was a different kind of feeling. On previous cases, he had always known what he was up against, but that had changed as of today. How could someone fight ants when there were millions of them that could attack at any given time? How were they being controlled to attack and, most importantly, who or what was that raving lunatic that had run him off the road and had come back to finish him off? He wanted answers to all these questions, and he had none. He would have to admit to the exterminator that he was wrong, but that minor point wasn't going to stop him from asking an awful lot more questions of him. Far off in the distance he could hear the faint sound of a siren wailing, and he breathed a sigh of relief. Finally, he thought, it would be good to see someone else in law enforcement.

As the police car approached him, he anxiously peered toward it to see if he knew the officer that was coming to pick him up or any other sign of familiarity. The car pulled up alongside of him. He stood up from the sidewalk and sauntered over to the car. The passenger side window was rolled down and the officer inside spoke.

"Hello there, I'm Lieutenant Jones with the state police. You look like you've had a rough go of it. Are you in need of medical attention?" he asked.

"No, I'm alright. I am just a little banged up from today's little adventure. Can you get me back into town and call out a tow truck for my vehicle? You are not going to believe what I have been through."

"Yeah, sure I can, hop in the car and I will call dispatch and get someone out here to pick up your car. If you need any medicine or first aid, it is in the glove box."

The voice reverberated in the air, coming from all directions. He continued.

"Yeah, I understand. I have had days like the one you are having, and I always try to forget them with a couple of stiff drinks later in the evening."

"Yeah, I need one about right now." he said.

He felt a bit reassured that he was going to get a drink in the evening after this ordeal was all over. Pausing a second he continued on.

"It's funny but I don't ever remember seeing your name on the state police list. Are you new?"

"Yep, I sure am. I just got reassigned to this area. It sure has been quiet up until the last day or so!"

Stan opened the passenger side door and got in. He could feel himself immediately relax and a deep sigh of relief made its way through the car, but goddamn did it smell like skunk! Glancing over at the lieutenant who had his cap down low over his head, he couldn't see much of his face as the sun was directly east of him, but the thought occurred to him that he looked awful sunburned. Closing the car door, he looked back at the building and saw ants pouring out of the building and from holes within the earth. He felt his adrenaline shoot up and he became almost frantic.

"Look at that! Jesus H Christ do you see them all! Oh my God . . . Let's get the hell out of here. They are coming straight towards us!" he bellowed out in his policeman's voice.

As he said this, he could see thousands of ants swiftly moving in unison across the ground in a massive black and maroon tidal wave of motion. He was scared beyond his worst nightmares after his last encounter and seeing what they had done to Roy. He turned to yell at his partner to get moving and his heart dropped in his chest. He heard the car doors lock shut at the same time that he got the first good look at the lieutenant's face. It was the man who had run him off the road! His face wasn't sunburned but rather red . . . from the paint that had been dropped over him. He could hear the laughter again just as he felt a sharp pain in his leg. Jerking his eyes downward to the spot of the pain, he realized even before he had seen it, that he had just been stuck with a needle.

A feeling of warmth started spreading from the point of the needles contact. He knew he had been drugged but who knew with what? He could hear screaming but was not even aware that he was the one making the noise. With one eye watching the ants getting closer to the car, and the other trying to see what the man in the driver's side of the car was doing, he frantically tried to pull open the latch on the door and escape. Things were getting blurry. His days of a civic call to duty with an English muffin, cup of Joe, and an easy beat around the burbs was coming to an abrupt end. The terror he felt was dizzying when mixed with the drugs he was feeling inside of his body. All of his struggles to fight the drug were useless. He was starting to feel lightheaded and sleepy from the tranquilizer. It was as if he was starring in a horror movie screaming (which he still was and did not know it), but not really there, like in the projectionist's box, looking down upon himself. He was above himself and not with himself. He was floating free of himself; even as he realized that for the first time in his life, he was the helpless victim. He was caught in the spider's web. The prey trapped by a web of treachery and drugs. Within a few more seconds, he began falling into unconsciousness as they whipped down the highway toward the deserted quarry which lay on the outskirts of town.

His hand tingled. Where was he, he thought? It was dark and damp. He couldn't seem to move although he wasn't in any immediate discomfort. He was strapped to something, and he could feel restraints around his ankles, wrists, and across his chest. It was really dark, and he could feel his hand tingling. Where was he and why was he tied down? He tried to remember what had happened to him but was having a hard time thinking of anything. What was wrong with him? It was cold and he shivered. He tried to adjust his eyes to the dark. What was he looking at? It was pitch black, but it appeared he was looking at rocks of some sort. Maybe he fell and hit his head and had amnesia, he thought. Why couldn't he remember? Who was he? Yes, he should concentrate on that and then he could track back his loss of memory. Oh, that damn tingling on his hand was getting worse. He wished he could scratch it. Why was he tied down and in the dark, he thought? Had he done something wrong, so that he was in solitary confinement or in a dungeon? What had happened to cause him to be in this situation? Maybe I should cry out, but wait he thought, that might be unsafe. He tried moving his lips and found it hard to speak. Both his mouth and lips were dry. He cleared his parched throat and managed to get out a gritty hello, which barely seemed to echo back at him. Well, that confirms it, I am in some sort of cave. God, I could use a drink of water, he thought. And where the hell am I, was his next thought. And within those two wandering thoughts, his inner dialog had inadvertently bespoke of the dire plight he currently faced between God and the devil.

He wanted to scratch his hand with a passion, since it felt like he had stumbled into some poison ivy. Moving his head to the right he could barely make out something attached to his wrist above his right hand. His eyes were finally adjusting to the darkness, and he could just make out that he was strapped to a long board which lay on top of a table. He must try and remember who he was, that was his primary concern. Why can't I remember? Why am I here? And why does my hand itch, and what is that dull ache in my leg? That is new, he thought, why does my leg hurt, like I have received a flu shot? He could feel that whatever sedatives he was under were wearing off. That was it! He had been stabbed in the leg by that madman, and he was a policeman! Immediately a black fear crept into his mind. The last thing he remembered was looking at the ants pouring out of the building and seeing the man's red face. He was beginning to put the pieces back together and he began struggling against the bonds that held him tightly to the table. The itching in his hand was beginning to turn painful. Straining to see what was around him, he was able to focus on his right hand. There was some sort of glass jar attached to his wrist. What is this thing, he thought, as the pain increased within his hand? What was happening to him he wondered and then he remembered the ants? The ANTS! They were inside of the jar and eating the flesh off of his right hand! He began realizing what was happening.

In abject terror, his screaming reverberated off the walls of the quarry he was entombed within. Now that his eyes had adjusted to the dark, he could see that his right wrist had been sealed off from his hand, almost as if with a tourniquet of some sort. Raising his fingers within the jar, he saw what looked like the hand of a skeleton attached to his body. Within the confines of the cavern, his sobbing echoed against the walls, like the laughter of the devil.

Chapter Nine

Texas Showdown

The ant that had struggled to live within the crown velvet bottle was finally showing signs of dying. It dragged itself about the petri dish that lay on the examination table in the basement of his house. This was an incredibly tough species, he thought. The ant was missing both antennae and three legs to the fire, but still was looking for some way out of the predicament it found itself in. Using a pen knife and tweezers, he held him down, and sliced off his head. The head bobbled around the petri dish. For a few more moments, the body continued to involuntarily squirm and wiggle about, but that was completely normal. Using a high-powered microscope, he began to examine the pieces of the dead fire ant. Having Sally around helped him immensely. As he talked, she would take down the notes, which saved him a lot of time and effort. He began by examining the head.

"Very large head with protruding eyes and two very large pincers. Perhaps forty millimeters apart."

"Reddish black coloring, with dimpled spots along the skin, across all regions of the body."

"Unlike any other fire ant seen alive in this era or time period."

"It has an extremely large body of almost an inch in length."

"Protruded eyes and abnormally large for the species."

He sat back from the microscope and leaned back in his chair. The florescent lights in the basement kept flickering on and off and between the lightning flashes. There were instances when the lights went out and only the lightning illuminated the room. He could hear the rain hitting the roof and the pitter pattering on the ground outside of the windows.

As the thunder boomed, he thought of the ancient ants from the distant past that in some instances were as big as hummingbirds. That was nearly ninety million years ago in the time of the Cretaceous period. He remembered when he had seen one in a museum, which had been preserved in amber for all of eternity, as he listened to the thunder booming in the background. Had this man somehow gotten hold of some ancient DNA from these extinct ants and created a modern-day nightmare? From where the antennae should have been to the end of the abdomen the ant was almost an inch long. He looked at the stings that had been inflicted upon him, the pustules starting to develop. The lights flickered off again and the lightning flashed. He looked upwards from his thoughts and found Sally's eyes, like green amethysts flashing out at him. He knew she was worried and scared. Getting up from his chair, he walked over to her and put his arms around her as the rain continued to pound all around them. He heard her whisper to him.

"Let's get out of here. He will know where you and I are, and it will give us some time to make a plan rather than sitting here waiting for him to show up."

Mick, still holding her, thought about what she said. It actually made sense to leave the premises and get a good dinner.

"Sally, I guess you have a point there. Let's get out of here, and make sure we get the jump on him, as opposed to him trapping us here. Why don't you get your stuff together, and we can find a place along the highway to stop and grab some chow. Maybe we can even find a place to stay this evening?"

Letting go of her, she kept smiling, gazing up at him, with the lightning flashes distorting her face. He got a weird feeling that she was somehow attracted to him with her head bent upwards into his. He suddenly felt a strong attraction to her. Was she was emitting signals to him or was he just imagining things? Had her bosoms become erect against him? He shook it off and tried to remember what he needed to bring for the trip as he began packing for their departure into the night.

She slipped a blanket over her shoulders and her purse around her arm and could not stop thinking about what had just happened. She thought of her boyfriend and how the attraction between them had gotten stale and boring. Really, they just used each other to gratify themselves, and weren't going anywhere and fast. Checking her phone, she realized that he had not even tried calling her. Well, that was it, she thought, I guess it came down to that old one liner, "I love you, but I am just not in love with you." It seemed to sum up her whole life and all of her past relationships as well. It was either her letting go of a boyfriend or lover or someone else letting her go. She never knew she held these feelings for him, or lack thereof, until she had been secretly drawn toward Mick and his hillbilly charm within the past couple of days. He had been a consummate gentleman in hillbilly gear locked within his own crazy caged mind. He was laughable in a peculiar sort of way. He compensated for his clumsy ways by charging into a cobweb like a bear and then trying to tiptoe his way back out of the sticky situations he found himself wrapped up in. It was comical but also adorable. In other ways, he was crafty and deliberate in his methods and deeds he accomplished, like in the morning when he set a trap and ambushed the devil.

"Come on, we had better get moving. I don't want to see that guy again for a while."

Grabbing his waterproof camouflage jacket, they headed out into the driving rain, and made a break for the truck. He had the GPS tracking device with him, his bow, a hunting rifle, bowie knife and an extra tank of poison in case he met up with those ants or their agent again. He stowed them behind the front seats of the truck and kept looking around to see if anyone was around. He didn't know it at the time, but their decision to leave was quite timely.

The devil was thirty miles away from them, driving furiously through the rain, and coming to kill them both. He had quickly realized that a GPS device had been implanted within him when he had examined the wound to his chest. He had subsequently duct taped it to the policeman's head, who was bound, gagged and unconscious from the drugs, deep within the depths of an abandoned mineshaft within the quarry. He knew this would keep the exterminator from knowing where he was located, and therefore he would be taken off guard, much like the trick that had been played upon him in the morning. Smiling with pure delight, he was looking forward to the payback he would inflict upon him for the pain and embarrassment he had suffered at the hands of this idiot. So, intent upon reaching Mick's house in the driving rain, he failed to realize the truck going in the opposite direction with them in it.

The driving rain and buildup of water on the highway kept them from going any faster than forty miles an hour and seeing as it was about fifteen miles to the nearest town, Sally felt that she could relax a bit. Thinking that she might be able to get a small nap she leaned her head against the truck's window pane until her thoughts were interrupted by Mick.

"Do you know what the difference is between humans and ants, Miss Sally?"

Knowing he was not looking for an answer, she continued to look out into the rain swept prairie land with its gray and brown grasses blowing in the wind.

"Well, let me tell you the difference. First an ant doesn't think like an individual because it can't. It can't think for itself. It is either a soldier, a worker, or in some instances a drone. They are born into a caste system that is something on the order of Huxley's Brave New World. They lead their lives like they were in George Orwell's Animal Farm, but only on more strict and rigid terms, when it comes to their duties. Everything they do is based around the propagation of their species. The queen ant lays the eggs and some of the workers care for the larvae. Others build the nests. Others make underground farms while still others forage for food. Day in and day out they work and follow. Work and follow. If one of them breaks the chain when it comes to looking for food, they get confused. They are continually touching each other's antennae to get the message either backwards or forwards in the chain of command loop. All of our different units of the military envy them for the way in which they follow orders without question. Does this all make sense, Miss Sally?"

Again, she knew he was not looking for a reply, stretched a bit and yawned, enjoying the heat from the air vents blowing into the cabin.

"So, if you look at the collective psychology of an ant's mind, it is truly 'all for one and one for all.' If one of them is flattened, they pick up their dead. When they gather food, you never see one ant eating on the job and taking back the leftovers. If the colony is attacked, they all take part in defending the nest and their queen. It is the queen that controls them all. They live for her and her alone. That is why there is only one queen per nest. Why it makes sense, Miss Sally. They are all her children or lovers, and she rules them with an iron fist. Nobody gets out of line or dreams of leaving the colony. The have a collective psyche like the Borg in the Star Trek series. They are not meant to function as an individual or in pairs, and in fact fail to function, unless their queen is alive giving the orders. Are you with me?"

After hearing the three references he had just made to Star Trek, Animal Farm and Brave New World, she shot him a look that said, are you kidding me? He continued to talk seeing as he had her attention.

"Now hear me out Miss Sally as I am getting to something here. Let's just say we have a bigger problem than we think. Since we already know that at the two places I showed up in town, he had easy access to control and manipulate the ants close by the premises, let's just assume he has many more. Let's just say he has about five thousand colonies and at five million ants per colony, then we are roughly looking at billions of stinging, biting, flesh eating minions of his, that he directs at anyone or anything he desires. With the rate of reproduction of a typical queen at the rate of sixteen hundred per day per colony, and if allowed to continue unchecked, he could control the whole planet within a few years if he logistically set things up correctly, and I am assuming he probably already has a plan in place. Are you following me now, Miss Sally?"

With her eyes wide thinking about it and the repercussions of what he was saying, she snapped out of it when he ended the sentence again with Miss Sally and threw a left hook into his arm.

"Shut up with the Miss Sally shit and get to the point you bug freak."

Mick smiled as he knew he had finally gotten under her skin with the Miss Sally stuff. He felt better somehow that she was finally playing around with him after he got smacked in the arm.

"So, this is the dilemma we are facing. Luckily for us, I have thought about this for some time and believe I might just have a solution. If we can somehow kill the devil, then we eliminate our problem; or if we can kill the queens in their nests, we can destroy the chain of command to her workers. Killing one of something or five hundred of something is a lot easier than killing billions of something, especially at the rate that they reproduce. What do you think . . . Sally?"

Once again, he had surprised her with his logic. Her gaze rested on the side of his face as he continued to drive the truck and talk about how they could possibly accomplish the daunting task that lay before them. As he continued talking, it slowly dawned on her that she was having very strong feelings for him and that she just might be falling for exterminator 69 as the rain continued to streak down the windows of the truck.

The parking lot of the diner he pulled into was deserted. It was your typical standard rectangular building, with a long counter that faced the short order chefs, and booths along the window side of the building that faced the highway. Dashing from the truck into the diner only took a few seconds, but the rain still managed to wet them down. The waitress, a woman in her fifties with her hair pulled back in a ponytail, smiled at them as they entered the building.

"How are you all tonight folks? Sit wherever you would like," as she followed them to the farthest table away from the front entrance next to the windows.

"Would you like something to drink while you look at the menus?"

"Yeah coffee please," Mick said.

"And me as well," chimed in Sally.

The waitress left to go get their drinks. Sally pulled out the menus and handed him one. He just put it down on the table.

"I have come here so many times before, the waitress knows me and what I'm ordering, the chicken fried steak with the mashed potatoes, brown gravy and peas. It is phenomenal."

The waitress reappeared with their coffees and took their order. Sally ordered the garden salad with grilled chicken on top and the vinaigrette dressing. Mick just looked at the waitress, smiled and nodded. She knew what he wanted and went to place their orders grateful to finally have some customers on this stormy night.

They were almost too tired to speak. When the food came, the smell of it revived them. They both ate as though they had not eaten in days. Between the coffee and the food, each of them began to feel much better, more alive and awake.

"So how do you think you can accomplish knocking off five hundred or so queens and still live to talk about it," Sally asked.

"That is a great point and I have been wondering that myself. First, I have to find out where exactly all their mounds are located, and then I need to try and ascertain how far down the queen is, since they are a genetic mutational ant species, and she could be a lot deeper down in the earth than a regular queen within a colony. If I can dig one up with a backhoe, I can get some kind of idea as to the depth of all of them."

The thought of Mick going after a queen ant with a backhoe while trying to fend off thousands of flesh-eating stinging ants struck her as madness. Then again, he was an exterminator. Mick continued on with his thoughts.

"I guess I can probably find the mound that is next to the office and dig that one up. I probably could do a little experiment with different poisons on them while I am there . . . Then again, maybe I should just drive down to the quarry and see what we can find out about this man. What do you think?"

Upon mentioning that he was possibly considering going to hunt him down at the quarry her eyes grew wide with fear.

"I am not going, absolutely not. You are not going to get me to chase after some spawn of Satan with you! You can just leave me off at your house. Really, why should we be trying to save the planet when we have law enforcement that should be taking care of this?"

"Well, I agree with you Sally. I don't want you to come along since it's too dangerous. And the police are bloody useless in my opinion. Just look at the one guy on the case who was going to arrest me, after I had shown him all the facts, and then had to save his ass! Why don't we go back to my house, and you can watch over the dogs if you don't mind, then I will just go check out the quarry, and I'll be back in a jiffy. The GPS System says he is still there."

Her lack of response was his answer. She was mentally exhausted, and felt in over her head, especially with all this devil stuff. After finishing up and paying the bill, they left the restaurant as the rain finally began to ease up. Mick, seemingly unbothered by the events swirling about them, turned up the radio and began singing to the country tunes that emanated from the speakers. He sang with gusto, and Sally really could not believe it, a bit annoyed.

"Are you for real, how can you be singing and be so happy after what you have just been through, and what is ahead of you. Are you out of your mind?"

"The devil's in the house of the rising sun, chicken in a bread pan pickin' out dough, granny does your dog bite? No child, no"

As the instrumental part of the song took over, he turned his head and grinned at her and kept singing, only this was his own made up melody she had never heard.

"I'm Gonna catch me a devil by the toe, wrap him up in cellophane and rain down on him blows. Teach him a lesson he will never forget. Drive him to his wasteland down below. Boot him out the door and let him go, so he'll drop off this land and fall below. Yee-haw!"

In his excitement, he stopped singing and spoke in excited earnestness.

"I want a piece of this bastard. All my life I have been afraid of this evil spirit, but not anymore, like I did a few days ago. He was always a figment of my imagination or in picture books or Bibles, but now he is real and fallible, just like us, and I swore to myself that if I ever got the chance to beat him, I would. If I die trying, at least I know I am going to heaven having fought the baddest, most wickedest, man ever. Does that make sense?"

The lyrics to the Charlie Daniels Band came back on the radio and he began singing again. His logic was so perverted, and backwards, that it actually was starting to make sense to her. I must be going crazy, she thought. As they began approaching his house, he began to get chills in his spine. He looked down at the GPS device and it still read that the raven-haired man was in the vicinity of the quarry, but he had an uneasy feeling like something was amiss. He decided to pull over on the opposite side of the road about two hundred feet from his house, and did so by driving his truck into the bushes out of sight of the main highway. He grabbed his pair of binoculars and zoomed in on his house and yard. He didn't see any cars about in his yard, and he began focusing on his house. Something was wrong, but he couldn't put his finger on what it was. The engine was turned off and the windows, from the combination of the cold outside and their breathing, were beginning to steam up the windows. He rolled down his window to get some air and that was when he heard them. His dogs were yowling at the top of their lungs while trapped inside the house. He recognized a low humming. He now knew that the demonic man was lying in wait for him, but just where he was hiding, was the question.

He couldn't necessarily trust his own dogs after witnessing what Edith Baxter's cats did to her, but maybe he could use them to try and spot him. Keeping his binoculars focused on the front window, he could see that they were running back and forth from the front window to the back-sliding glass door. He had an idea. From the dog's movements, he must be moving around, checking on the other side of the house. If he could get on the roof and put his back up against the chimney, he should be able to cover all the different angles below him. He grabbed the first aid kit out of the glove compartment and took out some ear plugs. Next, he got out his rifle and loaded it, checked on his hunting knife in its sheath, and attached it to his belt. He put on night vision goggles and slipped on his jacket. Grabbing a tank of bug poison from the back seat, he strapped it on. He motioned for Sally to roll down her window.

"What are you doing? Are you crazy? I don't' think you should be planning on going over there alone."

"Listen to me, the keys are in the ignition. I am going to get up on the roof. There is a ladder I left propped up against the side of the chimney, hidden by the apple tree, where I can make my way up to the roof. Use the binoculars and keep an eye out for anything strange. If you have to, drive out of here, if need be. Also, there is a handgun in the middle console of the truck that you can use to defend yourself. It's already loaded so be careful with it. I have to go."

Before she could stop him, he was across the street and making his way toward the house. He took a route through an adjacent field. She adjusted the binoculars to see how he was making his way up the roof. With the window partially down, she heard the dogs incessant barking. The gun lay silent in her hand. It was a small Smith and Wesson revolver that was as clean as the day was old. She had handled guns before at her father's farm, so it wasn't too big of a deal, and she liked the feel of it, but it felt cheap and an unworthy adversary for what she faced. Looking back over at the house, she could see that he was already on top of the roof and had his back up against the chimney.

From his vantage point he could see the black car about a quarter of a mile up the street hidden behind some creosote bushes and willow trees. He was a crafty bastard, he thought. He must be on the other side of the house, waiting for him to return home, or maybe he was hiding inside of the house. He wanted to peek over the lip of the roof which was about six feet away in a downward sloping direction.

With the wind swirling, and the rain still coming down in a steady torrent, he inched his way along the pitch of the roof. By the time he got to the other side, he was sweating from all the equipment he was carrying, and the slow laborious movements he had to make. His movements were like a turtle and just as awkward. Before he even looked over the side, he sensed he was near him. He could feel it. For all of his bravado he was scared shitless. With his night vision goggles on, he dared to poke his head over the edge of the roof. He wasn't there! Oh shit, where is he, he thought? Turning around he saw him. There he was, on the roof, and just a few feet from him! His heart jumped in his chest. He tried to get to his knife and had just enough time to remove it from its sheath before he felt a powerful blow knock him in the side of his head. It was a rock that clocked him in the head. He lunged with his knife to stop himself from falling. Luckily, he planted the hunting knife deep enough into the roof that he had gotten into the plywood below the shingles. But he was hanging on with one hand to the knife, his feet tenuously supported by the gutter, and the heavy canister tank weighing him down which was strapped to his back. The devil was making his way down the roof . . . drawing out a stiletto knife! The long thin silver needle like blade flashed in the night, as he struggled to keep his balance on the slippery roof. From the edge of the roof to the ground was about twenty feet, but Mick didn't feel he had any choice. With the stiletto flashing toward his face, he let go of the hunting knife.

Rocks, plants, and dirt shot backwards from the truck tires as she floored the accelerator. She had watched the whole thing unfold in front of her eyes. Mick had hit the ground awkwardly from the weight of the poison canister strapped to his back. His knee buckled underneath him, and he crumpled to the ground screaming in pain. The man on the roof, choosing not to jump after him, had made his way to the chimney at the far side of the roof and was starting to climb down the ladder. He would be there shortly. With her left hand on the steering wheel, and the gun clutched in her right, she sped toward the house. She smashed through the shrubs, and then stomped on the brakes skidding through the wet lawn, with Mick sprawled out in front of her, as one of the tires came to rest in the koi pond just inches away from him. She could just make out the man coming around the corner of the house. Startled to see her, he stopped in his tracks, with a look of surprised amazement on his face. The look of surprise soon changed to one of pure hate and then to one of pure evil and then astonishment. It was raining, but the direction of the water was coming upwards from the ground. The realization, stinging sensation, terror stricken frightening conclusion was that the exterminator had started spraying him with a stream of poison from where he lay injured on the ground!

"Aghhhh . . . you bastard" he roared, stumbling backwards back around the corner of the house and away from the stream of poison. His eyes and face felt like they were burning off. Barely able to see, he found a puddle that he was able to bathe his face in and wash the poison off.

Having almost run over Mick, who was lying on the ground just in front of his truck, Sally helped him to his feet. With one of his arms draped over her shoulder, she eased him gently into the passenger side of the truck. She nestled the poison canister between his legs and jumped in the other side, starting the engine. Out of the corner of her eye, she saw the black car approaching them at a high rate of speed. It was going to ram them! Somehow, he had managed to get back to his car. She stomped on the accelerator, crashing into the front porch so that the black car hit the back of the truck rather than the passenger side door saving Mick's life. The truck flipped up in the air before coming to rest on its roof, on top of the black sedans hood and rooftop, which was now wedged underneath the bed of the pickup truck. The pickup truck began rupturing fuel.

Sally, bleeding from a gash on her forehead, was upside down and in shock from the violent accident. Shattered glass was everywhere, and she wasn't sure what was happening, but someone was pulling her out of the truck through her window. Dragging her through the wet grass Mick propped her up against the trunk of the apple tree about thirty feet away from the accident. She didn't know what was going on but could sense some pressure being applied to her head. Mick had taken off his shirt and tied it around her head to try and stop the bleeding. She tried to focus her eyes and remember what had just happened. She could barely make out the scene before her or concentrate. She was suffering from a concussion, although she didn't realize it at the moment.

When the bed of the truck landed on the roof of the black sedan it wedged the car doors shut with over six thousand pounds of pressure. Frantically, the man inside the car was trying to open the car doors. Realizing it was useless endeavor, unless he got the weight of the truck off of his car, he tried putting the car in reverse and backing up. It was no use, he was stuck. The rainstorm had rendered the ground into mush and the tires just spun themselves into ditches. Sally and Mick could see him trying to climb his way into the back seat. He was going to attempt to go out the back window. Mick, pulling along his bad leg, was slowly making his way toward the scene of the accident. The devil in the back seat noticed him and became even more frantic in his efforts to kick out the back window. Grabbing his revolver and the poison from the truck, he pulled it along the ground until he was behind the rear window of the sedan. Their eyes locked.

"Ho, Ho, Ho and a Merry Christmas to you mother fucker. Does the little baby devil need some help with the window? Is it stucky-poo? Here, let me help you."

He opened the valve on the canister of poison, and with the remainder of the strength left in his body, heaved it through the back window, hitting him squarely in the face. Mick then limped away from the vehicle. The man in the car was still moving. His nose and mouth were gushing blood, although he was still trying to make his escape out the back window of the car. Mick turned and their eyes locked again. This

97

time when their eyes met, the devil for the first time looked uncertain with a tinge of fear in his eyes. Raising the revolver, he fired in rapid succession into the gas tank of the sedan. The first explosion was followed in rapid succession by two others. The sedan exploded in a ball of flame that blew the back axle off the car and propelled the car nearly forty feet off of the ground. The canister, filled with poison, moonshine and other combustible chemicals, flashed like a fireball within the inside of the car while the car was still rising in the air, and exploded like a supernova with shrapnel flying in all directions. Crashing back to earth, a third explosion went off as Mick's truck joined the conflagration in the front yard. Flames reached over fifty feet in the air. Sally instinctively had crawled behind the apple tree, shielding herself from the blistering heat from the multiple fires.

Mick lay flat on his back having been knocked off his feet from the shock wave of the first explosion. With his head raised just a few inches off the ground, he had seen the man struggling in the back of the car as the flames were burning him alive, that is, until the canister exploded. Afterwards, there was no other movement, except the flames consuming the interior of the vehicle. The next thing he knew his German Shepard was licking his face. Glancing at the house, which was on fire in multiple places, he saw that the windows of his house were shattered and blown out from the explosions. And then his dog ran off toward the street. Turning his head, he could see his neighbor Billy running up to the yard.

"Holy cow Mick! Are you all right, what's going on?"

"Yeah, Billy I'm just barely surviving, but I do have one whopper of a yarn to tell you later. Can you help me to my feet?"

Stretching out his arm, Billy helped him to his feet. He could tell that his knee was in bad shape. He must have sprained it jumping off the roof.

"What happened? Is anybody dead? Is that Sally over there?" Billy asked in bewilderment.

Not knowing what to say, even to his friend Billy, he just spoke what came to his mind. "There was a guy, no, maybe a demon, in the back of that flattened black sedan who I just exploded into smithereens a few seconds ago. He has been trying to kill me for the past few days and I just extinguished him, country exterminator style number 69, if you know what I mean."

"Are you kidding me, man!?" as he looked at him and the burning cars half askance. "Just what are you talking about? Are you pulling my leg?"

Mick looked at him with tired eyes.

"Trust me on this. He was a true incarnation of the devil or evil spirit."

They both walked around the outside of the flaming wreckage and located Sally who had managed to stand up. She looked pale and sick. Throwing her arms around Mick she hugged him tight.

"You did it! I saw everything. The way the both of you were staring at each other and the way you threw that tank of poison through the back window. You killed him. You did it."

While Sally and Mick were busy in conversation, Billy felt drawn to the scene of the accident, and went over to inspect the flaming wreckage. The gasoline that was fueling the fire, was almost spent, and the flames were dying down. Peering into the back of the black sedan he tried to make out the man's face and body. He didn't know why, but he felt compelled to get a closer look, even if it was just to satisfy his own morbid curiosity. The body in the back of the car didn't show any signs of movement, but he wanted a closer look at it. He decided to open the car door to see if the man was still alive. He wrapped his coat around his hand, tugging open the back door to the car which was still steaming.

The car door came off its hinges and fell to the ground. From inside of the vehicle a blistered red and black hand shot out and grabbed his arm! In that split-second Billy, with his mouth agape, felt the whole of his life flash before his eyes. Powerful emotions swept through Billy's body, memories flooded his consciousness, and angry thoughts from his past, when he had been hurt by others, filled his mind. The wife that had cheated on him with one of his best friends, the father that had beat him when he was drunk, and a mom that was too busy for him to show him any love, were his immediate thoughts. The thoughts began filling him with an uncontrollable rage. Thoughts of when the local priest, Ed Bagley, had touched him when he was only seven were as fresh in his mind as if they had just happened. He didn't even notice that the hand had dropped away from his arm, fallen limp, hanging halfway out the car. The pain, hurt and anger were overwhelming. Waves of rage were enveloping his whole body, and even though his eyes were open, he couldn't see anything but what filled his mind. He remembered when a couple of bullies had held him down when he was twelve, and another one had pulled down his pants and pissed all over him, while he was screaming and crying for them to let him alone. Dripping wet from the urine, he had run home in shame and humiliation, eventually crying in the bathroom shower. Afterwards, they had teased him incessantly at school and the nickname of "piss baby" had stuck to him for years after the treacherous incident had happened. He could feel his blood boiling.

Strange thoughts began to fill his head. A powerful uncontrollable rage filled his mind, while inside of his whole being a white-hot burning desire to exact retribution was overcoming him. The monstrous waves of revulsion for being a coward his whole life and not fighting back were over. He had held back all of the injustices that had been done to him throughout his whole life, and within seconds, they had crystallized into a steel javelin, replacing his backbone. He didn't know he was smiling as he walked away from the wreckage toward his house. He never heard Mick calling out after him as he walked down the street. He really wasn't even sure why he had thoughts of the old quarry just outside of town. All of those assholes that had wronged him during his life were going to remember this day as he gathered up his hunting gear.

Chapter Ten

Billy Has No Regrets

He knew what he was going to do, but unlike any other time in his life, he had no feelings or compassion. He was still Billy in the sense that he remembered all of his past, the humiliations and the deprivations, but unlike his old self, he was going to make sure that he settled any scores that had festered within him. He had no fear of reprisal. He had no fear of remorse. He had no fear of recriminations or whatever may come his way. His mind was split as though it was on two separate levels. The first level was his old life with himself in the downstairs of the house being scorned upon, laughed at, and treated as a second-class citizen. Now, there was a second level from where he now controlled himself (or something controlled him). The view from the upstairs of his mind was all powerful and the split between the two levels was absolute. He knew something had happened to him when the man in the back of the car had grabbed hold of him, but he was powerless to stop himself. He was possessed with hate, vengeance and the overriding need to control everyone and everything within his domain. He certainly wasn't going to take any shit from anyone today or ever more.

Leaving his house, dressed in hunting gear and a ball cap, he saw foot long earthworms wriggling along in the wet ground. In the past, he would always have made sure not to step on them, in his heart feeling sorry for the small defenseless creatures. Today, his boots never varied their path to his truck, trampling them without so much as an iota of consideration as to their life or death. Is this how a psychopath feels, he wondered? Two different realities were alive within his mind. He no longer felt compassion or guilt for any of his actions or for the feelings of others or animals. Billy's mind, which housed all of his repressed feelings of hurt and anger, was on the first floor and was feeding the second floor of his mind where some unknown force controlled his actions and current malevolent feelings.

The mind that was telling Billy to get to the quarry was distracted by another part of his mind that was rationalizing a few stops along the way. Pulling off of the highway, he could see the cars of Bobby Joe, Dale and RJ parked in front of the local bowling alley. Well, well this didn't surprise him a bit, he thought, seeing as how it was Monday night and the local bowling teams were having their regular tournament play. Later in the evening it would turn into drunken karaoke. He wasn't welcome here, and they had let him know it in the past, on the one time he had stopped there. It only took a few seconds before somebody recognized him. Bobby Joe, one of the gang that had held him down during middle school, elbowed his friends and yelled out across the alley.

"Hey everybody, look who showed up, if it isn't piss baby. Hey, isn't it past your bedtime; it's almost six o'clock?"

Hoots of laughter rang out through the bowling alley, with smug faces all around the bar and bowling alley smiling at Billy's face. Expecting him not to say anything, everyone was surprised to hear him holler back.

"I would ask you to fuck those two pussies next to you, but seeing as how I have already seen the size of your two-inch pecker, it is probably quite impossible with those fat asses you are next to."

Roars of laughter from across the establishment broke out, followed by a stunned silence, because everyone couldn't believe that he had the nerve to speak to him like that. Bobby Joe, in shock and embarrassment from actually getting belittled in front of everyone, shouted back at Billy.

"What did you say fuck face? How's about you coming over here and polishing my boots with your tongue before I kick your ass into another county, piss boy?!"

At this exchange, the rest of the place grew silent, except for his two friends Dale and RJ who guffawed at his reply. There was a fight brewing, and they knew Billy didn't stand a chance. It had turned serious for Billy and quickly. Then the amazement on their faces grew as he calmly strolled over to the three of them. Bobby Joe was standing up waiting to bowl while the other two were sitting down waiting for their turn. Nobody could believe it, since they had known Billy their whole lives as a coward, and the kid that got picked on incessantly. The closer he got to them, without saying anything, made it so you could hear a pin drop throughout the bowling alley. Bobby Joe's face was a pure grin from far away, fifty feet or so; but as Billy drew closer, it seemed to falter a bit as he saw the look on Billy's face. The look he saw was one he couldn't place. His face showed absolutely no fear, pain or anger, and his body and movements belied no emotion whatsoever. He was five feet from him. Whirling away from Bobby Joe, without speaking a word, he pulled out two, foot long hunting knives, from the inner pockets of his jacket and simultaneously, with a knife in each hand, drove them cleanly through each of Dale and RJ's respective left legs as they were seated. Each knife went clear through the leg up to its hilt and also through the wood seat they were seated upon. He left the knives sticking out of their legs as the blood began spurting from each of them. Looks of utter amazement, disbelief, and then horror spread across their faces. Billy had struck terror in their hearts as he smiled at them with a long smirking grin. Meanwhile Bobby Joe, in shock himself, had just enough time to drop his bowling ball and take a swing at Billy, but Billy was prepared for this. He was stoically calm even in the face of all the blood spurting from the femoral arteries of each of his victims and the general pandemonium and screaming that pervaded the air within the bowling alley.

"Oh my God somebody call the police!"

"He has a knife! Watch out! He's gone mad."

"Holy shit he's crazy!"

He was not distracted in the least. He anticipated a swing from Bobby Joe and was ready for him. As he swung over his head, he used the big man's momentum by grabbing his punching arm and turned him so that he was directly behind him. Grabbing a third knife that he had tucked into the front of his pants, which he pulled from its sheath, he drove it into Bobby Joe's anus and up into his stomach. The screaming was the loudest he had ever heard anyone make, and then he twisted the knife back and forth, and left it in his ass all the way up to the hilt. Across the bowling alley and bar all eyes were upon Billy, as Bobby Joe fell forward to the ground yelling and screaming like a stuck pig. His two friends, Dale and RJ, losing copious amounts of blood, were going into shock and soon Booby Joe would be as well.

"Why don't you two stick around until we can get your cowboy buddy a colostomy bag. Hey, isn't it funny, now?"

He laughed uproariously, since both of them were in a fashion, fastened to their chairs by the knives that protruded from the undersides of their chairs. The bowling alley had gone deathly quiet again except for the victims who were screaming. Jack, the barman, grabbed his rifle and swung it toward Billy from behind the bar, but Billy saw him first. Unfortunately for him, everyone knew he hid a gun behind the bar. Billy shot him square in the face, killing him instantly. Then with the gun in his left hand, covering anyone who was thinking about trying something, he unzipped his fly with his right hand and proceeded to piss on all three of them where they sat and lay. With no more emotion than if he had just picked up his mail, he zipped up his fly and strode out the door.

At his next stop, the morning sermon was taking place with about thirty parishioners attending mass. Entering the church, he noticed the priest looked up to see who had entered, and he felt sure he recognized him immediately. He hesitated with surprise for a few moments, so that a few of his flock turned to look at Billy, but he soon regained his composure and went right back to reading passages out of the Bible. Billy listened for a few seconds and could hear the words, "though shall not covet thy neighbor's wife," and at this, he began walking from the back of the church up the middle aisle. With his voice reverberating off of the walls, he spoke with an unparalleled authority.

"And thou shall not covet thy parishioners' children like the beast that you are. Nor shall he keep hidden his evil misdeeds by way of the holy cloak. Nor shall he prey upon the young and the weak that have no one to protect them. Nor shall the priest receive from his flock money to support his hypocritical sanctimonious filth of a lie life. Nor shall your sin be forgiven since it was done to me, Billy Watkins, at the age of seven."

The sunlight that had been illuminating the church through the stained-glass windows went away. In the darkened church, lit by only a few candles, scared faces of those in attendance looked back and forth between the faces of the priest's and Billy's. Caught by the truth, the priest blinked, as his face fell with the knowledge of his evil ways. Attempting to somehow sway Billy's thoughts or actions, the priest tried to muster a strong voice to defend his false honor, but it was a meek reply with his voice cracking.

"Billy, so glad you could join us today . . . um can I have the pleasure after Mass of seeing you privately?"

"Stripped of your false holiness, you will never see anyone alone again in order to do your acts of blasphemy. You are a rapist of children and a deceiver of all that come before you. Bow down on your knees and ask forgiveness of your false lord."

By this time Billy was a mere ten feet from him and his hardened gaze and spoken truths had driven the priest to his knees. His voice had commanded him to his knees. His dark secrets had been spilled to his flock, and he began sobbing and weeping with his head bowed down to them all, as a queer silence captured them in the unfolding drama before their eyes. Ascending the steps to where the priest was in penitence upon his knees, Billy walked past him to where a chivalric shield and sword from the Middle Ages was positioned upon the wall. Grabbing them from the wall, he walked back to the priest who was still prone in the same position and threw the shield face down in front of the priest.

"Here you surround yourself with those that are strong and valiant and gave their lives in sacrifice to upholding just virtues. And yet you have the audacity to commit your perverse sins in your father's house and to hide from the law by invoking his name. But I am going to help you!"

At this the priest, with tears streaming down his face, looked up in hope and amazement. He was wondering what could be done for his salvation, how he was going to be helped, but the voice was so strong and wrought with conviction that he believed him. Inquiringly, he looked into Billy's eyes but did not see the forgiveness he was looking for; instead he saw the flames of hell burning brightly within his pupils.

With a quick smile of death, the sword came down and severed the priest's head so that it rolled around within the underside of the shield. Gasps and screams erupted from the church, but nobody dared approach Billy, as he turned on his heel and walked out of the church. They had felt his omnipotent power. Billy, finished with his earthly business, was going to help the lifeless body on the altar for all of eternity continuously remembering the evil he had done in his life. It was time to go to the quarry.

He arrived at the quarry. It was crystal clear in his mind what he needed to accomplish. Parking the truck at the rim of the quarry, he began his descent down the steep slope to where the entrance of the mine shaft lay at the bottom of the pit. Side stepping his way down the rocks and stones was difficult due to the recent rain. It was hard just trying to keep his balance, but eventually he made it to the opening of the shaft. Pulling out a flashlight, he made his way to the command center created by his predecessor. Billy had never been here before, but in his controlled mind he knew exactly where everything was located. Flicking on the lights within the main control room, he went to the panel that showed all of the different ant colonies that were active around the county. There were over a thousand different individual colonies that he controlled, and with just one flip of the master switch, they could be activated. The ants would be hummed to, louder and louder, until they were an uncontrollable voracious army of fire ants of over a billion strong. It was time. He flipped the switch. The humming that one would usually hear from an electrical transformer began humming across the county. Seconds later the ants began making their way out of their mounds to attack any living thing that happened to cross their path.

Chapter Eleven

Fire Ant Frenzy

The paramedics and ambulance crews were attending to the victims at the bowling alley when they received a call from the parishioners of the First Baptist church down the street. A hysterical woman told them that the priest's head had been lopped off by Billy. All that could be done for the priest was to say a prayer and notify the local mortician, Ed Sneed, which they instructed the church members to do. The situation was critical at their current location. At the bowling alley, chaos ensued after Billy's departure. Nothing like this had ever occurred in the small ranching and oil drilling community, for as far back as anyone could remember. Most of the patrons were in a state of bewildered shock that Billy had snapped, many believing he must have been tied to the other murders that had splashed across the front pages of their morning newspapers. The only good thing to come out of today, was that they all felt with certainty that they knew who the murderer within the town was. Most of them were angry for the carnage he had inflicted upon the innocent victims, like Edith, Roy, Louise and Jack, the barkeep, although the same could not be said for the three gravely injured men the para-medics were attempting to keep alive. These three had been bullies to Billy their whole lives, and secretly many of them felt a sense of relief that he had finally stood up to them. Life certainly would never be the same again within the town of Bishop.

The first person to hear the humming noise was Bobby Joe. Crying and moaning in agony, with the knife still stuffed up his ass, the para-medics propped him up on his side on top of the metal gurney, ready to wheel him into the ambulance. With the front doors of the bowling alley wide open as they wheeled him out, a strange, almost humming bee-like vibrational sound pervaded the air, and a most peculiar sight presented itself. In the parking lot a massive swarm of insects covered the ground and were rapidly moving toward them. It was reminiscent of autumn cricket season in west Texas, but these weren't crickets. Furthermore, instead of seeing thousands of them, there appeared to be hundreds of thousands of them. They approached like a dark wave flooding across the parking lot.

"What is that infernal noise?" Bobby Joe cried out in sympathy for himself while trying to look out the windows of the ambulance from the gurney he lay on.

"Better yet what are those things? Are those locusts?" answered the first paramedic, knowing even when he said it that they weren't.

"Hey, those are humongous ants! There must be millions of them!" the second paramedic cried out in disbelief.

They managed to get Bobby Joe into the back of the ambulance before the ants were upon them. Aggressively attacking, they stung and bit the two paramedics who frantically tried to get into the ambulance, but with each biting sting, were driven back inside the relative safety of the bowling alley. With everyone crowding around the doors to get a look at the spectacle, they watched in horror as the ants converged upon the vehicle and front doors of the building. That is when the screams of Bobby Joe began. Through the two small upper windows in the back doors of the ambulance they saw him trying to whack them off of him but to no avail. Seconds later, he was covered with ants, his body erratically jerking about in all directions. The screams of Bobby Joe being eaten alive by a thousand ants was followed by the sound of the hum getting stronger as his pitiful cries for help died out.

The surreal scene was broken by a scream. The patrons at the bowling alley turned in unison. The ants, which were barred at the doors from entering the building, had found their way through the vents in the walls and were pouring in between cracks between the walls and through unseen holes in the floor. There was no escape for any of them. Within minutes thirty-one picked clean skeletons lay strewn about a deserted bowling alley.

Across the land, the marauding ants vanquished any living thing in their path. Skeletons sat behind steering wheels of tractors. Barnyards, that were once full of corralled horses, sheep and cows, became wastelands. Supermarkets were stripped of everything but canned goods. There was nothing that walked in the town of Bishop, Texas that was left untouched. Circling high above the multitudes of ants, only the birds were safe from the marauding killers. People who were lucky enough to be driving in their cars were able to avoid the carnivorous orgy that ransacked the town. The ants satiated from their wild feeding frenzy, descended back below the ground, bringing sustenance to the colonies. An eerie stillness settled over the long prairie grasses that rustled in the wind. The silence of the land, occasionally broken by the cawing of a few crows or by the sound of the wind tickling some wind chimes, lay uninterrupted across the barren landscape.

At the main control center of the quarry, Billy enjoyed himself for hours listening to a police scanner jammed with thousands of unheeded emergencies. Yawning after all of his evening's excitement, he felt drained and exhausted from his day of debauchery. Even the devil needed some time to recharge his batteries, trapped as he was within his human host. After shutting down the humming mechanism, and allowing the ants to return to their respective colonies, he laid down on a cot in a small back storeroom and decided to rest. The body he inhabited was strange to him. It had taken time for him to figure out how to control the host, and he had been distracted by getting revenge on Billy's old enemies. It was all new to him, this process of transmogrification.

Realizing it would take a bit of time to adapt to his new situation and control the thoughts of his host, he thought back on the day's events. He had been killed, and by that nitwit of an exterminator, no less. With his last bit of dark energy, a bit of mind control and luck, he was able to get Billy to approach him. He had to be more careful. He knew he would need to be fresh and alert for the next stage of his master plan.

A hundred feet below him at the end of a nondescript mining shaft, Stan struggled to free himself from the table he was strapped to. The ants were not interested in his picked clean skeletal hand anymore and had retreated out of the jar. They had scurried down a plastic tube that was connected to the jar attached to his hand which ran into the face of the rock wall. Momentarily, everything was quiet. It was different a few minutes prior, when he had heard the faint sound of footsteps and machines whirring somewhere within the labyrinth of caves and tunnels. For hours, he had heard noises and now it had grown silent. If he was going to escape, he reckoned this was his opportunity. Wriggling against the straps that held him, he could tell they were too tight to budge, except for when he inhaled his chest strap. When he did that, the strap appeared to loosen up a bit. What could he do, he thought? With as much effort as he could, he inhaled and brought his head up as far as it could along his chest and was just able to reach the strap across his chest. For the next hour, he would breathe as deeply as he could, and then chew on the leather strap that held him tight. It was exhausting. His jaw and teeth were soon sore and hurting from continuously chewing on leather. Slowly a small rip was made in the leather and then he proceeded to make it bigger. Next, he tried to inhale and put pressure on the strap with his chest puffed up while chewing on the strap. This strategy was nearly impossible. He went back to work on chewing through the leather rather than trying to make it snap. After what seemed an interminable amount of chewing, he broke through his chest restraint, his mouth bleeding from the effort. It felt great to partially sit up, but his hands and legs were still strapped firmly to the table. He also got a better look at his hand in the jar. It was an awful sight to see. The bones stuck out of his hand. It was like he was looking at a skeleton from a graveyard. His wrist must be cauterized somehow, or wouldn't he be bleeding at the moment, he thought? Leaning over to his left, with the sorest jaw he had ever felt in his whole life, he began chewing on the leather strap that encircled his wrist. Angrily, at times savagely, he tore and ate at the leather that kept him prisoner. He could feel the warm blood in his mouth, but he didn't care. He was scared and needed to get free before that monster revisited him. It took just a few minutes, although it seemed like forever. Disattaching himself fully from the table was easy after he got one hand free. He kept the glass container over his right hand after disconnecting the tube that ran to it. He didn't want to even look at his hand much less touch it. He was in a state of denial and shock.

In the dimly lit room, he found an exit. Snaking his way along the corridors, the only thing he thought to himself was that if he was heading upwards, then eventually he should be able to reach the top of the quarry. It was his only chance to reach the surface and freedom. Thirty minutes later he saw moonlight! Climbing the steep embankment was twice as hard with only one working hand. Exhausted, he reached the top and found a truck parked with the doors unlocked. The keys weren't in the ignition, but that wasn't going to stop him at this point in his struggle to escape. He had been a police officer for the past twenty years, but that didn't mean he wasn't aware of the tricks of the criminal trade. After hot wiring the truck, he settled down to getting used to driving with his left hand. His right hand, enclosed in what appeared to be a huge glass pickle jar, lay awkwardly on the passenger seat.

Driving toward the hospital, he was a mix of emotions. He was scared of the man that had mutilated him. He was in shock, angry from the events of the day, and yet he no longer felt like a helpless victim. He was angry and hurt knowing that he would never be the same man again. Then the realization struck him that he would never be a policeman on duty again. Perhaps they would offer him a desk job. He hadn't lost his life, but he had lost a big part of his masculinity. Anger and hurt emotions flooded his brain. He thought of Mick, how he had mistakenly almost arrested him, and how he had saved them. He thought of Joe and wondered if he would meet up with him at the hospital. Wouldn't he be surprised by the turn of events since when they first met in the morning? Seeking a break from his bleak stream of thoughts, he turned on the radio. Static was the only noise that came from the speakers no matter what channel he tried. Disgustedly he turned the radio off. He wondered what the hospital staff were going to say to him, once he unveiled his right hand or lack thereof. He looked around for something to cover the pickle jar encompassing his hand and saw a towel in the back seat of the truck which he could use. He didn't feel like getting gawked at or drawing any attention to himself. He felt ashamed and embarrassed. Yesterday, had been the worst day of his life, he thought, that was until today came along. Off in the distance he could see the multistory hospital complex and breathed a sigh of relief. Finally, he could get some help, or so he thought.

Walking the empty corridors of the hospital, he found himself stepping over skeletons in the craziest of places. Many of the victims had been trapped in the stairwells trying to escape the ants when they died. The victims clothing, rings, jewelry and whatever else they were carrying were scattered among the picked clean white bones. Anything that wasn't edible was left strewn amongst the carnage. Still other skeletons, he found in hospital beds with no hope of escape, while still others had died trapped in the confines of the hospital elevators. It was the most ghastly and surreal sight he had ever seen in his life. He found himself walking the halls of the hospital in a trance, much like a zombie.

The sound of a crying baby snapped him out of his trance. Running down the hallway, with his skeletal hand wrapped in a towel enclosed inside a pickle jar, cradled by his left hand, he reached the sound of the crying infant and the maternity ward. It was sealed off from the rest of the hospital. The babies had miraculously survived. There were bones all along the outside of the glass walls that separated the maternity ward from the rest of the hospital. The parents hadn't survived. It was easy enough to understand what had happened. Those inside must have had to watch as those on the outside were eaten alive. Surveying the scene, he realized that the doors were sealed off, or they would have died in the same gruesome manner. He could see the newborn infants neatly lined up within the ward, but there weren't any attendants visible. He could hear many of them crying. He knocked on the door and then on the glass windows. From the back of the room a door opened, and a woman's face peeked out. Cautiously, a young woman approached the door responding to his motioning. He figured it was the police uniform he was wearing. Cautiously, she opened the door and let him in. Immediately, her gaze rested upon his right hand, and she backed away from him, her eyes growing wider with fear and suspicion. He turned and locked the door behind him, and without any further ado, pulled the towel off his hand and asked if there was a doctor left alive to treat him. It was a chilling sensation to see her faint before him with the sound of multiple babies crying around them. Her eyes that had been wide with fright rolled back in her head as she collapsed to the ground.

Chapter Twelve

Awakening

Mick was so busy taking care of Sally that he didn't have time to think about the way that Billy had left them. It certainly was peculiar, but for the past few hours his main priority had been addressing the gash on Sally's head and tending to his own injuries. After putting a dressing across her forehead and bandaging up some small cuts mostly across her legs and arms, he had begun examining himself in the mirror. For as bad as he looked, he felt pretty damn good inside, that is except for his sprained knee which had swollen up. Any immediate concerns about being hunted by a demon were over, and it felt as though a huge weight had been lifted off his shoulders. But he was bothered. Thoughts about what had transpired kept floating around in his head and his mind kept racing back to Billy. Why had Billy left without saying anything? It was curious, he thought, since it certainly wasn't like him to leave in the midst of an emergency. His mind raced back to what had happened after he opened the car door and then left so suddenly without even saying a word or checking on them. An ominous black foreboding filled his thoughts. Had Billy been infected by the evil spirit! He had his suspicions. The more he thought about it, the more he became convinced that is what happened. Surely, that was the reason why he hadn't answered his shouts, while he casually walked away from the accident. The thought was terrifying. He wondered where he had gone and what he was doing. It was maddening to think that he had beaten the devil in battle only to have come up a loser. Fears were creeping back into his mind, as the heavy weight of stress settled back down upon his shoulders. Sally could see it in his face.

"What's wrong? What's going on?"

"I don't know; maybe nothing. But I don't like the way that Billy left without saying anything. It is very strange, but I feel like the evil spirit somehow got him to go over to the car and open the car door. It then somehow transferred itself to Billy! I know it sounds like hogwash, but it is the only explanation I have for Billy acting so weird."

Sally, her shoulders slumping, began to cry. Silent tears flowed down her face that she couldn't stop. Mick sat down next to her, handing her some tissues and wrapped his arms around her. She felt warm inside of his arms and she snuggled into his shoulder. Minutes crept by as the two embraced. He could smell her lightly scented perfume. She could smell the scent of his dried sweat and breathed it in deeply. She wanted him. She wanted him now. Quietly, they both felt for one another. Her lips joined his, and they felt for one another for the first time. All of their past was behind them. Slipping her hand down onto his groin, she began massaging and pulling on his cock. Mick moved his hands up to her breasts and began grabbing and massaging them, fingering her nipples as they hardened between his fingers. It was all happening so fast that neither of them had any time to think about what they were doing. Inside of her hand his dick hardened within seconds. The tension that could have split the air seconds ago was replaced by the heated passion of two new lovers. The love making was both intensely climactic and animalistic as the events of the past few days had driven them together in a force more powerful than either of them had realized.

Once finished, she slipped off to the bathroom, and turned on a steaming hot shower. The water felt amazing as it ran down her hair, neck, shoulders and back. She was in a state of pleasant disbelief with a smile on her face. She couldn't remember the last time she had sex like that. It was so raw and sensual that she almost couldn't believe it. It was so good, that for a few single moments, she felt completely satiated and didn't care about any future consequences. If it was going to be like this, then that was fine with her. It was wild to think that all of this had developed within the span of just a few days. As bewildering as the events were for her, she soon began to wonder what he was thinking. Was he serious about her or had he just taken advantage of her vulnerability. Deep down she felt compelled to believe that, for him as well as her, each had undergone a transformation in their feelings for one another at a basic level. In the past, he had always toyed with her about how much he wanted to be with her, but she knew he had been just kidding around. Everything was different now.

While toweling herself off, she happened upon some skin cream in the bathroom that had a nice smell. It had a lavender smell, and she applied it generously to her body. She felt pretty and refreshingly alive. And she hadn't felt this way in a long time, certainly not since she had been with her last and most recent boyfriend, who was now officially her former boyfriend. Combing her hair, her thoughts ran to how it would be to have Mick as her lover. If the sex was anything like what she had just experienced, then everything would work itself out just fine, she told herself. Looking in the mirror she examined the cut on her forehead and breathed a sigh of relief. It didn't appear too deep. Hopefully, she wouldn't have a permanent scar, she thought. She looked for some vitamin E oil in the water closet, but failed to find any and wondered if she had any in her purse.

Walking out of the bathroom to find her purse, she called for Mick, and got no answer. As she searched from room to room, she soon realized he wasn't there. Where had he gone? She thought of Billy and knew exactly where he had gone. He was going to try and find him without her! Frantically she ran to the garage. The only car remaining was an old dust covered pickup truck. He had taken his black 1973 Monte Carlo fastback on the road without her. She was perturbed for him not letting her know. She made her way back to the bathroom and found taped to the outside of the bathroom door a note. It read, "Sorry for having to leave without telling you, but I didn't want an argument and know what has to be done. I have to find Billy and stop him from whatever he is going to do. Please take care of the dogs until I get back and make sure you have an exit plan in case of anything. I really hate to do this, but I want to keep you safe albeit for selfish purposes of my own." At the bottom of the note a drawing of a big smiling face was looking back at her. She pulled the note off of the bathroom door. That was when she noticed something on the back of the note. Two stick figures in a sexual position were drawn. Scrawled above the picture were the words, "see you soon Miss Sally—be safe". She folded the note and stuck it inside her wallet within her purse. She was keeping that note.

Being on the outskirts of town, Sally had no idea of the Armageddon that had been unleashed upon the townspeople. She found some dog food in the cupboards, fed the two dogs, and let them out. Then she started cleaning and sweeping up all of the glass that was in and around the house. Thousands of dollars in property damage had been done to the house, not to mention the vehicles that were total burnt out losses in the front yard. And she certainly wasn't going to venture out of the house with the way she felt, although, instinctively she felt that the evil presence wasn't around anymore. She was right.

Chapter Thirteen

What the Flock

From over a mile away he could see the smoke rising into the cool dusk air. Ed Sneed, the local mortician and funeral home director, had suddenly become one of the busiest men in town. His latest call had been from an hysterical parishioner, who had let him know that George Bagley, the priest, had been murdered by way of decapitation. God almighty, what was the world coming to, he wondered. The haze from a burning fire was getting thicker as he approached the Baptist church. As he turned the bend, the flames were in front of him. The church was completely surrounded by a ring of fire that was anywhere from three to six feet high! Stopping his car just outside the ring of fire, he could see the people hauling the church pews down the front steps of the church. Old Man Johnson, a local corn farmer in his seventies, had an axe in his hands and was chopping the pews up, while still another man was using a sword to do the same. Still others were gathering the pieces to feed the raging ring of fire. They all seemed to be in a state of panic yelling and screaming at one another. Had they all gone mad, was his first thought? Honking his car horn, a few heads popped up and turned in his direction. With sweat pouring down their brows and crazed looks in their eyes, he was beginning to wonder if he shouldn't just come back at another time for his own safety. Old Man Johnson put down his axe and made his way over to the edge of the fire. Managing to get a pew across the fire in a low spot, he motioned for Ed to come across. With some trepidation, and then a quick dash across the pew, he was inside the ring of fire with the others. Bert Johnson spoke first.

"Did you see any of them?"

"Any of what?" Ed asked.

"Why, any of those huge ants, of course!"

"I really do not know what you are talking about. I got a call from someone at the church to come here because I was told that Billy snapped and killed George. Then I get call from the paramedics from the bowling alley that they can't handle the job, because they were too busy with multiple stabbing victims, and that Jack the bartender was murdered, also supposedly by Billy. I figured he must have left the bowling alley and came to the church to settle another old score of his. Anyways, when I call back the ambulance service, it just rings without anyone answering the line. Finally, I decide to drive down here to see if I can help, and forgive me if this sounds callous, but you are all engaged in some sort of messianic occult church ritual. It is frankly incredible to see you all burning the pews in a circle around the church. And now you are talking about giant ants?! I mean Jesus H Christ Bert, just what is going on around here, has everyone gone mad?"

The collective terror that had run their lives for the past few hours had begun to wear off. Bert explained how everything had happened. He began with Billy barging into the church and the priest crying in shame, up until he lopped off his head with the sword, which seemed to be part of a play involving George and the Dragon. Then, after Billy left, they had called the paramedics, police, and him. They didn't have any luck getting hold of the police. That is when they had started hearing a funny humming noise that kept growing stronger. Bert had been the first to see it, a mass of humongous reddish black ants converging on the church from all directions; thinking that it was a part of the apocalypse, he urged them all to keep the ants away from the church by ringing it with a protective barrier of fire. Ultimately, this act saved all of their lives. For hours, the ants had tried to breech the wall of fire, and then just as mysteriously as they appeared, they had vanished. With everyone's adrenaline at sky high levels trying to defend themselves, they had failed to notice the ants had receded just prior to Ed showing up. Ed wasn't sure what to make of the whole story, but upon examination of the two separate pieces of George, he decided there was certainly some credence to at least half of the story.

As the ring of fire began dying down, the churchgoers were coming to the awful realization that it was not only them that had been attacked. Husbands couldn't get hold of wives; wives couldn't get hold of children and panic struck them once again. Each of them began driving away from the church to try and find their loved ones while facing their own private hells. The only two remaining at the Church were Bert Jackson and Ed Sneed, both without any family members anymore, relinquished to a world that many older people find themselves. Almost as if purgatory was alive and well, right here on earth, without the living seeing any part of what was going on around them. Only those within its realm knew of its existence, a place where one wasn't dead, but if one was dead, nobody would notice either. The two looked at each other, and without saying a word, each of them knew they were a part of this silent realm. Grabbing a pine coffin out of the back of Ed's hearse they proceeded to put the remains of George in it, while each of them mulled over their own private thoughts.

Chapter Fourteen

The Battle Continues

Mick zipped down the deserted road in his black Monte Carlo, and even though he had been wracking his brain, he still didn't have a good plan in place to defeat the devil within Billy. The transference of the evil spirit bothered him immensely. A transference or possession could happen to anyone, including himself, and it scared him. How was he supposed to vanquish an amorphous body without getting too close to it, while also trying to save his buddy from down the street? It seemed impossible. If only Billy hadn't been drawn to the wreck, he wouldn't be worrying about any of this, he thought. Then again, maybe that act somehow held the solution. If he could draw the demon outside of Billy by making the devil believe that he was in imminent danger, perhaps then he could trap him into some other being that could more easily be disposed of, like an animal. As he continued to try and think of ideas, with his knee still aching from earlier, he noticed something out of the corner of his eye. On the opposite side of the road Billy's truck was parked at the hospital!

He wasn't ready for another confrontation, but he needed to find out why Billy was at the hospital. He pulled his car into the parking lot and decided to wait and observe. He hid his car three rows away from Billy's truck, but in such a position so that he couldn't be seen, but he could clearly see the truck between two cars. Slouching down in his front seat he waited. And he waited. After two hours passed, the fact that he didn't see anyone else in the parking lot, or any activity at all began to bother him and poke at his curiosity. His better judgment told him to lay low, like he was in a hunting blind, and so he continued to sit in his car.

Then he remembered he might have something to ease the pain in his leg within the glove box. Much to his delight he found a couple of aspirin and a half a bottle of crown velvet. Ten minutes after taking two aspirin with a few slugs of liquor, the pain in his knee had eased a bit and his head felt better.

Finally, he saw some movement! A man was walking out of the front entrance of the hospital. He strained his eyes to see if it was Billy and his mouth opened in amazement. It was Stan the policeman, who had tried to arrest him earlier that morning. Furthermore, it appeared he was missing his right hand! He was heading straight for Billy's truck. Not knowing what to think, he silently exited his car with his pistol in his hand and inched closer to the truck while staying out of sight. Could Stan have been infected by Billy and was he now the devil? He couldn't be too sure and wasn't taking any chances. Stan reached the truck and Mick stepped out from behind where he was hiding. Stan looked like he had seen a ghost when he got a glimpse of him and then he smiled. Not in a malicious or evil way but in a good-natured way. He was truly glad to see him. For a moment neither of them spoke until Stan raised his right arm.

"I guess you are probably wondering how I lost my right hand since we met this morning."

"Yeah, and also why you are driving my neighbor's truck, if you care to let me know?"

"What? Well, that is interesting seeing as how it was the only vehicle at the quarry where I was held captive and tortured by that maniac."

"Oh, well I killed that man a few hours ago, but he transferred his soul into my neighbor Billy, who's truck you are driving."

Everything had become very convoluted. They spoke about their experiences over the past twelve hours. No longer was it the questioning policeman and the country dolt, but a serious face to face talk amongst warriors battling the unknown. They understood they needed to combine forces in order to survive. When Mick told Stan about how he killed the man with the black hair by blowing him up, Stan's face beamed with joy. His hatred for that abominable monster ran deep within his soul. When he told the story of what transpired afterwards with Billy, he grew serious and knew now why the truck was at the quarry. And when Stan relayed what he had seen inside the hospital, it registered with Mick why the town was for the most part so quiet and deserted; the ants had been unleashed upon the townspeople eating everyone and everything. They also knew something else for certain. Billy was alone and without a vehicle at the quarry. If ever they were going to have an edge over him it was now, and they had to act.

"You want to do what?" Stan exclaimed in disbelief.

"I know it sounds a bit crazy, but I think it will work. If I can trick the demon into transferring its presence into the body of an animal, I can save Billy. Once that happens, I can with a clear conscience kill the animal. I was thinking a coyote would be our best bet in terms of capture, by tranquilizing it and transporting it to the quarry."

"Oh sure. Let's give it a shot. Are you as crazy as you sound?"

Stan amazed himself by eventually agreeing to the plan. He couldn't think of anything better, and he knew they didn't have much time either. What they needed were some supplies and bait to catch a coyote.

"Follow me down the road a few miles and we can stop at Hunter's bait and tackle shop. It should have everything we need," Mick said.

Within a few minutes they were foraging through the shop. Mick grabbed a few dead frozen rabbits, which luckily weren't eaten since they were in a freezer, ammunition for his rifle, some explosives and blasting powder. He also found a CD mimicking the sound of a rabbit in distress that would help draw the coyote to them. Before he left the store, he put the dead rabbits in the stores microwave and heated them up a bit so that their smell would be more pungent to the coyote's sensitive nose. He knew that time was of the essence and that the plan hinged on them capturing the animal and getting to the quarry before Billy left.

They set up the dead rabbits, positioned as they were, downwind along the trails of some hills. These were the same trails used for centuries by men and animals of all sizes. Then they sat back and waited in the waning hours of the day. It was over ninety degrees even in the shaded portions of the tall grass as they sat and watched, but the quiet time did them each a favor. It gave them some time to think, rest and talk about their last few days. Just having someone to talk to rationally about the last few days' events, released some of the stress from the both of them. Mick could sense that Stan was in a state of shock and withdrawal, and although he wasn't a psychologist, he realized he was feeling victimized, with a profound sense of loss. Unfortunately, there was nothing he could do about it. The diagnosis was accurate, just without any cure available, except for maybe time.

An hour later they caught a glimpse of a skulking coyote coming over a ridge. It had picked up the scent of one of the dead rabbits. They had set up two rabbits downwind of the ridgeline and had played the soundtrack of a wounded rabbit over the car speakers. Watching the coyote, its ears perked up high upon his head listening to the cries of the rabbit, its eyes kept darting back and forth, wary of the situation. Mick turned off the car speakers so as to not confuse the coyote, now that he had caught wind of its scent. The two rabbits were spread about a quarter mile from each other. They could tell by the track that the animal was taking that it was going for the one on their left. That was fine, since it would enable a clear shot for Mick to use his tranquilizer gun. Slowly he began to position himself, lying flat on the ground so that the gun rested on top of a large rock from which he could hide behind.

The coyote was almost upon the rabbit. He would have to make his first shot count. He would probably only get one good chance. It appeared to look right at him before dropping his head down to grab the rabbit in his jaws. He squeezed off a round aiming for its hindquarters. It was a hit! After initially shrieking in surprised pain, the coyote whirled and ran with the rabbit clenched in his mouth. He was over the ridgeline within seconds and both of them scrambled to follow. It took them an eternity to get to where he had gone in less than a minute. Panting and wheezing Mick and Stan weaved their way through the rocks, cactuses, and tall grasses as small lizards dashed away from them in fright. The coyote was out of sight over the ridgeline. Mick was nervous they were going to lose him. Upon reaching the summit, Mick pulled out his binoculars and began scanning the horizon. He was winded and his knee hurt. Some movement off to the west caught his attention. There he was. About three hundred yards away, next to some rocks under a juniper tree, the distressed coyote lay. When they got down to him, they could see he was nearly passed out from the tranquilizer. He barely raised his head and snarled as they approached. Three quarters of the rabbit lay next to him. He must have been famished.

Soon enough the tranquilizer had taken effect. Mick proceeded to pick him up and begin the journey back up the hill. By the time they reached their vehicles, they were both panting and out of breath. Mick placed the drugged coyote inside a cage which was in the bed of Billy's truck. Looking at one another, they both sensed the easy part of their journey into some dark netherworld was upon them. It was easy enough to trap and tranquilize a coyote, but now they had to try and use it to trick, trap, and kill a demon. And the day was getting late. The sun was edging lower on the horizon pushing its faint rays between the Pinon's and tall pines that dotted the landscape. Holding his fingers up to his eyes and peering above them toward the sun Mick could see that the sun was only three of his fingers from dipping below the horizon. That gave them less than an hour to reach the quarry. It wasn't enough time before nightfall.

"Stan, we don't have enough time to get to the quarry before dark. I don't like our odds," as he kicked his boot into the sand in frustration. He was tired and sweaty.

"I agree. Let me try and get hold of someone from the next county again and see if we can get some help."

Stan called out on his patrol radio for the umpteenth time, but no one answered his calls for assistance. After a few more attempts he stopped trying. They were in a dead zone in more than a few ways. They both agreed to meet the next morning on the outskirts of town prior to the sun rising. One handed Stan would bring the coyote and Mick would bring a fresh batch of his ant poison. Together they would try and stop this madness. The plan was to tie the coyote down near the entrance of the quarry and, when Billy came out, they would shoot him with animal tranquilizers. Hopefully the demon inside of Billy would realize his dire situation, transfer over to the coyote, who they then hoped to kill. Mick was trying to save Billy's life while also outsmarting the devil. It was a dubious plan at best. There was a multitude of factors which made the plan far-fetched, and obviously many things could go awry, but neither of them could think of anything better. They agreed on the plan and left each other in silence.

Stan wasn't the same purpose driven man from just a few days earlier. He was no longer the cocky policeman with an agenda. He was a shell of his former self. In truth, he was a wrecked man. Both physically and mentally he had been crushed. He felt he wasn't up to giving orders anymore, and really just wanted to just drive away from everything and go hide somewhere. The man he had been intending to arrest for murder, was virtually giving him orders, had saved his life, and all within the span of a day. He hadn't given much thought to the existence of God or the Devil prior to the past few days, and now his mind was filled with supernatural fears, knowing what he now knew, that demons coexisted alongside humans on this earth. How was any of this even possible, he thought, and just how could they beat such a powerful force by themselves, he wondered? He couldn't seem to shake the thoughts from his head and clear his mind. He was in a state of consciousness that was hazy at best and beyond making rational decisions. Most of all he was scared. He couldn't think clearly and had lost his grip on his duties to the police department he served. Clutching the steering wheel with the only hand remaining to him, while sweating profusely, he drove through a town devoid of any life or even sound. Quietly he drove onward and that was when he made a fateful decision. He began driving as fast as he could back toward his hometown in the next county over and away from the insanity that had engulfed him for the past few days. He was a copper copping out. He drove knowing that what he was doing was wrong, but he couldn't seem to stop himself. Soon he would realize, like many people who try and escape their problems, that as fast as he drove away from his immediate concerns, the more his mind would be haunted by his fears which inevitably he would have to face.

Mick made his way back to his house while contemplating what to do next. Pulling into the driveway, he saw Sally waiting for him on the porch. Surrounded by two burnt out cars, a house with no windows, and black fire damage everywhere he looked, especially on his new white satin paint, it was comical to see a smiling face peering back at him. Nothing else mattered but her smile, but the carnage was messing with his obsessive-compulsive disorder. It was a natural unforced smile that overcame her face, and he knew from just seeing her radiant face, that she had fallen for him. He felt prouder than a rooster with a flock of hens. Before he had even managed to get out of his car, she was there by his side, helping him out of the vehicle. His knee was in bad shape and running after the coyote hadn't helped. She locked onto his lips with a big kiss as soon as he got out of the car.

"Hey, I was worried about you. What happened?"

"Well, I thought about getting a jump on Billy by surprising him, but actually was surprised myself. I ran into the lieutenant, and we concocted a plan for tomorrow. I will fill you in on it, after we get inside."

God that felt great, he thought. His mind was so frazzled from everything that had transpired that afternoon, that the fresh wave of her tongue upon his, guided him into a much different and nicer reality. It was smooth and fresh, not too complicated and sweet to the touch. He reciprocated by grabbing her ass cheeks with both hands and squeezing them with vigor. This may just work for a bit, he thought. He had never considered her in the past, other than just someone to toy with; but after what had happened, he was willing to reconsider the situation. The sex had been marvelous, erotic, spontaneous, and all together fantastic. There was something to be said for great sex, he thought. At the hardest time of his life, he felt strangely invigorated by his new-found love, who had been waiting for him at his doorstep.

Chapter Fifteen

Lucifer

Billy found himself mumbling to himself in trancelike sleep. The thoughts were not his, nor the words he spoke either. He was channeling the demon's thoughts.

Billy's thoughts were his thoughts. Billy's actions were his actions. Billy's mind, like a caged animal at the zoo, was silently watching the actions of others and also those of himself, subject to the whims and desires of the demon inside of him. The sleep had served Lucifer's servant well, although he felt a bit constrained by the mortal vessel he found himself trapped within. For now, the vessel would have to serve his purposes. It was time for another phase of his plan. He strode over to the control panel. Switching one of the controls, he grabbed a microphone attached to the board and began to speak. Across the town emergency broadcast speakers squealed into use. Originally set up as tornado warning system many years past, he had spliced into the wires just recently, and he spoke to the townspeople in a calm monotone voice.

"This is an emergency. There has been an outbreak of highly virulent fire ants and help is on the way. Everyone should gather at the church until help from the neighboring county arrives. The police, along with ambulances and medical personnel, will be available within a few hours to help those injured. Please proceed with caution and gather at the church. And God bless."

He couldn't help but chuckle to himself about those last words he spoke, since he knew that was the last type of help the townspeople could expect. Hopefully, all of those remaining within the small town received the message. It was going to be so much easier if they all congregated together, like the sheep they were, for him to begin the next step of his plan.

Stepping out from the bowels of the quarry, he looked up to the ridgeline and could see the sun was almost below the horizon. The next thing he noticed was that the truck was missing. Furiously, he bounded up the side of the quarry, hoping that it wasn't true, but it was. Someone had stolen his truck, left him without a vehicle, miles away from town. Slowly he made his way back down the steep rock sides of the pit and went to check on his prisoner Stan. Stan was gone. The leather straps were hanging from the sides of the table, chewed clear through, like a rat had gotten ahold of them. He was mildly surprised to find that Stan still had enough fight left in him to escape. It was no difference to him, except that one less guinea pig had been lost for experimentation purposes. His plans would have to be changed to take into account these unforeseen circumstances.

It did not take long for him to settle upon a new and more suitable course of action. Smiling with pure wickedness, he packed a backpack and began the trek into town. Prior to leaving, he activated two tons worth of explosives he had previously positioned to blow up the town's water supply. The dam, which was directly east of the town, held back over two million gallons of water. He set the timer for a few hours. He had made sure the dynamite was in place months prior to the execution of his plan. This was just one of his many contingencies that came in handy after all these years of planning. Inwardly, he mused that it was very unfortunate for the humans that fire ants were masters at swimming.

Chapter Sixteen

Jesus Has His F150 Stolen

Mick was working in his basement mixing together a batch of his special poison when he thought he heard something. It sounded like someone had switched on a radio, but he knew it wasn't either of them, since she was working with him in the basement. Quickly rushing up the basement stairs with Sally right behind him, they managed to catch the last few sentences of the announcement over the town's loudspeakers. They both looked at one another and mouthed the word Billy to each other.

"Goddamn it. It's a set up. He is trying to get them all to gather together for him," Mick spewed out.

"Yeah, but why does he want them?" Sally replied.

"That is a good question, and I don't have any answer for you, but I bet it isn't to feed them milk and cookies, and tend to their medical needs. That bastard is going to try and kill the rest of them, is my guess, and it is easiest if they are all in one spot. Christ almighty, over half the town has already been killed by those ants of his, and he probably just wants to finish them off, is what I reckon."

Sally nodded her head slowly in agreement. Mick continued with his train of thought.

"That doesn't leave us a whole lot of time seeing as how we need to get these canisters filled and then drive out there to try and stop him from God knows what."

Understanding the urgency of the situation, they hurried back down into the basement to finish the work they had started earlier. Working as fast as they could, while delicately handling dangerous chemicals, had them both dripping with sweat and exhaustion at the end of another hour. But they had done it. They had a total of four canisters mixed and ready to use. Now the problem was getting them upstairs and strapped to the top of his Monte Carlo. Sally helped with some of the heavy lifting since his knee had not gotten any better. He was pleasantly surprised that for a skinny blond chick she was pretty strong. Maybe it was the adrenaline, but she managed to hoist up each of the sixty-pound tanks to him while he strapped them down tight to the roof of his car. With a rigged ski rack, bungee cords and copious amounts of duct tape and cordage, he strapped them down as best he could. He remembered what he had done to the devil the last time he had met him and didn't want to go up inadvertently in that same type of fire ball. When they finished, they jumped into the car and began the drive to the church.

With all of the work they had just labored over for the past few hours, they didn't even have time to think about what they were doing. They were going to try and meet the devil, holed up within Billy's body, on his terms and at his meeting location, and kill him. But they didn't have time to think about it, since time was a precious commodity they were desperately short of. Driving at dangerously unsafe speeds toward the town church was when they heard the loudest explosion either of them had ever heard in their lives. In fact, it was so loud that it was as though they had gone through a sonic boom and temporarily lost their hearing.

Out his driver's side window a wall of water over one hundred feet high was barreling toward them. The dam had been blown apart. Rushing directly at them and the town of Bishop, Texas was over two million gallons of water. It was just seconds away from overtaking them. They now understood why Billy had called them to meet at the church. It was a trap.

An hour earlier, Billy had found himself walking towards a gas station along the side of the main highway leading into town. Parked at the gas pump, with the fuel nozzle stuck in the gas tank, was a brand-new black Ford F150 pickup truck. Billy jerked the hose out of the truck and let the fuel spill all over the ground and the surrounding tanks. Then he dropped the hose on the ground but not before wedging a penny within the handle of the gas pump in order to keep it open and flowing. He walked up to the driver's side door and opened it. The keys were still in the ignition. Good, he thought. Turning the engine over, he noticed a large man with cowboy boots, jeans and a large wad of tobacco in his mouth come walking out of the gas station looking directly at him.

"What the fuck! Get the hell out of my truck you little shit. I'm gonna kick the fucken shit out of you when . . ." He was yelling all this while he was racing toward him with his fists raised. Billy proceeded to lock the doors of the truck and pulled out a cigarette. By the time the man, who was perhaps in his mid-thirties, had come around to the driver's side door, Billy had finished lighting the cigarette, taken a long drag, and was proceeding to blow out the smoke within the cabin. By now the man was pounding on the door and fumbling with the door latch trying to get into his own truck. He was furious, as he saw Billy nonchalantly smoking in his new truck. Then Billy turned his head and smiled at him, a crooked malicious smile.

"Get the hell out of my truck, asshole. Let me in. I swear when I get hold of you, I am going to rip you from limb to limb you piece of . . .

Billy opened up the small back window of the truck that separated the cab from the bed and with one flick of his finger, arced the cigarette he had just been smoking high up into the air. The man stood there with a curious and confused expression on his face until he looked down at the ground and noticed he was standing in gasoline. By the time his brain had registered that he was in deep shit, the cigarette was a foot off of the ground. As he turned to run, the last words he heard came from the skinny car thief behind the wheel of his truck.

"Didn't your mother ever tell you not to smoke at a gas station?"

Billy punched the accelerator, squealing the tires, just as the cigarette hit the ground. Instantaneously, the area around the gas tanks was on fire as well as the surprised, hurt and very angry cowboy. Turning on the radio, Billy found Johnny Cash was singing the Folsom prison blues, and he proceeded to turn up the volume. He liked the way Mister Cash told stories in a no-nonsense fashion. As he sped off onto the main highway, he watched through the rearview mirror as the gas station blew up in a thunderous explosion. Smiling, he watched as the man, still ablaze and rolling around on the ground, was picked up and blown across the road from the concussive effects of the explosion. Well, there should be some water along any minute to cool you off, he thought, if you are still alive. Laughing, he cranked the radio up and headed for the east hills, which looked down upon the town of Bishop. He wasn't going to miss this spectacle for the world.

Jesus Gonzales, who's truck was just stolen, was a third-generation Mexican American rancher, and had just bought himself his first new truck, a black Ford F150 pickup, at the age of thirty-two. He had worked hard for the past four years and saved enough to pay for the truck in cash. The town he lived in, right next to Bishop, was a close-knit community, and one without really any crime to speak of. He and his extended family lived on the outskirts of town, where his nearest neighbor was over ten miles away. In the community everyone helped one another out, especially in times of need, and they had your back if you were in trouble.

But he had just been robbed of his truck, laughed at and made fun of, square in his face, burned, and blown up. Any normal person would have been dead at this point, but Jesus was just stubborn enough to live, kind of like a cockroach that doesn't realize that it should be dead after being partially squashed. He was not going to let this man get away with what he had just done to him. The Gonzales family were bull riders, ranchers, cow punchers and farmers that worked the land with an intense savagery just to make a living. The large, calloused hands the family members sported were badges of honor and were a testament to the hard work they proudly inflicted upon themselves on a daily basis. It was this type of determination that had finally landed him his new truck after years of scrimping and saving. He sure as heck wasn't going to let death get in the way of him getting his truck back, and then beating the piss out of this scumbag, out-of-town thief. He had been run through a gauntlet of emotions all within a minute. From surprise at the stranger's audacity, to anger at someone attempting to steal his truck, and then to rage at being denied access to his own truck while this man calmly smoked inside of it. Then he had been surprised and dumbfounded by the flicking of the cigarette, and back to anger, as he saw what was happening to him. Then he was caught between fearing for his life and the anger from what had been said to him. Nobody plays games with me and talks about my mother, were his thoughts, as he was frantically rolling around on the ground trying to put the flames out across his body. Luckily his instincts were good, and he was wearing cowboy boots and jeans.

The next thing he knew, he was being hurtled across the street once the gas station exploded. It was an extraordinarily free feeling to be flying through the air, but the force of hitting the ground felt like he had been drop kicked by a Brahman bull. The wind had been knocked out of him, but luckily he had landed into some bushes which had cushioned his fall. And in the midst of it all, he was still attempting to put the fires out on his clothing. He was fighting desperately for survival. He rapidly pulled off what was left of his smoldering shirt and could feel the burns across his chest and back. Most of the hair on his chest and top of his head had been burnt off of him. He had to keep smacking himself all over the top of his head to stop the fire from burning his scalp and the remainder of his hair off, while throwing dirt and sand over his body. At least he knew how to take a dirt bath in an emergency like this. He knew from working the land for his whole life that dirt, just like water, could put a fire out.

Slowly rising to his feet, he looked over at the station which was engulfed in flames. He knew there was no hope for his friend, Sonny, who had worked behind the register. Sonny was a simple old man, a friend of his, one of the nicest guys he knew. The mounting anger inside of him felt like a volcano about to explode. He was hurt and needed medical attention but all he could think about was finding his truck and the man who had stolen it from him. The man's face was ingrained within his memory. With no shirt, third degree burns on parts of his chest and back, and hair that was still smoking, he began trudging down the road in his charred blackened jeans and boots. Determinedly, he told himself that by the Good Lord's grace he was going to catch this man and when he did . . . even the Lord was not going to be able to help him.

It was an awe-inspiring sight to see full grown seventy-foot popular trees completely swallowed up by a gigantic wall of water. Trees, farmhouses, telephone poles and everything in its path was flattened by the humongous wave that was washing down upon the town of Bishop. The only problem with taking a second to watch it, was to know that you were next, in terms of its deadly power and destructive force. Newton had given mankind the equation of force equals mass multiplied by acceleration. It was something to the nth power to try and gauge what force was rumbling down the mountain toward the tiny town, where almost everyone had gathered at the church for help and assistance.

Mick's eyes grew wide as he saw what was happening and his only thought was to get away.

He floored the 1973 Monte Carlo, knowing their only chance was to try and outrun the rushing water. Yanking the car hard west at the first major thoroughfare, with the tires squealing and the car nearly tipping over from the extra weight, he somehow righted the car. His mind had gone blank when he saw the wall of water approaching them. That was close, he thought, as he breathed a sigh of relief, while glancing over at Sally, who's eyes were the size of half dollars. The water was nearly upon them, a towering brown wave chocked full of every imaginable thing the wave had picked up over the past few miles! Thankfully, he had a straightaway in front of him. He pushed the gas pedal as far as it could go. With his foot to the floor of the car, giving it all it had, they still couldn't seem to outrun the wave. The roiling wave was so close that its rushing sound blocked out all other sound, as if they were trapped in some sort of vortex. When it got to within fifteen feet of them, he yelled at Sally to hold on tight. Flipping on a nitrous oxide switch, he had installed years ago in his younger days as a gear head, the vehicle was given a breath of fresh air. They hit speeds of well over one hundred and eighty miles an hour. The wave of water, matching their pace, had decreased some in height, although it was still well over thirty feet high. That was when Mick knew they were in trouble.

They were coming to a slight incline in the road, where it met railroad tracks, right before a bridge that spanned a dry riverbed. He couldn't slow down at this point, and knew they were going to be airborne with the speed he was traveling at. The bridge was only fifteen feet across, a relatively small river that ran through the west of the town, but none the less it was a major problem at this time. He had a decision to make. With no other choices available, he pushed the accelerator of the car to the floor, and watched as the speedometer pushed past the gauge's limit as they roared up the inclining ramp to the bridge. For the next few seconds, they were flying through the air above the bridge, feeling the effects of weightlessness and looking at each other. They both were in awe of what was happening, but Sally had more of a look of horror on her face as opposed to his, which was a mixture of oh shit, determination and grit. They flew through the air for over forty yards and came down perfectly on the other side. But the car was too hard to handle at those speeds. When they landed, both of them smashed upward in the car, hitting their heads on the roof despite having their seat belts fastened, and were thrown back and forth a bit like rag dolls. Upon hitting the bank on the other side, the car jerked to the left, went off the road and into a grove of pine trees where they raced between the trees at speeds of over one hundred miles an hour, just narrowly missing some of the larger pines. Mick could feel the undercarriage of the car getting ruined as he just tried to keep from hitting any of the big objects directly in front of them. Behind them the wave of water had reached the bridge and the river. The wave naturally found the lowest point of gravity, which was the riverbed twenty feet below the bridge.

After skidding past at least a hundred trees, Mick jerked the car to a smoking stop in the dry dirt. Looking in his rearview mirror, he could see that the wall of water was being diverted downstream and away from them for the most part. His heart was beating so hard it hurt his chest, but at least Sally's screaming had subsided, giving his ear drums a bit of respite, although it sounded like she was beginning to hyper ventilate. Soon enough, the water began sloshing around the tires of the car, but luckily it didn't seem to be going any higher than about a foot. The chasm where the river occasionally ran, was funneling the majority of the water downstream and away from them.

Jesus Gonzales had walked with charred boots and burnt pants for too long. He was finally within sight of the small town of Bishop. He was in agonizing pain. And the more that the shock and his adrenaline levels subsided, the more that the burns were beginning to hurt. His mind was collapsed within his own world thinking about the man, his truck, Sonny and what he was going to do when he found that man. Otherwise, he probably would have been wondering why there was no traffic on the road and or any people or animals anywhere to be found. That was when he heard it. A sound, like a monstrous lightning strike, crackled all about him. And then simultaneously the sound changed, into what can only be described as a giant crashing and flushing sound, as though a thousand waves had been unleashed upon his ears. His eyes darted to where the sounds were emanating from. He could hardly believe what he was seeing. Plainly, he could see that the dam had been obliterated. All of the water stored up behind it was crashing through where it used to stand. And for just one brief second, he looked off to the east, where he glimpsed his black truck high up on the East Mountains, with that murderer and thief man standing next to it, calmly smoking a cigarette, watching the whole scene unfold. Intuitively, he knew he was the cause of all of this. His inner rage boiled a bit higher at that moment and he vowed to survive, if only to get revenge upon him.

Frantically, he looked around for anything that would put him on higher ground. He was in the middle of high grass country caught out in the flats. He was not fast enough to get uphill where the mountains lay and was seemingly stuck out on a desolate stretch of road. The only thing high above the land that was near him was a tall popular tree. He made a dash for it. He had at most a minute to get to the heights of the tree, and even then, he might not make it, but at least if the tree didn't come down, he had a chance. He had no other choice. He was having a hard time walking, much less running from the explosion and burns he had suffered, but managed to ignore the pain, sprint to the tree and jump up to the crotch of it. With the bark tearing away what little bit of skin he had left on his arms and torso, he forced himself to hug it and work his way up its massive branches. It was a torturous climb. By the time the water hit, he was about twenty feet above the ground. But the water was thirty feet and rushing at over one hundred miles an hour. He had hooked his arm in between a crook in the tree where it had branched off, and retied his belt to include a large branch, but even that was useless. He felt himself yanked away from his haven and immersed in water tumbling over and over. The tree couldn't stand up to the water either and before long was floating with the current.

Right before the water smashed into him, he had held his breath and turned his back to the water, but to no avail as the force of the water knocked the air out of him. But he kept his wits about him. He knew that he was close to the surface of the water, initially being twenty feet above the ground, and he desperately clawed his way toward what he felt was up. It was difficult when you were being thrashed around in high speed water, getting hit with things you couldn't see, and unable to see. It's like his head and chest were going to explode as time continued on without him catching a breath, until he felt he couldn't take it any longer. It was all over for him if he opened his mouth, and he knew it. He felt his right arm out of the water and his head went toward it in a last-ditch effort for air. Gasping, his head made it above the water line. He had no idea where he was headed, and if he would ultimately live, but for the moment the sweet breaths of air he was sucking into his lungs were all that he cared about. Grabbing a tree that was caught in the torrid current next to him, he knew he was going along for the ride.

At the Baptist church, Old Man Johnson was trying to get everyone to calm down. Many of the townspeople were to the point of hysteria.

"Who is coming to meet us? I never heard that man's voice before," yelled a woman from the back of the church.

"I'm not sure, but we all heard it over the town's loudspeakers," Old Man Johnson replied.

"I don't trust any one of you at this point," shouted a man from the back, "I saw with my own eyes what those ants did to my wife and son in a matter of seconds and how Billy was possessed. The Lord's wrath is upon us I tell you! We are all going to die."

"Now, let's not get ahead of ourselves. I believe we are all good church going folks and there is no sense turning on each other."

"We need to run as far away from this town as we can, the devil is here amongst us! Look what happened to the preacher," another voice from the back of the church yelled out.

"Now folks, what we need to do is not panic like what we are doing right now. The voice over the loudspeakers said that help was coming soon. So, they must be aware of our current situation."

Throughout the congregation little groups of people were praying together as more survivors from the day's events showed up.

"I think we should put some people outside the church to be on the lookout for Billy and if any of those hordes of ants should try to attack again. We successfully fended them off earlier with fire, and I was thinking that we should do the same thing right now so that they can't get near us. Why don't we build a perimeter around the church and have a few men with guns stationed outside just in case that madman comes back and tries anything. That way we are protected just in case he shows up again."

There were a few grunts and acceptances of what was said, and a couple of the townspeople, who obviously were in agreement with him, began making decisions between themselves.

"I agree with Bert Johnson and think we should start right away in order to protect ourselves," a voice from the back of the church yelled out.

"And me too. I brought along a gun."

It was decided. Bert Johnson started giving orders.

"Harvey, you get the rest of my guns out of the truck. Hank and Tom, can you take the backside of the church? I will stay up in the church tower while Stevie and Sid can watch the front."

"Harriet, will you help get some of these remaining church pews outside to get ready to burn?" Bert asked.

Harriet hurried over to where Bert was standing to help with the pew.

The ensuing explosion and collapse of the dam shattered their plans. Looking east through the windows, the townspeople sighted a wall of water three times higher than the church barreling toward them.

The water surged over land; land that hadn't been touched by a major rainstorm in years. It was rock hard, dry, parched earth. An earth that let the water move practically unimpeded, as it instantly filled the little holes in the earth where the ants lived. The water that had been backed up behind the dam came from on offshoot of the Pecos River and had been the town's water source for over fifty years. There had been over two million cubic meters of water sitting behind that dam, and it was all set free at once. But it wasn't going to take long for all of that water to actually make its way through the opening of the crumbled concrete. Within the earth, any hole or crevice was being filled; and riverbeds that had not seen water for over a half a century were funneling the water whichever way that gravity flowed.

The ant colonies that surrounded the town of Bishop, Texas were hybrid fire ants. These were some of the toughest creatures that inhabited the earth. In the case of a disastrous water problem, such as a flood, they instinctively knew how to survive. As the water penetrated into their lairs, they escaped to the surface and connected themselves into balls of floating fire ants, periodically switching who was at the bottom of the ball and who was at the top. They knew their place, took orders, would sacrifice themselves if needed, and moved as one to the rhythm of nature, all as one cohesive unit. They floated together, legs entwined at the water line until they met land, or anything floating that they could grab. They had been constructed by God, and in this case manipulated by the demon's spawn in just a certain way to enable them to live in the harshest of conditions. One by one, they connected to each other in an emergency with the queen in the middle of the ball and moved along the water until it landed them at another suitable spot for colonization. This was the ingenuity and survival adaptation of the fire ant. And species 202 was stronger than any regular fire ant.

In this particular instance, he expected over twenty-five percent of the special fire ants to perish due to their proximity to the dam. He knew sustainable losses were inevitable in certain situations. Some things could not be avoided. The force of the water rushing down upon them was too quick and cataclysmic even for the ants to recover and rally around their queen. On the other hand, this still left the majority of species 202 ants alive! And most of them would be floating toward the town of Bishop.

Perched up on top of the East Mountains, Billy, with a pair of binoculars, had seen everything. He had seen the man who was at the gas station, who's truck he was driving, get swept away after trying to scramble to the heights of a tree. He had watched a car drive away from the onrushing waters and leap a bridge and get lost in some pine trees. He had seen a church ringed by fire awaiting his arrival. A pity, he thought, that he could not go down and greet them in person. He would have loved to make another entrance. Unfortunately, his plans had been altered by that infernal nuisance exterminator, who not only had a solution to kill his precious fire ants but had the audacity to strike out and lay a trap for him. That exterminator would find out who was in charge soon enough, he thought. He had not initially planned to kill all the people in the town, since he wanted to make some his personal slaves, but he could wait for the next town to put that plan into action.

The master plan had gone awry, and he had been forced to switch to a contingency plan. Knowing the ants would float downstream following the contours of the land, he thought of the repercussions, if any, of the dam bursting and killing thousands of people. Natural and manmade disasters happened all the time, he told himself. There would be no witnesses to any devilish actions, murderous ants, possessed people and murders. There would be no witnesses. There would be nobody left to speak out about what happened to this quiet little town in west Texas. And even if there were a few stragglers who survived, who would believe them? Certainly not any rational person.

Content with his work, he pulled out a smoke from the cigarette pack and realized that he didn't smoke, but Billy did. He felt the urgent need to smoke a cigarette. Curious that he had total control over this man's body but the urge to smoke was still there and compelled him to light up. Amazing that the human body could be controlled by such drugs, he thought. Dragging the tobacco into his lungs, he was surprised by how satisfying to the body it felt. Well, what did he care? He was the devil. He smoked and laughed to himself while high up on the hilltop looking down upon the death and destruction he had just wrought. He watched the tremendous wall of water approach the church, thinking about that bastard exterminator that had tried to vanquish him. He believed he had gotten rid of him as well as every other person within the town. Nobody should be able to survive what he had done to this town. He smoked and felt good about his evil deeds. Soon, he would gather himself up and move on to the next town. His ants would be waiting for him; waiting for him to sing them a song of death.

With the muddy water sloshing and swirling around the tires of the car, and thankful to be out of any immediate danger, there was nothing else to do but sit tight and wait it out. Sally was still breathing hard, although she had calmed down a bit so that she wasn't hyperventilating anymore. She had seen her life pass before her eyes when they had jumped the bridge and become airborne. Everything that was happening was surreal. The problem was that there did not seem to be an ending to it. At one point, when they had killed the raven-haired man, she had felt as though they had won, and the saga had ended. Now, she didn't see any end in sight. Deep within her own thoughts and fears, she finally looked over at Mick. She couldn't believe what she saw. He had his hands down his pants and was fumbling around. He was massaging himself while he stared out the window seemingly in a trance.

"Uh Mick, what are you doing over there?"

"Huh, nothing."

Awoken from his trancelike state, she had brought him back to reality.

"I was just thinking" and then his voice trailed off as he noticed he had been massaging himself, and she was aware of it.

"Oops, I guess I had spaced out there a bit and forgot where I was at."

Sally had caught him red handed and laughed. She reached over and put her hand on his cock.

"Next time you can let me help you out with that, Ok big boy?"

She said this with a smile and a bit of a southern Texas drawl, and his embarrassment melted away.

"Sometimes when I have gone through a stressful situation, my mind blanks out and I don't even realize what I am doing, and I find some strength in relaxing my boy, if you know what I mean. You know what? I was thinking about that old biddy with the cats acting so shocked about me masturbating. You tell me anyone that says they have never done it, and I will show you a goddamn liar. That sanctimonious hypocrite calling me a pervert. I tell you what, if we can get through this alive, we are going on a long vacation somewhere the hell out of here."

Listening to him, Sally didn't even realize she was smiling to herself. Mick was off on one of his tangents, and she had to laugh inside. In some instances, he was so crude about things, but he was truthful to a point. And he had made her mood brighten up at the thought of escaping the nightmare they were involved in with thoughts of tropical beaches and palm trees dancing in her head. Immediately she felt better. Yes, that would be nice if they could survive. Reaching out her hand, she stroked his hair. Breathing a sigh of relief, she was thankful for not having to run from a mountainous wall of water anymore and in her gut, she felt like they were going to make it. That is, as long as Mick was there to protect her. Sure, the town had been wiped off the face of the earth, but they were still alive, perhaps the only two within the town. With nothing to do but wait for a bit until the water receded, she found a John Denver CD and their minds floated away for a few minutes to the distraction of a rocky mountain high. Unfortunately, the reality that everyone who had gathered at the church were more than likely dead, and that Billy was responsible for it, was prevalent in the back of their minds. Even inspirational music had its limitations.

Chapter Seventeen

Chaos Across the Land

The ease with which the water ripped him from the branches of the popular tree surprised him. He thought he would be strong enough to withstand the assault of the onrushing water, especially with his belt tied around him as well as the tree. He had been swept along with the onrushing water, like a leaf in a storm. Mother Nature was a beast, he was a man, and he should remember that, he thought. He was being tossed about within the water with every other thing that existed on the plains of Texas, and it didn't feel too good. He had been smashed by something extremely hard a few seconds prior, maybe a tree trunk, and he had felt some ribs give way. He was in bad shape. He struggled with every breath to keep his head above the water while holding on to the log. He was continually pushing his legs and swimming, while making an upward motion. He saw the town center. He was having a hard time believing his eyes, but it appeared as if there were about fifty people outside the church, which was ringed with fire, awaiting his arrival by way of a massive wave.

As he and the wall of water approached, he could see Bert Johnson screaming at the top of his lungs.

"All the woman and children get up to the second floor of the church as fast as you can. We need to open up the church doors both front and back. Smash all the windows within the church. We need to make sure that this church has a chance of standing after this water hits. The more openings we have in the building the less resistance to the water and power of it we will encounter. If we let the water pass through the building, it just might stand."

A young man in his twenties began shattering the stained-glass windows and was screaming and yelling at the others as he raced to smash more. He had gotten the message loud and clear. Shocked out of their collective torpor, that had enveloped them once they heard the dam burst, each of them raced either up the stairs to higher ground, or were busy smashing windows and propping open the doors. In less than twenty seconds, they had managed to knock out all the windows before the wall of water hit them.

Jesus was unceremoniously deposited just upstream of the bridge. He was having a hard time staying afloat and was getting battered by the debris that was caught within the wave. Each breath of air was painful from the broken ribs he had suffered, and something had been jabbed into his right hand. For the first time in his life, thoughts of death began creeping into his mind. He was exhausted to the point where his legs were cramping up on him. He was ready to let go. That was when he saw that he was approaching a bridge which was just barely sticking above the water line. It was his last chance. With all of his remaining strength, he readied himself to try and grab hold of the bridge railing. He hit the bridge hard. But it had stopped him. After steadying himself for a bit to regain his strength with the water pinning him to the side of the bridge, he was just barely able pull himself up and onto the bridge.

Exhausted, he lay there on his back panting and wheezing. Finally, able to get a look at his hand, he found out what was causing the pain. Embedded within his hand was a prickly pear cactus, its spines embedded deep within his flesh. Some of them had gone in the front and come out the back of his hand. He had been skewered like a kabob. Delicately with his good hand, with his back against the bridge railing, he began pulling the prickly pear out of his hand.

When the water swept him away, his cowboy boots had abandoned him. Which meant he was now done to one sock and a pair of jeans. His hand throbbed and was puffed up, but he had finally managed to get the cactus spines pulled out. He lay on his back shivering, staring up at the cloudless blue sky, listening to the water rushing just below his head. He thought about his morning. Two hours ago, he had a breakfast sandwich in his hand, a new truck to his name and was looking to buy some bait and go fishing. For once he was going to enjoy a day to himself. All that changed as he had said goodbye to Sonny at the gas station.

Moving himself on to his elbows, he peered over at the East Mountains to see if he could see his truck, but he didn't see anything except a flattened and washed-out town. It looked like a war zone. Hardly a tree was standing, and those that were still upright, were ripped apart twisted wrecks. Mud covered just about everything he could see. He felt sick inside from what he was witnessing. As his concerns about his own well-being began to subside, he realized that there were probably people in town in much worse shape than he was. Struggling to his feet, wincing at the pain inside the right side of his chest, he slowly began to make his way off of the bridge and back toward town. As he approached the beginning of the bridge, he stopped for a second and said a prayer for whomever might be in need of help in the town and hoped he could find some help himself. And then he heard it. The sound of a car engine behind him. Turning around, not knowing what to expect, he saw an old black Monte Carlo with a man and a woman inside of it crossing the bridge. It slowed down as it spotted him and stopped. The driver rolled down his window and he heard the magic words he had been praying for.

"You need some help?" Mick called out.

They used the first aid kit Mick had in his glove box. The burn ointment tube had never been used before, and never would be again, as all of it went across the pinkish red skin that proliferated across his torso and back. Thankfully Mick always carried a spare change of clothes in his trunk. He never knew when something was going to happen on his job especially with skunks popular in the area. Although the clothing was painful to the touch, Jesus was able to muster a grin across his face feeling the warm touch of a flannel shirt, dry socks, jeans, and flip flops. And he even had a ride into town.

Mick drove the car back onto the road and headed toward the town center. Driving slowly across the mudded rock and tree strewn highway, they began to learn about Jesus and his day. With a Mexican American accent common to the area, he proceeded to tell them what had happened.

"Well senor and senorita, this gringo diablo just helps himself to my truck, while I am filling it up with gas and getting myself a breakfast sandwich. I come out of the station and start yelling at him to get the hell out of my new truck, and I start pounding on the door. So, he looks at me, takes a puff on a cigarette and smiles. And I don't allow any smoking in my truck, so I am getting really pissed off at this skinny mierda. Then, he slides open the back window, and flicks that little cigarette into the air, and that's when I notice he has dumped gasoline all around the tanks and my truck. The whole place lights up in flame while he peels out and leaves me with my ass on fire. I will never forget the dark eyes of that dirty bastard so long as I live. There I am rolling around, trying to save myself from the fire, and not paying attention to too much else and the gas station proceeds to explode. Luckily, I had rolled away from the gas station toward the road or else I would be dead by now. So, I am lifted up off the ground by the force of the explosion, get thrown like fifty feet across the street, and hit some bushes and rocks while I'm still on fire. That is when I remember, this cat has the audacity to yell something like, didn't your mother teach you not to smoke at gas stations, and I want to kill him so badly. He has my new truck, killed my friend Sonny, and tried to kill me while making fun of me. Oh, and the story gets even better from there . . ."

Mick and Sally looked at each other in amazement. They knew exactly who the bastard was that Jesus was speaking of. By the time he had finished his story, they were approaching the place where the church should have stood. The place looked like a tornado had touched down. The building was still standing, but it certainly wasn't standing straight up. What was left of it was bowed backwards at a thirty-degree angle. They could tell from the way the church was bent backwards, that the wall of water had hit the front of it. The support timbers were tilted backwards and broken in some places, but miraculously the back wall supports were still holding up the majority of the building, even though the structure was smashed beyond repair. It appeared to be the only building in town that was even partially standing. The rest of the town was flattened. There was one reason why the church was not flattened. The original builders of the church had poured a thick slab of concrete at the base of the church and had used hickory logs that were driven seven feet below the depth of the concrete.

As they surveyed the wreckage, they started to see weird looking mounds within the mud. That is when they saw a hand. And then a shattered leg. It dawned upon them that there were human beings scattered amongst them and buried under the mud that covered the landscape. Mick stopped the car amidst the wreckage and muck. Turning off the engine is when they first heard the faint cries of pain and suffering surrounding them. Each of them forgetting about themselves, jumped out of the car and began rushing to aid the remaining survivors. The loudest cries of pain were coming from the direction of the leaning church.

The cigarette was Billy's third within the last hour. He had watched the destruction with detached disdain. More intent on the survival of his precious fire ants, than the town's people destruction laid out below him, he witnessed how the ants had formed themselves into floating balls and rode along the top of the water, masterfully changing places amongst themselves to ensure their survival. They were a thing of wicked beauty, he thought.

At one point, he witnessed a man trying to escape by boat, only to unavoidably make contact with one of the ant colonies floating atop the rampaging waters. In vain he tried to stop them from boarding his small wooden boat, but once they made contact with something solid, the fire ants did not let go. Within seconds, the boat was a crawling mass of ants. The man had no other choice but to abandon his little boat and place of refuge to the ants and jump into the raging waters. Taking a final long drag on the cigarette, he threw it to the ground and walked back to the pickup truck. It was time to move on to the next town, although he had to stop at the quarry first. For now, he knew his ants would go to wherever the river flowed. As the water gradually subsided, they would make contact with the riverbanks and establish their presence within a few days in the towns just south of Bishop.

After an hour of driving, Stan had stopped at a roadside motel. His mental exhaustion combined with the loss of his hand were too much for him. Getting out of Billy's truck, he made his way to the night attendant on duty at the motel.

"I would like a room for the night."

"Sure mister. Just need to see some ID. Do you want a single or a double room?"

"I just need a single."

"Great. I got a room just outside where you parked. The rooms cost fifty-nine dollars a night plus tax, and if you have an animal, it is an extra ten dollars a night. I see you have a cage in the back of your truck.

We accept master card or visa." The night manager smiled at him while trying not to glance at his rumpled uniform and missing hand.

"Well, I'm not bringing any animal into the room, it's just a tranquilized coyote that I'm leaving in the back of the truck. The varmints are used to sleeping outdoors. Um, by the way, I am in serious need of using a telephone. Do you have a payphone? My cell phone isn't working."

"Uh . . . ok. Yeah, I understand. Cell phone service has been knocked out. I can't get hold of anyone on my cell phone either. Not sure what is going on, but I do have one land line here in the office that still works, if you want to use that?"

The night manager wasn't sure what to think about the whole situation, and although he had seen some strange things in his days, this one was beginning to pique his interest. It was not too often when one got a visitor such as this one, a dirty, one handed, crazed looking law man with a sedated coyote in his personal vehicle. He led him to where the phone was located, a small office behind the front desk, but only after he had paid for the room. He wasn't completely sure about this guest.

Stan closed the door to the office, slumped into a high back wooden chair, and dialed the number to the station. After a few rings, a panting Desmond Beauregard picked up the phone.

"Hello, police department, what can I do for you?" he drawled out in his Nawlin's accent.

"Desmond! Why the hell are you picking up the phone? This is Stan McCormick. What is going on over there?"

"Stan is that you! I can't believe it. We have been trying to get in touch with you for almost two days! Where have you been? Why haven't you contacted us? How did you make it out of the flood alive?"

"What the hell are you talking about? What flood!?"

"Why it's all over the news stations. The dam burst and the whole town of Bishop has been wiped off the map. All law enforcement, medical personnel and even National Guard from the neighboring county are on their way over there. You just caught me, before I was due to leave. I was locking up the station."

"Jesus Christ. This is insane! Do you remember the case we were working on with Roy the half-eaten policeman, the dead woman, the two arrested pussy cats and a lead on that exterminator? Well, it turns out that there is a psycho or demon of some sorts, who carried out the killing, and he attempted to kill us all over at Dinkin's Exterminator's headquarters with ants that attacked us. I mean, I was just at the hospital after chewing my way out of being held captive by this madman down at the quarry, who by the way had ants eat my left hand off, and there were hundreds of skeletons filling the hallways where the ants had attacked and finished everybody off!"

The silence on the other end of the telephone line was telling.

"Now just take it easy Stan. I know you have been under a lot of pressure and stuff from this case, but I want you to just relax. Where are you at now? I can have someone come and see you."

Stan could tell by the way the doctor was lilting his words and talking really polite that he assumed he had gone off the deep end.

"Goddamn you Beauregard! If you think I have gone nuts, I am going to stuff my handless stump up your ass. We have a demonic man on the loose, and he is going under the alias of a town bumpkin, known as Billy. He assumed his body, after he had gotten blown up by Mick, which is why I am driving his truck now, because it was the only vehicle left at the quarry. We are going to try and capture him with the coyote I have in the back his truck by having his spirit transfer over to it, that is if he believes he is in mortal danger. So, you understand we have a plan, but I am going to need some help."

After a slight pause, he asked.

"So how did the dam give way? Was it accidental or on purpose?"

After hearing the profanity laced tirade that sounded like some of the wackos that they incarcerated typically for being strung out on PCP or heroin, the doctor was stretched a bit thin trying to think of what to say next. He decided it might be best if he went and visited him on his way to Bishop.

"Listen Stan, I believe you, but I have to get to Bishop. People are hurt and dying. We don't know how the dam burst, but I have to leave. Where are you at? I can come help you. We can try and get everything sorted out. Does that sound good?"

Stan could tell that the doctor was still using that placating bullshit language on him, and he was getting angry, but if the dam had burst, then that truly was top priority, and furthermore he did need to see someone about the past few days. Furthermore, he needed help with the coyote as well.

"I am at Steven's roadside motel on highway fifty just north of Bishop. Come to room eleven and bring me a rifle and a colt 45 while you are at it. Billy took mine."

"Ok sure thing Stan. Now just take it easy until I get there and try and relax. I should be there in about an hour. Bye."

Stan slammed the phone down on the receiver and hit the wall with his good fist. As he did this, he heard the night manager stumble into something, groan and fall down. He should have known. He had been intently listening with his ear up to the wall the whole time. Stan exited the manager's office to find him lying on the carpet in the act of getting up. As their eyes met, Stan already perturbed by the medical doctor's lack of belief in his story, could tell by the fear in the night manager's eyes that he felt the same way about his mental state. And to make matters even worse, he was pissed off that he had been eavesdropping on their private conversation. Raising his left stump toward him, he jerked it up and down.

"If anybody tries to take my coyote, I am going to be one pissed off lawman. Do you understand? I expect that beast in my vehicle when I am ready to leave."

The night manager from his position on the floor just nodded at him. Then, as he turned to leave for his room, he happened to see Gideon's Bible sitting on a shelf next to a wooden cross hanging on the wall.

"By the way I am going to have to confiscate these items due to a police emergency. I will make sure you get them back. Ok?"

With a scared look in his eyes, he just nodded with a puzzled look on his face, while Stan, armed with a confiscated Bible and cross, headed for room eleven. When he made it to the room, Stan turned on the television and looked at the news reports of what was happening in Bishop.

He knew that the way he had been talking to Desmond had only exacerbated the situation, but he didn't have much time and needed to get his message across to him, even if he knew the story sounded absurd. He thought back as to how he had not believed Mick at their first meeting, with all of his talk about evil demons and ice-cold houses, but now he knew it was true. Looking down at his arm, he knew it was all too real to just be a bad dream. He had seen with his own eyes the ants attack and the evil within the man that had tricked and drugged him before imprisoning him in the depths of the quarry. He had seen the bodies of Roy and Edith Baxter and the skeletal remains of everyone at the hospital. There was no longer any doubt as to who or what he was up against, but even so, he was as nervous as he had ever been, and he found himself pacing back and forth within the room looking at the digital clock, waiting for the medical examiner to arrive.

An hour later, the medical examiner arrived at the motel. Desmond saw the truck and parked alongside of it. Before he knocked on the door, he glanced at the coyote in the cage. Not knowing what to expect, while shaking his head in disbelief, he began walking toward the room. He noticed a man peering from behind a window at the front of the motel, presumably the night manager. Stan pulled open the door before he could even knock. Desmond was aghast.

Looking back at him was a hollow-eyed vision of a man, certainly not the same man he had seen and conversed with just a few days ago. Stan hurried him into the room, closed and locked the door behind him. Stan proceeded, in an incoherent gesticulated and half crazed manner, to explain everything that personally happened to him as well as what had transpired within the town. The medical examiner couldn't help but keep glancing at where Stan's left hand used to be. It was quite a shock to see the lead detective on the murder investigation talking wildly about a devilish man with black eyes, ants that were controlled killers, and a town with thousands of victims that had been wiped off the map.

Even though the medical examiner believed in God, he only partly believed in the existence of the devil and was having a hard time believing the far-fetched story that Stan was spinning for him. Sure, he had to believe that the town had somehow been wiped out, but that was merely a dam bursting, he said to himself. But . . . Stan was missing a hand, and there were other strange happenings, such as how they found Roy the policeman and also how Edith Baxter had been killed. As he mulled all of the strange occurrences in his mind, he was becoming more apt to believe that there was some sort of evil spirit or demon behind it all. The thought of Roy, steaming and half eaten, was an image he could not get out of his mind.

"So, you have a plan to apprehend this man?"

"Apprehend him shit—I'm not talking fair justice and a trial here, Desmond."

Desmond's eyes widened a bit realizing what Stan was talking about. Pushing his shoulders up, while bringing down his head with a smirking grin on his face, he gave him the shrug that asked Stan, without saying anything, well then what are you going to do?

"Mick and I have a plan. It involves a coyote, some surgery, a few sticks of dynamite, a detonator, the use of animal tranquilizers and utilizing the element of surprise. I am actually glad you are here, since you can perform the surgery on the coyote and insert the dynamite in its belly prior to us getting to the rock quarry. Are you up for some motel surgery?"

Stan couldn't help himself as he began laughing at the medical examiner's facial expression, go from one of amusement to sheer terror, as he was brought in on the plan that sounded like something out of a cheap horror film. The plan was set to be launched just before the break of dawn and that gave them just enough time to do the operation.

The surgery was a success. Cutting open the coyote and inserting the two sticks of plastic dynamite was the easy part, even if his medical skills on living things were a bit rusty. What was going to be difficult was keeping the animal alive long enough for it to serve its purpose.

Unconscious but alive, the coyote was blissfully unaware that it was going to play the lead role in the destruction of the demon that inhabited Billy's body. With a long pull on the syringe needle, the doctor was able to measure out enough morphine to make the animal not feel the effects of the surgery, and also not put it to sleep, permanently. It was a delicate procedure. Pushing the needle into the animal's abdomen, he forced the contents very slowly and gently into the inside of the animal and then proceeded to retract the syringe. Wiping the sweat from his brow, he glanced backward only to find the lieutenant fast asleep in a corner chair.

It was nearly time. He made a final check of the animal's breathing and heart rate, and found them to be high, but nothing too abnormal given the recent surgery.

After splashing some water on his face, he emerged from the bathroom and shook the lieutenant by the shoulder.

"Time to wake up and smell the coffee. We got a coyote to deliver and a demon to smite. It will be light in a few hours."

With a small grin, he turned back around and finished knotting his belt. He really didn't believe much of the story he had been told a few hours ago, but he wasn't one to not obey orders and not go along with what he was told to do. Besides, he reckoned, if ever things did calm down and things went back to normal, this was going to make one hell of a story to be told for the rest of his life. Although, he had to admit to himself, the events of the last few days were beyond the scope of pure coincidence. How could a dam burst and wipe out a town just after a policeman was found eaten by ants? And how could a woman be murdered by her pussycats? And then later the lieutenant lost his hand while being held captive by a madman that imprisoned him within the depths of a quarry? None of it made any sense.

He could hear Stan groaning while attempting to rise from the chair. He sounded horrible.

"What the hell time is it?"

"Three thirty in the morning. Grab a cup of coffee; you will feel better."

The medical examiner watched as he shuffled over to the bathroom dashing some water on his face. He proceeded to get himself a cup of coffee. Even this early in the morning it was hot in West Texas. And window air conditioners in cheap motels never quite cooled anything down.

As he gradually came to his senses, he looked at the drugged coyote with the incision in its belly and settled back into his chair with the cup of coffee in his left hand. He found himself staring at the bandaged stump that made up what used to be his right hand. This wasn't the way that things were supposed to have happened. Without ever raising his eyes from his stump he started to ask the doc questions.

"How did the surgery go?"

"Fine . . . just fine. The animal certainly won't be running around anytime soon, but I reckon it will be alive for the required time we need it to be."

"How are we going to get it to the quarry without blowing ourselves up in the process?"

"Well, that is a good question. I figure if we put a few blankets on the bottom of that cage and a few over it, and bungee cord the cage down to the bed of the truck, we should be ok. Besides, it should be knocked out for another hour or so."

"Alright, then I guess we should be hitting the road. Let's go back over the plan while we drive there so we are both on the same page. I just hope Mick shows up and that bastard is actually at the quarry. As you can see, I won't be able to take the shot. I never was one to be able to shoot with my left, but Mick can. How are you at shooting?"

"I used to be pretty good, but my eyesight isn't what it used to be. We both better hope your previous number one suspect shows up. For all we know, he was wiped off the face of the earth with the rest of the town."

They both looked at each other. There was a lot to think about and very few answers.

Prior to them driving away from the motel, the hotel manager had watched them strap down the animal crate to the back of the truck's bed. The medical examiner left his vehicle in the parking lot as they drove off together toward town. He wondered what he would find in the room and made a mental note to make sure he charged extra for the coyote. It had been in the room.

Chapter Eighteen

Picking Up the Pieces

The night was pitch black except for a few stars visible between smoky clouds that had been drifting eastward away from the town. Coupled with the soot from the fires, the air was scented with a mix of burning pine trees and a moist almost peculiar smell. A smell, which only water can unlock when unleashed upon an arid parched land beaten down for thousands of days by the sun. Billy looked down upon the ruined town. He wondered if the exterminator and his woman accomplice had been killed in the deluge.

Grabbing his last cigarette from the pack, he reflected on the day's events. It was a strange thing to be addicted to smoking cigarettes, he thought. It was also a very strange, not to mention exhausting, to be controlling the mind of this hillbilly Billy, while he went about his business. Unfortunately, he did not have any choice but to borrow someone else's body since his body was spread about in a million little pieces. His mind was simmering with hate for Mick, who had destroyed his body and had momentarily thwarted his legions. He realized he needed a more suitable host. Taking a last drag on the cigarette, he proceeded to grind it out on his arm. He could smell the burning flesh, feel the searing pain, but the sensation did not matter to him. Deep inside of him, he could hear Billy's locked away mind screaming for him to stop. Chuckling to himself, he made his way to the bottom of the quarry. He needed rest. It had been a long day. In the morning, he would search for a new host. There was a prison just a few hours away by car and he was sure there would be better suited hosts available to carry out his plans.

Billy, the real Billy, hidden within his own body somewhere deep inside his mind, knew everything that was happening and everything he was doing, but he had absolutely no control over his actions. It was difficult for him to keep the outsider's thoughts from being his own thoughts. He felt like a gorilla trapped behind a pane of glass at the zoo. The one that you could see and view, but that no one could hear, separated from everything within its walled enclosure. At other times, he was part of the killing and the mayhem, especially when it intimately involved his emotions. He could feel the cigarette burning through his flesh, cauterizing while it burned away his skin, and yet he was powerless to stop his hand from causing it. The mind control was nearly complete. He was the passenger in the back seat of a car going for a ride at a hundred miles an hour. A ride that was testing the limits of his sanity as the car moved faster and faster down a long dark tunnel.

The revulsion Sally felt staring at the child's hand, which was sticking out of the mud, was the final straw. Up until that moment, she had handled the sheer madness that had engulfed her life over the past three days, but now the reality of it was too horrible for her to except. The little bit of lunch she had eaten was violently vomited, splattering across the side of Mick's car and embedding itself within the rim of the front tire. Her body continued to try and throw up, even though her stomach had been emptied, and soon she found herself dry heaving while leaning against the puke spattered car. She was on her knees. Her head felt like it was going to explode. In her mind, she experienced visions of the man with the red eyes, exploding to pieces, only to find he had transferred his spirit into Mick's hapless neighbor, Billy. She felt a hand on her back, and from the soft touch upon her, knew that it was Mick. He set a water bottle down next to her and let her know he had to check and see if he could help any of the survivors. She could hear his feet sloshing through the mud as he proceeded in the direction of the church.

At the church, which really was not much more than a collapsed building, he could see that a few people were attempting to extricate themselves from the mud. Mick and Jesus helped the survivors, including Old Man Johnson, clean themselves of the mud and administered first aid as best they could. Off in the distance, they could hear the wail of sirens, and see the faint flashes of red and blue approaching. Thankfully help would arrive soon. Once the ambulances and medical personnel arrived, Mick went looking for Sally. He found her in the passenger seat of his car staring straight ahead. They drove back to his house in silence.

He knew the plan and needed to prepare for the following morning. His knee hurt, Sally was reeling to the point of not functioning, and he wasn't sure if Stan was even going to show up at the quarry. He had his doubts about him when they had last parted, by the look of fear in his eyes. It was a scared look, and his gut told him that he wasn't going to show up with the coyote, that they had worked so hard to capture. In his mind, he couldn't shake the feeling that he was going to run away. He knew that would leave him stuck at the quarry without a plan and facing the devil. He did not like the odds.

Arriving at the house, he noticed that his dogs were not around. He assumed they must have fled when they heard the dam break. Looking at his once pristine beautiful house he cringed. The house had been through an explosion and had fire damage. The front windows were blown out and two junked burnt-out cars were on display in his front yard. He winced at the scene, but knew it really was immaterial compared to what he faced, and that he should count himself lucky for the house not being in the path of the water. His obsessive, compulsive disorder was still in place, but it had to take a back seat to more immediate matters. He helped Sally out of the car. She made it to his bedroom where she lay down and went to sleep. He could have slept as well, but he knew he had a few things to get ready prior to him driving to the quarry. He double checked the tanks on the top of the car and found they were loose. He secured them. He salved down his knee with CBD oil for the pain. Then he got to the real important job. He raided the refrigerator and found some fried chicken. It had been sitting in his refrigerator for a few days, but he didn't care. He was famished. He wolfed them down with a couple of cold beers and thought over the plan that he and Stan had concocted earlier in the day.

It wasn't much of a plan, he thought. They would get to the quarry and stake down the coyote on a rope. The coyote would be rigged with some dynamite surgically placed inside of its body, and when Billy came out of the quarry's entrance, they would shoot him with animal tranquilizers and attempt to disable him. Once Billy and the demon inside of him realized that he was trapped, they hoped he would recognize the animal near the entrance and move to transfer his demonic presence to the animal. In this way, they could save Billy and then detonate the dynamite within the coyote and be done with the son of a bitch once and for all. Mick knew it was a weak plan, but it was the best he could come up with. He drank the last of his beer feeling the tiredness in his mind and bones. He needed some rest even if it was for only a few hours. He made his way to his bedroom and lay down next to Sally. He knew his brain was not working well, almost if he were drugged or comatose, like most of the people around town. He was asleep almost as soon as his head hit the pillow.

Chapter Nineteen

Ready, set, action.

Even the roosters were asleep at this time of the morning. Amidst the smoke-fog that covered the ground, brought about by the previous day's deluge from the broken dam, visibility was poor. A person couldn't see more than ten feet in front of them, without the landscape becoming hazy and objects becoming indiscernible. And yet the plan was in motion and there was no turning back.

Mick was first to see the faint yellowish hues from the headlights of the truck. Flicking his headlights on and off a half a dozen times, he knew he had caught the attention of the other vehicle as it slowed and eventually stopped. They were on the only road that ran into the quarry. Mick pulled up alongside and recognized the lieutenant in the passenger seat but didn't recognize the man driving. Glancing at the back of the truck he could see that they had the cage strapped down.

"Is it done?"

"Yeah, the doc here was able to perform a little operation last night," as he pointed involuntarily with his stump at the man behind the wheel.

"Hey, if this all works out, I promise to get you an eye patch and a hook for that hand of yours, ok pirate?"

The doc's eyes grew wide at the ribbing by Mick.

"That's just great. And if we get through this, I will make sure you get an occasional extra bologna sandwich during your three squares a day."

Mick got a big smile on his face. It was returned in full. Realizing the two of them were on better terms than he imagined, even the doc got a smile on his face.

"So . . . how's the patient?" Mick asked turning toward the medical examiner.

"The coyote is drugged and is doing just fine, but the animal should be coming out of it real soon," he drawled in his thick Louisiana accent.

"I placed those two sticks just outside his stomach cavity next to his intestines. It doesn't take too much to set those sticks off . . . so the quicker we can get him staked down, the better off we are. I got a rope, a real long one, that will attach to the collar."

Mick nodded his approval and moved around to the back of the truck. Pulling up the blanket he could see the animal with the bulge in his belly where a wicked cut had been incised and then sewn back together. Its breathing was heavy and labored. He unstrapped the restraints, and with the help of the medical examiner, gently lifted the cage down from the bed of the truck. It was approaching five in the morning and there was very little time left. Between the doc and him, they cautiously and silently moved down from the ledge of the gravel quarry. Meanwhile, the lieutenant carried the collar and stake in his good hand, while the rope which was wound in circles was slung around his neck and shoulder. Twenty feet from the entrance, they staked down the animal and slogged back up the rocks in the quiet predawn darkness.

Once they reached the top of the quarry, they got inside the truck to discuss the last minute details of the plan. It was then that they realized they had a major problem. The thick fog, almost California Tule fog in nature, had rendered the plan unworkable. Mick couldn't see to shoot accurately, either Billy or the coyote, without almost being right on top of them, and that certainly wasn't going to work. The original plan was to shoot the animal tranquilizer into Billy, have the demon spirit realize it was in trouble, thereby forcing it to look for another host, and consequently transfer to the coyote. After the transference, they would then blow the coyote to kingdom come.

"So, besides not being able to see anything, just how are we supposed to know when the demon spirit has transferred from Billy to the animal?" the doc asked.

They all looked at each other as it dawned on them that unless Billy said something, or did something that would alert them that he was back to normal, they wouldn't know.

"Ah shit, shit, shit shitty goddddddam plan. Wa, Wa, Wa What the fuck!"

Mick's turrets and stuttering issue went on full display for them as he began pounding his fist on the dashboard.

"May, may, may maybe," he stuttered "We coo, coo, could have someone near the coyote with a light to flash us, if, if, if they notice a change in the animal's or Billy's s s-state?"

The doc and lieutenant stopped and stared at Mick as he struggled to recoup his regular functions. The lieutenant spoke next.

"Well, we can't see anything anyways, and I reckon one of us has to be down near the entrance. I can let off a flare once I see Billy come out of the entrance of the quarry, and I guess I can let off another one if I see a change in Billy or the animal. Then you shoot him with the tranquilizer. What do you think, fu fu fu fu fucker?

Mick and the doc with huge grins on their faces, began laughing uproariously, having been made fun of by the lieutenant.

"Deal, let's shake on it!" Mick said.

The twisted look on the lieutenant's face made them laugh even harder, knowing he had no right hand, and ultimately, even the lieutenant began laughing uncontrollably with them. It had been a long couple of days, and they were all a bit loopy. That was when they heard the coyote begin to howl.

Sally awoke with a start. She could tell it was still dark outside, but something had brushed up against her nose, and she felt the presence of something staring at her. In a state of pure terror, she madly attempted to adjust her eyes to the dark. Two brown eyes were staring directly at her. Unable to form words, she began to hyperventilate, and then it moved toward her and licked her. Comprehending it was only Mick's dog and not some demonic killer, she grabbed it and hugged its big head. The other dog jumped on the bed, and for a minute a love fest ensued at the house of Mick.

The digital clock on the nightstand read four thirty-three. After calling out for Mick a few times, she realized he had lied to her. He had left without her. Damn his machismo! She thought something like this might happen. They had discussed the plan the night before, and he had tried to dissuade her from going, but she had been adamant and finally he had relented. Now he was gone. He had slipped away while she slept. Whipping through the house, she accomplished her mental list in minutes. She went to the bathroom, splashed water on her face, tied up her hair, pulled on her blue jeans and a grey sweatshirt she found in his drawers, popped two aspirin, since the bottle was on the sink and her head still hurt, and grabbed the keys to the only available vehicle, an old pickup truck. The dogs were wagging their tails and waiting in the bed of the truck, seemingly already aware she was going on a trip. She didn't have time to argue with them and she liked their company anyway, but she made sure they sat in the front of the truck with her. Turning the truck over, it belched smoke and backfired. Wiping her hand over the dusty dash, she could see it had not been run for quite some time, but to her surprise there was three quarters of a tank of gas left. That was more than she needed to get to the quarry. Squealing out of the garage, she swerved around the mess in the front yard, as the dogs danced next to her, trying to keep their legs under them. It was quarter to five in the morning, she was madder than hell for having been lied to, and minutes away from the quarry.

As the medication wore off, the rising pain from within the coyote had become unbearable. Somehow it had become tied down and its belly hurt but not from the usual hunger pains. Howling with hurt, anger and confusion, it was trying to shake the cobwebs out of its head and figure out what was happening. It didn't recognize the area or know why it hurt so much and felt so weird, like it had swallowed a rock of some sort. The drugs were wearing off.

"Ahwoweee, ahwoowee, ahwoweeee . . ." it yelled into the darkness.

Billy, the real Billy, could hear the noise of the coyote howling in the darkness, as he lay in a state of stasis, at the back of his own mind and body. Trying hard to concentrate, he knew it was a cry of pain rather than one of hunger, having heard coyotes many times before during the evenings. Something was wrong. What was wrong? Is there something more to this than just a coyote making noise? Could his friend and neighbor Mick be behind it? He didn't know what was causing it to howl in pain in such a weird, distorted manner, but he was determined that whatever bit of who he was and whatever control he had, to be vigilant if an opportunity presented itself to be free of this demon. He listened intently to the screams and steeled himself to jump at any chance he might possibly have at regaining his freedom.

The demon was disturbed. The caterwauling racket that was entering his ears was infuriating. He could not sleep with this awful sound emanating from outside his sleeping quarters. With the unsteadiness of a man just waking up, he slipped his legs over the side of the cot, fastened his boots and made his way toward the entrance with deadly intentions to quiet whatever beast was making such a racket.

Staring through the misty fog, he was having a hard time comprehending what he was looking at. Was that an animal tied down howling in pain? Also, there was the outline of a man nearby whom he could faintly smell, with his memory racing to try to remember that smell, and there were others present at the top of the quarry. It was a trap and he realized it quickly. They would all die, and he would see to it quickly. His eyes blazed red, instantly alert.

And from his throat came the sound of the hum, so loud and striking with its intensity, that everyone was caught off guard. It drowned out the cries of the animal and Mick's shouts to fire the flare gun, as he desperately tried to locate them through the fog. Meanwhile, the medical examiner began making entreaties to God as he dropped to his knees, while keeping his face upward toward the heavens. And as the lieutenant tensed, so his trigger finger shot the flare directly into the ground, its discharge dancing along the ground like a loose fourth of July firework. There were intermittent seconds of pink light created from the flare, where eyes locked upon eyes, Mick's upon Billy's, and Billy's upon each of them, except the praying doctor who had seen enough. The demon that was Billy smiled. He wanted the satisfaction of these kills. He began walking toward them.

From underground, millions of ants began crawling their way to the surface, alarmed and agitated, as the high-pitched hum drove them forward. The ants were triggered to be famished with hunger, based upon a certain inflection within the humming sound he was making.

The ground was seething with what appeared to be a rippling black water pouring out of the entrance to the quarry and from other holes in the ground. Mick wanted to shoot but couldn't locate the target. The plan was unraveling faster than a ball of string rolling downhill. And then suddenly, a loud screeching noise caused everyone to jerk their heads upward toward the road. A pair of headlights came roaring out of the mist, crashing down upon all of them.

Sally, still steamed up from being left behind at Mick's house, had made it to the quarry in record time. She rounded the bend of the road, the wheels of the old truck screaming against its own rims and shot into the loose gravel. Not able to see much of anything in the heavy fog, she aimed the truck at the dancing lights from the flare gun. Unfortunately, she could not see where the road ended, due to the thick smoky fog that lay across the land. Coupled with not being able to see where the road ended, and a severe lack of brakes on the truck (which is why Mick had not driven the truck for months), she realized too late that she was not going to be able to stop. The truck flew straight off the road catching air and began bounding down the steep quarry walls directly at Billy and the lieutenant. The two of them, as well as the coyote, looked up at their impending doom stricken with horror, their mouths wide open in disbelief. The doctor and Mick turned to see what was happening, and found themselves staring at the flying truck, Sally gripping the wheel, furiously pumping the brakes.

The scene played out in slow motion. The demon inside Billy instantly stopped his humming, causing the converging ants to pause in their tidal wave of motion, as he dove back toward the opening of the quarry trying to avoid the front grille of a truck. The lieutenant dove in the opposite direction, also trying to avoid the front of the truck as it barreled directly at him. The coyote, who was in the middle of the two men, curled up tight in a ball beside a large stone trying to make himself as flat as possible.

The front wheels of the truck, jerking left and right from hitting the uneven rocks, erratically determined its path down the side of the slope. The right wheel cut the rope that staked the coyote down as the vehicle bounded just above its head, while the left wheel clipped Billy's left foot and catapulted him like a spinning top through the air and deposited him about thirty feet down the slope. Meanwhile the lieutenant felt the rush of air as the truck swooshed by him with the tailpipe blowing exhaust into his face. Seconds later, and three hundred feet down the slope at the base of the rock pile, the truck skidded to a stop enveloped in a cloud of dust.

Mick reached Sally first. He didn't know what he would find, but he certainly did not expect to see her laughing hysterically.

"Woo-hoo that was incredible! Did you see the way that damn demon within Billy went flying!? I bet he pissed his pants when he saw me flying down the hill at him. I got him, Mick. I got him," as the laughing began turning into tears. He put his arms around her and let her cry tears of joy and relief into his shoulder as she kept repeating the words, I got him. Soon thereafter the medical examiner reached them.

"Goddamn little lady, I don't know who you are, but you were the answer to my prayers. I never seen anyone drive like that in my whole life. And my God, with no fear, no fear at all, just straight off the side of the road and down the hill right at them. Unbelievable. If I live to tell this story, nobody is going believe me! Just incredible what you just did."

The sound of a truck engine starting at the top of the quarry, made them stop talking and turn to look back up at the road. Through the mist, the sight of red taillights was all they could see as it disappeared into the distance. Billy had left.

Johnny Cash blared through the crew club cabin as he floored it heading south. His left ankle, already swelling, lay twisted on the floor of the truck. It did not matter to him as the body had served its purpose. Beside him on the seat, lay Max the coyote, with its thick rope leash. It was his coyote now and he had decided he would call it Max. The prison wasn't far ahead, about another twenty-five miles, and Max would be useful.

Minutes later he found himself pulling up to the main gate of the prison. He could see the overweight guard reading a magazine . . . Lazily, he pulled back the sliding glass window that separated them, with a much-maligned attitude for having to work.

"ID please."

His eyes grew wide as he saw the coyote in the passenger seat.

"Hey buddy, you can't bring that animal in here. What the . . ."

He was looking down the barrel of a colt 45.

"Open the gate."

The guard stared at his own mortality at the end of that long chamber screaming his name. He was afraid. Very afraid. And he knew this one was going to shoot. He could see it in his eyes. Crazy forbidding, dark pools without any light, eyes. Not daring to look away, he nodded and backed upped toward the lever that opened the gate. The only question was when he would try to jump out of the way of the open window. He would have a chance to unholster his gun . . .

"NOW!"

"Please mister I got a wife and kids."

He didn't.

As he pulled on the lever opening the gate, he jumped backward out of the gunman's line of sight. Grabbing for his gun, he fumbled with opening his holster. After an eternity of perhaps a few seconds, he realized he didn't have any bullets. He might as well be dead, he thought. He had forgot to load his gun since target practice last night. The faint sound of footsteps had him in a panic. Like a cheap Western movie, the bad man walked in with a gun in his hand, but this time with a live coyote attached to a long rope, that walked alongside him like it was some sort of pet.

"Sit down."

The guard and coyote obeyed immediately. He also involuntarily began wetting his pants.

The guard was tied to his chair with the rope from the coyote collar, which was then tied to the building. Then, pulling out silver electrical tape, the man physically taped the coyote to the front of the guardhouse windows. What the . . . was happening, he thought? This man was certifiably crazy.

"Call your superiors and tell them you are a hostage. Let them know you opened the gate. If you say anything else, I will watch you die and come visit you every so often in hell. DO it NOW!"

The call was made. He did exactly as he was instructed.

After the call was made, he proceeded to tape shut the guard's mouth all the way around his head, then continued onward by continuing to tape his forehead from front to back. By the time he was finished he had covered the guards entire head in silver electrical tape so that just the eyes peered out from between the silver strips.

The prison came to life as soon as the call was made. It officially went on lockdown, as loudspeakers began issuing a call for all prisoners to return to their cells. Sirens began blaring. The sound of metal clanging against metal rang through the prison yard while search lights were turned on. Men in uniforms were instantly running in all directions. About twenty of them, slowly, began converging on the guardhouse. They could see the guard, propped up on his chair, his large eyes peering back at them through strips of silver tape. But what they couldn't stop staring at was the coyote splayed against the window snarling at them. Its belly was huge. The body was distended in an abnormal fashion, protruding up against the glass, with the recent incision dripping blood down the exterior of the guardhouse window.

Inside the prison yard, the inmates who had been exercising and doing their morning calisthenics, were now looking around in confusion. With the klaxons blaring and the onslaught of sensory overload from the prison going on lockdown, they became excited and agitated as the guards attempted to round them up. A good lot of them were looking at a strange man they had never seen before, dressed all in black, just outside the two prison fences, holding a gun in his hand.

Slowly, inch by inch, the prison guards made their way to the guardhouse until they finally stormed the entrance. By the time they secured everything, there were a total of seventeen of them, either inside the building or just outside of it. They found it empty except for the one guard. Ripping the tape from his mouth he began screaming at them.

"He is over there behind the black truck looking at us! See!? Right there, in front of the fencing, near the recreation yard. Wait, he's waving at us? Oh my God. He is pointing that gun at us. Hey, help me out of this chair . . ."

The bullet from the Colt forty-five gun was straight and true. By the time the guards had locked on to his position with their eyes, he had already fired. One shot. That's all that was needed. The bullet smashed against the belly of the coyote with enough force to trigger the dynamite. And trigger it did. The explosion was deafening. Body parts and people began flying in all directions across the area as the building disintegrated before the prisoner's eyes. The guardhouse was gone, obliterated, and nothing but a pile of smoke and ash was visible from where it used to stand. Everyone in the recreation yard had stopped and some had begun cheering. The guards were no friends to these men. Five men were dead including the tied-up guard, whose head had become unattached and was rolling around like a silver soccer ball. Five more of them were critically wounded, two of which were without their legs and would die shortly thereafter. That was when a distinct humming began in earnest, mixed with the sounds of the sirens and klaxons blaring out at full blast.

Hobbling to the fence line, Billy noticed that most of the guards and inmates were struck by the sounds emanating from all around them, rendering them helpless and ineffective. Amidst the chaos, his ants began rising from the ground, forming attack groups. With a pair of bolt-cutters, he made a hole in the two chain link fences and began shouting at the prisoners, in order to get their attention. Then he got back in the truck and awaited their arrival. The prisoners, realizing there was an escape route, ran toward him and freedom. He watched as his legions of ants indiscriminately attacked guards and prisoners alike.

By the time the prisoners had gathered around him, he had already chosen his next host. The largest alpha male was impressive. At roughly two hundred and fifty pounds of pure muscle and over two meters in height, he was a giant of a man. His name was Sven Torgsen. He was in prison for assault with a deadly weapon, kidnapping and the rape of his ex-wife.

Sven, prisoner number one thousand six hundred and sixty-eight, was a newly divorced contractor and not your regular prisoner. Up until just recently he had been an upstanding citizen of the community who owned his own business, building houses in Texas. On Valentine's Day a year earlier, he had come home from work early in order to surprise his wife, but it was he who got the surprise. In disbelief, he found another car parked at the house. His wife was inside fucking an old friend of his, whom he had given a job, and had the audacity to take the day off. In the divorce, he had lost half his retirement and the house he had built with his own hands. Needless to say, he felt extremely mistreated by the judicial system. A few months later, he arrived to pick up his nine-year old son for visitation. He found him with a black eye, bruises to his face and his arm in a sling. And the man who had caused it was smiling at him with his ex-wife nestled up behind him through the screen door of his old house. He didn't remember anything after that. He was convicted by a court of law of beating his old friend nearly to death, sodomizing his ex-wife in front of him, all while his son was told to stay in the car. The court didn't go into the more lurid details.

Sitting behind the wheel of the truck, with his left arm partially out the window resting on the door frame and the gun in his right hand, Billy motioned Sven over to the window with his gun. Once Sven was at the truck, Billy grabbed his immense forearm with his free left arm, and the transference of the devil's presence began. It was nearly instantaneous. To the surrounding prisoners, it appeared as if nothing had happened. They thought it was comical when Sven grabbed the scrawny guy from behind the wheel and threw him to the ground, broken foot and all. Billy was Billy again. And Sven was now Sven, as well as Sven the devil. Adjusting the seat in the truck, he put the car in drive and squealed the tires as he made his way back through the front entrance, driving over bodies as he went. He had payback on his mind, some personal scores to settle and a split personality to make it happen.

Chapter Twenty

The Grand Plan

"What, are you crazy! How many did you say?"

"We are going to need ten million of them. No, make it fifteen million of them."

"That is one tall order Mick. Who is going to pay the bill for that many humpback flies? Hell, this is the biggest order I have ever gotten in my whole life by about ten. Why do you need so many?"

"The fire ant infestation we have right now in this part of Texas is deadly this time of year, literally. We have the support of the local sheriff's office, and they are willing to move funds from dam maintenance to support buying them. You may have possibly heard, but we no longer have a dam holding back the lake water."

"Yeah, what is going on down there? I heard rumors but they are a bit beyond belief."

"Really, what have you heard?"

"Well, I was talking to Old Man Johnson about some ants, and he said that the dam collapsed in an explosion, on purpose no less, and that mutated fire ants came charging out of the ground, attacking the whole town and eating people down to the bone! Can you believe that story?"

Mick paused.

"Leroy, it's true story. And the worst part is that and some goddamn guy, devil, or anti-Christ is running around town controlling a new genetic species of fire ant, which he has been secretly breeding for years around these parts. If you told me it was 2025 and that aliens had just landed from Jupiter right now, I would believe you at this point. Ever since I got a call four days ago for a simple extermination job, every-thing has gone haywire in this town."

"Wow . . . and here I thought Bert Johnson had finally lost his mind."

"No, unfortunately he is of sound mind, just maybe not body, after that wall of water ripped through the town and destroyed just about everything. By the way, did I tell you I need the flies, like yesterday . . ."

"Of course, it's always that way when you call. But you know I will do anything for you bug dude . . . When this is all said and done, I am going to need a solid. OK?"

Mick laughed.

"Only the best for you. So, at a reproduction rate of a larva every six hours how soon do you think we can get that order?"

"Give me some time to see what I can do. I am going to see if I can round up a few other commercial entomologists and split the job. If all goes right, I think I can maybe be able to deliver within three to four days. Let me call you back."

"Leroy, you rock, even if you never would let me see your sister. After this is done, I promise I will get you a solid so sticky that you will be riding as high as Lucy in the sky with diamonds. OK?"

"I'm salivating already. I will call you when I see how many of these little buggers I can round up. I have got to go now. Talk to you later."

Mick hung up the phone and looked around him. Sally had discerned for herself how the conversation had gone and the treat he had promised his friend Leroy. Mick smiled. He was aware subtlety was not his strong suit.

"Ok. So, here's the plan I have been thinking of," Mick said.

"Wait just a second there chief. That last plan you had to put it mild-ly, sucked. In fact, it damn near got all of us killed. I mean seriously, you expected to put dynamite in a coyote, drug it, and get the demon to transfer its soul or whatever life force it has to the animal, and then blow it up while we are being attacked by millions of carnivorous ants under his control?"

The lieutenant with a look of derision on his face stared at Mick. He continued.

"If your girlfriend hadn't come barreling down that slope like a bat out of hell, at that exact moment, we would all be a pile of bones. I think we really need to think this one out a little bit better."

Sally and the medical examiner nodded their heads in agreement as they looked at Mick.

"I agree. That last plan went off the tracks once the coyote started howling, although the fog didn't help anything either."

A breaking news story on the television made them all stop talking.

"A prison break just outside the town of Bishop Texas has been confirmed. There are multiple fatalities and unconfirmed reports of an explosion at the site. At this time, we don't have much information, but we have been instructed to tell people to stay away from the facility, as there are armed and dangerous prisoners on the loose. From a local source, we have been told that a man approached the facility armed with a gun, took the guard at the entrance hostage, and then proceeded to blow up the guard and multiple members of the prison staff. In another unconfirmed report the man is said to have been transporting an animal with him that appeared to be a pregnant coyote. Again, these are all unconfirmed reports,

folks. Stay tuned for breaking updates as we get
them."

Each of them looked at one another. They knew where their archenemy had visited after leaving the quarry. The devil controlling Billy had been visiting the local penitentiary. An hour later, they had decided upon a rough plan of action. It would involve procuring millions of phorid flies, commonly called humpback flies due to their unusual anatomy, which they would use to attack the fire ants. The issues involved were numerous. How to get the ants all to the surface at the same time, while they released the flies, and also how to keep themselves alive while they put their plan in motion, were just a few. The lieutenant floated the idea that the police department had some helicopters they could use, not only to release the flies, but also to stay above the ground while the ants were attacking. Still another issue was going to be that the plan would take time. Once the flies deposited their eggs upon the unsuspecting ants, it would take a few weeks for their heads to drop off, and for them to die. There was nothing that could be done, they presumed, about the time involved with the incubation period of the humpback fly. At least that is what they thought at the moment. Mick knew Leroy would have the answers on possibly speeding up gestation periods.

Furthermore, Mick required mass amounts of chemicals in order to manufacture thousands of gallons of his high-octane flammable pesticide, so as to burn away the nests and queens once and for all, while the male drones were above ground in battle. This would involve getting ahold of mass quantities of moonshine. That in itself was going to be a tricky task as the two known moonshiners in the county, were currently behind bars. Deals would have to be cut in order to get the hooch and Mick let the lieutenant know it.

Sally began calling poison distributors from the contact list she used while working at Dinkin's. The lieutenant was able to arrange to have a few helicopters flown over to Mick's house and was even able to make arrangements to have the two local moonshiners transported inside of them. Time was of the essence to get everything in place and securing enough moonshine was an essential part of the plan.

Chapter Twenty-One

Sven's Revenge

Sven decided to park just outside the prison, next to a small stream that meandered along the prison's perimeter. He may need some help with the next phase of his plan, he thought. He had accomplished so much in just a few days but wasn't satisfied. Yes, he had destroyed the town of Bishop, the ants had survived the flood with ease, and he was now a hulking bastard of a man, and yet, he felt uneasy about the exterminator that was now seemingly trying to track him down, with his crazy bitch girlfriend to boot. He had never been hunted before. It was unsettling, and a very different feeling to think that someone was plotting his demise. While listening to the radio, he thought of who he was going to kill next. It would be his ex-wife and her lover first, then Sally, and finally Mick. He might even visit the judge who presided over his case if he had the time. He wanted to bring death to each of them in his own special way. It really was his specialty. The hate, the torment, the terror, and the palpable fear that he drove into his victim's eyes was the best drug the world had to offer. And he and Sven wanted to get high. He could feel that the man, Sven, had quite a bit of pent-up anger within him. Between both of their combined angers, he would make their victim's final goodbye's special. If he had been a dog, he would have been drooling by now, as he fantasized about just how he was going to carry out the murders, while inflicting the most amount of cerebral pain possible prior to their executions. He wanted their souls to be continually and forever tormented, concentrated agony within those last few precious moments of their lives. Over and over again, he wanted them to feel his ultimate power. He would make them relive their deaths for eternity. He wouldn't have it any other way, he mused.

Glancing at the truck's rearview mirror, he witnessed mayhem transpiring beyond the prison gates. Prisoners and guards were fighting each other to the death. He could see his cellmate Chico Alvarez, a convicted murderer, making his way past the body parts and concrete pieces that were strewn about where the guardhouse used to stand, along with Sonny "Fat Stuff" Rubio, a pimp and pedophile that weighed about three hundred and fifty pounds. He just might be able to employ their special talents. Getting out of the vehicle, he honked and waved at them to come over and join him. He could see their faces light up with joy at the thought that each of them had transportation, no less a getaway vehicle with which to escape. Chico got to the truck first and jumped into the passenger side while "Fat Stuff" climbed up into the back of the pickup. They sped off from the prison area, leaving quite a few other prisoners disappointed, who were attempting to make their way to the truck.

"Hey, man, am I glad to see you. Where did you get the fancy truck?"

In the bed of the pickup, Sonny was holding on for dear life, but smiling like a Cheshire cat that had just swallowed a canary.

"I borrowed it from that guy who blew up the guardhouse, but I will make sure to give it back once I'm done. I promise."

Chico grinned at Sven. They both knew he was talking bullshit.

"Where are we going?"

"I know of a quiet little house in the country."

"You mean your ex-wife's house."

"Exactly. You're exactly right, Chico. We just need to clean out the squatters first. Then, we will have the place to ourselves to hole up for a while."

Fat stuff who had been listening in the back started banging on the back window while smiling with his thumb up in the air. He wanted to be part of this plan of retribution and was smiling from ear to ear.

Sven roared with laughter, so loud that the sound reverberated around him, shaking the car windows and sucking away all other nearby noises. As if brought about by the laughter, a crash of thunder and a bolt of lightning exploded in a nearby poplar tree, shattering the ground with sparks. His eyes blackened with rage. Little red coals began spitting and burning at the pit of his pupils, as he turned and bellowed out a hideous chortling cackling at his astonished prison mates. Both of them, who just seconds earlier had been enjoying their deviant thoughts of the debauchery that was to take place at his ex-wife's house, suddenly found themselves taken aback, bewildered and shocked, afraid of the man behind the wheel. The sky became black in seconds. Lightning crackled and exploded all around them, snapping off limbs and exploding trees and barn roofs, that stood amidst the periphery of their path. The prison gang revelry, quickly turned to a sweating palpable fear for their lives, as "fat stuff" held dearly as Sven went faster and faster. Both of them knew that Sven was causing these changes in the weather with this madness, and while they understood this and realized what was happening, they were very well aware that this was not humanly possible, and that Sven had metamorphosed into someone else.

"I shall put them on the cross, these squatters that infest my property, like they did to my wretched cousin thousands of years ago. I will crush their souls, for using these puny human laws to incarcerate me, steal from me, and laugh while I rotted away behind bars. They will rue this day and forever more, that they ever dared cross Sven, spawn of the devil."

Slamming his fist on top of the dashboard while laughing uproariously, he accelerated at speeds exceeding one hundred miles per hour.
The mix between the pent-up anger within Sven, and the rage inherent
within the devil, was like mixing alcohol, gasoline and dynamite together.

And that was when they noticed the poor soul walking alone
amongst the raging elements. Far up ahead in the distance, along the
side of the road, bible in his hand, they could see a young man drenched
from the rain, with his shoulders slumped, fighting against the storm that
had suddenly overtaken him. In his ill-fitting dark suit with the pant legs
obviously too short, nearly halfway up his calves, he stuck out like a sore
thumb, along the overgrown country road that ran due west from the
prison. From the forlorn look of him, he was unmistakenly a proselytizer
for the Lord fulfilling his missionary duty. A boy approaching manhood,
all of twenty years old.

Slowing down Sven pulled up alongside the young man. He was
young and of a fair complexion with light brown hair that was plastered
to his head from the rain. Motioning with his hand, he instructed Chico
to get out and let the man inside the cab of the truck, soaking wet and all.
Before the slightly built young man could even protest, he found himself
wedged between the two prisoners, having been grabbed inside the truck
by Chico. Sven punched the accelerator and was back at speeds approaching one hundred before the boy could get his wits about him.

"Well now, what brings you out to this god forsaken town?" Sven
bellowed.

Upon hearing these sacrilegious words, the boy's spine straightened.

"Oh, I disagree. God is everywhere. He lives within everyone. He is
our father and our savior." As afraid as the boy was of the men surrounding him, he felt strongly in his convictions and breathed a sigh of
relief that he started off with professing his beliefs.

"That bastard you pray to is not my father! He is a very, very distant relative. Have you talked to him recently or was he too busy for you? Which one of his minions are you? Mormon or one of those crazy ass Latter Day Saints? Or are they both the same nowadays?"

Chico let out a hoot of laughter and turned to see fat stuff with his eyes bulging out of his head not believing what he was hearing.

"I am a Mormon and the prophet Joseph Smith has spoken with the Lord . . ."

"Ah that crackpot. I have heard of him but never spoke to him personally. My father has that condemned killer pulling worms out of his orifices twenty-four seven while he makes him conduct a meet and greet with the newly departed Mormons. He thinks it is amusing to see their initial shock at seeing their false prophet at the door to hell. You know how many people that guy murdered in Ohio? Anyways, that is beside the point. What I need to know is how much money does that Mormon church have? How many followers is it nowadays?"

The young man's head swam with the horrible vision that had been placed in his brain. Sensing he was in trouble, he could feel his empty stomach churn, as he listened to the two other prisoners laugh at the outrageous statements of the driver. Quietly he said a silent prayer and then spoke, not as loudly as at first, and with the caution of a man sensing he was in trouble.

"Money? I have no idea . . . the church is not concerned with money! I . . ."

Lightning exploded off to the left of the truck as they swerved to avoid a falling tree that came crashing down upon the road. Sven was getting angrier.

"So, you are telling me they are not concerned with money?! And not power either, right?!" Sven roared above the storm. "They take ten percent of everything you make as a promise of your good faith and reprimand you if you don't make your donations. And then hound you if you try and leave the church. Are you trying to bullshit me that they don't care about money! It astounds me how you weak brainwashed idiots get involved in cults, and with pride do another human's bidding just by holding out the promise of salvation in front of your faces, like a carrot stuck in front of a horse's mouth and a whip behind its butt."

With his massive right hand, Sven grabbed the young man's hand with his and curled it inside of his huge paw. The intensity of the young man's reaction was a surprise to the others. The negative charge of feelings, rage and hate that ran upward within his arm were so intense it catapulted the boy up off his seat, and if it wasn't for the rearview mirror, he might have been ejected through the front windshield. His head smashed into the mirror with such force, that the mirror cracked into two separate pieces as a humongous stream of blood erupted from the boy's head, spurting across the windshield and dash. Chico instinctively pulled back from the commotion, staring in disbelief at Sven and the man who was now yelling in pain, while profusely bleeding across his shirt and pants. Sven slowed down and motioned with his hand for Chico to get rid of the boy. He was of no use to Sven. He was too low within the church organization to get any useful information, and so they left him bleeding under a torrential rain at the side of the road.

Unceremoniously left, clutching his head in dazed confusion, he watched as the devil sped off. Later, after his initial shock wore off from the encounter, the young man noticed burn marks in the shape of fingers from where the driver had grabbed the top of his hand. The permanent burn marks would remind him for the rest of his life of his encounter with the wicked spirit he had met while preaching on a quiet country road in west Texas.

Pulling off the main highway they snaked along a slippery mud road for a mile until they found themselves looking up at a large white house perched high upon on a ridge. They had reached Sven's old home. The first thing they noticed was the large "for sale" sign in the front yard. Sven started talking out loud to himself.

"Why that bitch had plans to sell my old house while I was locked up in the pen. Leave old Sven high and dry, without a clue as to where she was, when I finally got out. Just another way to backstab me with her new man. I see exactly what is happening here. She was going to take the sale proceeds and run away with my son so that I was virtually wiped away from her life. Unbeknownst to me, I would come wandering back to my old house only to find it occupied with an unknown family, and then I would be left to wonder about how my son was doing or where he was for the rest of my life. Well, I am going to show them eternity!"

Back in the town of Bishop, the ambulances loaded with the injured and the dead, for the most part, had cleared out. There were only a few survivors from the flood and two of them were talking to each other, Old Man Johnson and Jesus.

"I am telling you the ants were attacking us! And not only that, but they were cognizant of their surroundings. They moved like a pack of wild dogs. Hunting and pecking at the defense of their opponent and then attacking at the right time and spot. The only thing that saved us was the ring of fire that we constructed around the church."

Jesus nodded his head in agreement.

"I was paying for some items inside the convenience store when my truck was hijacked. And then the man that stole my truck tried to blow me up! I was gassing up and then this SOB jumps in my truck, locks it, and spills fuel all along the ground before he flicks a cigarette at me through the back window and laughs. Before I knew it, I was blown across the street from the explosion. Probably won't ever regrow the hair that was burned off of me and I didn't have that much to begin with. This joker has to die."

The two of them locked eyes, and with the burning desire for revenge that is born from hatred, they realized they had a common enemy.

"How do you figure you're going to get your truck back?"

Jesus went to scratch his head and realized how much hair he had lost to the explosion. His resolve hardened. It was just another reminder of how much he owed that thieving murderous bastard.

"Well, it is a good question, and I don't know the answer. I don't know this fella Billy, although I have heard of him from his neighbor, Mick. According to him, it really isn't him because he has lost his mind and it has been replaced by some other guy's mind who is the devil, which I kind of believe based upon all that has happened of late. So, what I am saying in a nutshell is that I have no goddamn idea! You got any ideas!?"

"Yeah, I got an idea. Why don't we talk to his neighbor Mick and see what he has in mind? I knew Billy before all this happened and he wasn't in the least bit dangerous. Heck, he was the runt of the town, if you get my drift."

Jesus sat down on a massive pine tree that had been deposited from the flood. He was exhausted. His adrenaline was no longer sustaining him, and his body ached from the ordeal he had been through over the past day. Old Man Johnson sat next to him. Both of them were bruised, battered and beaten down.

Out in the distance they could see a truck headed their way. After a bit, Old Man Johnson slapped his hand on Jesus's knee and nodded at him.

"I believe the good Lord just answered our prayers."

Jesus, with his hand up above his eyebrows shielding the morning sunlight, cast a glance at the old man and nodded back.

"Senor, I am sure glad to have met you. And even more thankful that we are on the same side in this fight."

Before they could speak again, Mick and Sally had driven up to where they sat. Producing thick stacked ham sandwiches and a couple of sodas, Sally helped them both into the car. They rode back to his house, while Mick explained how they planned to defeat the demon spirit that had hijacked Billy's body, and consequently left it for a gargantuan prisoner named Sven. They explained how they had seen footage of the prison break on the television. The two men sat in the back of the vehicle and listened, wolfing down the sandwiches and sodas that had been brought for them. The food made them realize just how hungry they were. By the end of the drive, it was with considerable effort that they kept themselves awake while Mick and Sally spoke of the new plan.

With a small sip of the freshly made lemonade, she paused long enough for it to slip to the back of her throat and tickle her taste buds. It was perfect. Loretta Schwann was pleased with her concoction. It was Sunday and she was happy. Someone had just made an offer on the property that was ten thousand below her asking price, but it was more than she had been hoping for, and she couldn't wait to move. She had just finished a call with her realtor who had let her know they could realistically have the paperwork completed by Thursday. Finally, her nightmare would be over. Goodbye Texas and hello California!

Grabbing the tray that held the glasses and pitcher of lemonade she turned and started to make her way to the back porch, where her fiancé was cutting the grass. She could hear the power mower with its rhythmic grinding permeating the air and it fell gently on her ears. Somehow the whirring grinding sound made her feel secure knowing her new man was working out in the backyard. Coupled with the joy of knowing she was leaving the horrors of Bishop behind and her abusive ex-husband Sven, she was as high as she had been in a long time. Setting the tray on a counter, she opened the sliding glass door to the back porch, grabbed up the tray again and backed out of the house. She had on a new dress and the sun felt joyously warm on her bare shoulders. Turning to place the tray on the patio table her heart was struck by a dagger that sliced her dreams into shreds. The tray, pitcher and glasses crashed to the ground in a cacophony of broken glass that shattered her tenuous hold on reality. Sven, and two monstrous looking men she didn't know, and didn't want to know, were all staring at her with malicious grins of ill intent. A scream, that must have emanated from her, filled her ears, although she didn't remember uttering a sound, and somehow it seemed disconnected from what she was looking at. Sven had the biggest grin of them all plastered on his face. Her dreams, from just a second ago, vanished like a morning mist in the midst of Texas heat wave. Off in the distance she realized the whirring of the lawn tractor had ceased to percolate in the back of her head.

"Well Honey, it sure is damn good to see you. I see you have your new "fuck" working hard for you, huh? Hmmm . . . I don't recall you ever letting me know you were looking to move and take my son away from me, but I guess it slipped your mind, didn't it? Such a busy woman, what with making plans and getaways, it must not have occurred to you that good ole Sven might want to know where his boy was when he got out of the pen, right?"

She stood ramrod straight, held hell bound by her thoughts and spellbound by the man in front of her. He was playing with her. He was controlling her. Just like when he had played with them prior to his incarceration. She was so afraid she couldn't speak, although audibly she could hear herself letting out a low whining sound that sounded like an animal crying out in fear. She found herself trapped and indecisive. Much like anyone who has witnessed a horror scene and screamed for the victim to run or do something to protect themselves, she was help-less, caught fast to the place where she first saw him, lemonade dripping down the front of her legs.

"Well boys, isn't she 'purdy', just like I told you about back at the jail, huh? Now at first, she may act like she doesn't want it, but don't let that bother you none. She is as horny as they come. And seeing as how her man was kind of 'broken up' after the last time I encountered him, she probably needs some good hard loving at this point in her life."

Sven was smiling from ear to ear relishing the words he spoke as he glanced over at Fat Stuff and Chico. He watched her cringing in fear, while her eyes got wider, realizing what he was proposing.

"Loretta! Loretta Run! Run Loretta run!!!"

The voice came from way off in the distance from where the lawnmower had stopped. Momentarily, everyone looked over to see her fiancé waving his arms and yelling for her to run. And in the next instant she did. The voice broke the spell from which she had been held. Sprinting down the stairs of the back porch she ran in terror, knowing full well she would never escape.

"Get her boys!"

In the very next instant, Chico and Fat Stuff were bounding after her, each wanting to be the first to reach her. All of them reached the spot on the grass where the grass lay uncut at about the same time. Quickly the teams paired off. Each of them knew in the back of their minds that it was only a matter of time before the man got separated from the woman and then it would be over, but first the Mexican standoff had to begin, prior to its ending. The grabbing and the punching and the dragging had already started.

From his perch on the backyard patio Sven was enjoying his view of the melee. Within a few minutes it was all over. Her fiancee had been knocked out cold, with some teeth lying about him, and she lay face down on a section of newly cut grass with her sun dress getting hiked up in the air. Straining his vocal cords to the limit he was able to mimic the humming sound necessary to call the devil's sheep to pasture. The grassy ground began bubbling with thousands of ants. Stealthily they surrounded their four, very busy, and very unaware victims.

Loretta was biting Chico's hand while trying to fend off his penis from penetrating her, when she felt the first stinging bites all along her neck and legs, causing her body to rise from the ground in pain, even with the weight of the two men upon her. It was like she had been burned by a hot stove across her body. Next, it was Chico fighting them off with his hands. Then they attacked the rest of them. Each of them, soon enough, were covered in a thick black tar of ants as the bubbling cauldrons of fire ants raced out of the ground searching for prey. From the porches elevated vantage point, Sven watched as the four of them crawled and ran and fell, screaming for mercy and help, of which neither was to come. Sven sipped on a fresh glass of lemonade he had retrieved from the house and enjoyed the action, until eventually they had all stopped moving. A while later, amongst the picked clean bones strewn about the yard, he noticed pieces of the grass-stained sun dress blow across the yard, eventually getting caught in the barbed wire that bordered the property.

Behind him peering out the kitchen window, his son Lars had witnessed everything. Unlocking the gun safe, he had managed to take down the family's shotgun. Now, loaded with a few cartridges, he had stealthily made his way back to the kitchen and stood at the sliding glass door. He loved his mom and his dad, but after what he had just seen, the love for his dad had died and been replaced with hate. The door was still slightly ajar, and in that opening he pointed the barrel of the gun at Sven's backside. He was scared and didn't want to do this, but he told himself he didn't have a choice. His father wasn't his father anymore.

That monster had stood casually sipping lemonade, while watching his mother getting massacred on the back lawn. He had to die.

Sven and the demon inside of him felt empty after the killings but unremorseful. It was his will and right to kill whoever got in his way or just annoyed him enough, like Chico and Fat Stuff. The two sexually deviant prisoners were used for his purposes and then disposed of just as easily. Almost as an afterthought, he remembered he had a son, only to hear the click of a trigger. The sound of the gun going off and the searing pain came at the same time. He had been shot in the ass, the left buttocks to be exact, ripping his flesh apart and tearing into his pelvic bone. It threw him against the wooden railing smashing at his ribs. He crumpled to the deck of the patio. The burning white flash of pain was like a hot wave through his body and was something he had never experienced before. It was not a pleasant feeling. His blood ran freely across the porch, dripping silently between the pine boards, onto the soft dirt below. As he fought to stay conscious, fighting the inevitable onslaught of shock, he wondered why he hadn't heard the child. Why hadn't he heard the child? He heard everything and could sense people and animals from far away. Something was different now. Was it because it was his own flesh and blood that he hadn't heard or noticed him? It was troubling development, he thought. These were his last thoughts prior to passing out from the blast that had shattered his back-side.

After pulling the trigger and watching his dad crumple in pain on the porch, Lars had scampered away, disgusted he had shot him from behind, and horrified by what he had done. And yet, he knew it was the only way that he would have been able to shoot him, and possibly save himself. He gathered up the car keys he found in the house, including the unknown set he found on the kitchen table, and dropped them in the toilet tank. Then he left. He grabbed his bicycle from the garage and pedaled away from the house of horrors. He had no plans, other than to escape from the evilness and death, that were now a part of his old home. He rode as fast as his legs would pedal him just to get away, and when he stopped miles away and much later, he found himself looking at one of the strangest things he had ever seen. In front of him was a shattered prison for violent offenders with over a dozen emergency vehicles, lights flashing, and numerous emergency workers attempting to help the many injured and wounded. It dawned upon him that this must have been where his dad had escaped from.

People were rushing around, attending to the wounded, while others were securing the area. Nobody was paying any attention to the boy on the bicycle. He sat there watching the scene for a good hour before someone approached him. A police sergeant in a grey uniform, ironically named Dirk Gray, had noticed him a few times, and finally decided he had enough time to shoo him away from the area. He walked over to where the boy stood with the bicycle straddled between his legs.

"Hey Sonny, you can't be around here. This place is a restricted area and dangerous. You are going to have to leave the area and go on home now."

Mournfully the boy looked at the officer with sad pained eyes and began blurting out his story by way of confession.

"My dad just escaped from prison, and he killed my mom and her fiancé as well as two other guys I don't know. So, I snuck up on my dad and shot him in the backside and left him on our back porch to die. I can't go home."

Lars just stood there looking at the policeman, who by now was gawking at him, not believing what he had just heard. Comprehending the situation, his heart went out to the small child, with the tears streaming down his face. Just another part of this crazy day, he thought. He put an arm around the child and let him know it would be alright. He then took him under his arm, walking him back to an office within the larger prison building. There he could speak with him in more detail about what had happened.

Chapter Twenty-Two

The Beast Takes a Walk

Mick awoke with a start, and, for a few moments, dreams floated around in his head like a white fog he could see but couldn't grasp. Images of Sally flying down the hill in the truck, the surgically repaired coyote, television scenes of the destroyed prison, all sifted through his mind in a jumbled stream of half-awake consciousness. Taking a deep breath while attempting to clear his mind, he could sense that it was early in the morning by the amount of dew in the air, its fresh crispness within his nostrils. Fumbling his way to the bathroom, he began to think of what day it was, but what did it matter, he said to himself. Still in a fog, he could feel the stiffness in his knee. Splashing water on his face, he looked in the mirror and was aghast at what he saw staring back. He looked exhausted and a bit thin around the face. He hadn't been eating or drinking like he usually did and the stress was evident upon his face. He had crow's feet lines spreading out from the corners of his eyes and huge black bags underneath them to boot. He looked horrible.

Rounding the corner of the kitchen, he caught sight of Sally sitting at the table. She was staring out of the house where a window used to be with a cup of coffee cradled in her hands, its steam rising into the chill morning air. He could tell she hadn't heard him, and not wanting to startle her, he cleared his throat. Snapped out of her trance, her eyes swept over and met his. She found a warm smile on his bedraggled face. Walking over to where she sat, he kissed her on the lips, and then proceeded to pour himself a cup of joe.

"How are you feeling?" she said.

"Honestly—I feel like shit. My knee is stiff, my back is sore, the plan we have is hurting my head and we don't even know where this Sven guy is. Not to mention my humble abode looks like a scene from a terminator movie, and with my obsessive-compulsive tendencies, it is literally driving me nuts. Other than that, I am fine. How are you feeling?"

Sally reached out and placed her hand over his.

"Honestly, I have visions that we are going to die. Nightmares actually. I see the man with the red eyes and his ants, and I don't see a way out. Only by the grace of God have we been able to stay alive over the past few days, and I don't see how we are going to be able to keep it up. I think our plan is as rational as can be for someone trying to slay the devil, but I feel getting it to succeed is a long shot."

"I agree, but what else are we going to do? I am not going to lay down without a fight. I am not going to think that the forces of evil can triumph over the forces of good. We have each other against him, and so far, that has held up. What we need is a little luck in order to turn the tide."

Mick's phone rang. The phone number identified the caller as the lieutenant.

"This must be important. It is 6:17 in the morning."

"Mick, there is a kid down here at the police station, who an officer friend of mine, Dirk Gray, brought in yesterday from where the prison was attacked. He claims to have shot Sven. He says he is his son. That is, after he watched Sven activate ants in his back yard in a killing rampage including the kid's mother."

"Goddam that is big news! So, has anyone gone to see if Sven is dead?"

There was a pause on the other end of the line.

"Well, seeing as we are not equipped with your special poison, we figured you might want to be part of the investigating party?"

This time it was Mick who paused.

"Yeah, well I guess we are way past you trying to pin Edith Baxter's and Roy's murders on me, but I want some type of assurances that, if I get out of this alive, I'm not going be brought up on any charges, seeing as how I am helping you out."

He heard a chuckle on the other end of the line.

"Come on Mick, we are way passed that point. I promise no criminal charges will be brought against you by my department for your actions over the past few days. Now, I can swing by your place and we will both go over there together with some back up troopers just in case, and see what there is to the kid's story. What do you say?"

Mick snorted his reply.

"Yeah, come on by."

Mick hung up the phone and looked at Sally. She had overheard the conversation and there was a faint glimmer in her eyes and a half-smile on her face.

"Just can't say no to anyone, can you?"

Mick moved one eye over to look at her while he contemplated what lay in store for him that morning. He needed to get some of the poison transferred to his wearable tanks, then go confront a wounded beast that could switch identities by way of touching, with a one-handed policeman and a few of his buddies as protection.

"When this is finished Miss Sally, we are going on vacation. I mean a real vacation to Hawaii or Tahiti or Australia or something. A nice long vacation just to get the hell out of Dodge, if that's ok with you?"

Sally could feel the muscles in her face relax for the first time in a long time. She found herself grinning at him.

"Yeah, that sounds great," she heard herself say.

A police van drove up an hour later. Mick was ready with the poison. Two hours later they found themselves driving down a long dirt road staring at a ranch house perched on top of a hill. It was Sven's last known residence. There was four of them in total in the van, and Mick began suiting up as they approached.

The house and its surroundings were quiet, deathly quiet. A few newspapers lay wrapped in plastic, unopened on the driveway, and they noticed that a thin coating of pollen covered the cars in the driveway. They appeared not to have been moved recently. The four of them fanned out and circled the house looking for any movement. There were no signs of any movement. Climbing up the back porch, which they found covered in blood splatter, drops and stains, they noticed the sliding glass door was wide open. The police were communicating by using their fingers to signal what their intentions and next movements were going to be. Silently, the two officers proceeded to enter the back of the house while Mick and the lieutenant watched for any movements off the back porch and in the grassy fields that surrounded the house. A few minutes later, the officers came back and pronounced the house empty.

It was hard to fathom, but somehow Sven had left the house without using the car that sat in the driveway, whilst being injured. One of the officers fished the keys to the cars from the toilet tank and placed them on the outside patio table. The boy's story was holding up. So where was Sven? Turning their attention to the blood evidence on the porch, it appeared, based upon a trail of blood drops found on the stairs leading off the porch, to indicate he had managed his way into the backyard only to disappear. Did he go off into the woods?

"Lieutenant, do you want me to call in to the department and see if we can get Max and Rosie out here?" one of the policemen asked.

These were the department's two prized bloodhounds.

"Yeah, that's a good idea. In fact, let's get two more troopers out here and have them bring along horses for the four of you. Call me immediately if you get a lead on him. I am going back to the station after I drop Mick off at his house."

After Sven regained consciousness, he managed to sterilize the wound with a bottle of Wild Turkey whiskey he found in the house, and bandage his shredded buttocks with some gauze and tape. Between the pain of the open wound, and the anger he felt at having been shot from behind in the first place, his frustration kept mounting as he was unable to locate the car keys. In the back of his mind, he could hear the real Sven almost laughing at him about how he had been duped by his small child. It was maddening to him. Arming himself with the gun that had shot him in the ass, he decided to leave by way of foot. He had no other choice. They would be looking for him, and, without a way to get away, he knew he was at a disadvantage. He knew better than to fight when at a disadvantage. If he could slip away for a bit while he recuperated, he knew he would be better off, and perhaps, he might just meet a hunter out there in the woods and transfer himself.

Taking with him a bottle of aspirin he found in the medicine cabinet, a week's worth of food which he put into a satchel, and the rest of the Wild Turkey to help deaden the pain, he set off. He walked slowly and in great discomfort, but used the lay of the land to his advantage. Intermittently, he would take a slug of the whiskey to help deaden the pain. For over a mile he walked upstream in a creek, thereby hopefully throwing off any animal that they could use to track his scent. When he left the stream, he left by way of a dead tree sprawled across the water, so that no tracks were left on the banks. He knew it would only delay them for a spell, and inevitably they would catch up to him, but he needed that extra time to heal and work out a plan to get back to the quarry.

"That little bastard kid really did a number on him," he thought.

And so, half-drunk he found himself wandering through the tall brown grasses and poplar trees that were prevalent in that area of Texas. Eventually, physically exhausted, he stumbled upon a small uninhabited cabin where he was able to lay down on the right side of his body, eat and rest. With the body strapped of its strength, he realized it took more effort to quash out the thoughts of Sven, who was futilely battling to regain control of his mind and body. He slept for a long time. When he awoke it was due to the throbbing pain in his ass. It was pitch black. Looking up through the gaping holes in the abandoned cabin's roof, he could see a few stars. He had a headache from the effects of the Wild Turkey. He searched for the bottle next to him, hearing its remnants slosh about in the dark. It was enough for a few slugs. He downed it knowing it wasn't good for him, but he needed something to dull the pain. Then he popped four aspirin and went back to sleep. In his sleep, the conversations began.

"So, what is it that you want?"

"Power and control of everyone."

"Over who? And why?"

"I am the dark Lord of Hell and feed off of the misery of others. I am ordained to rule the world, and I alone shall control the simple minions that walk upon the face of this earth and make them do my bidding. Just like you shall die when I am finished with you, as did your wife and soon your son."

"It appears that your condition for an almighty is less than ideal. How tragic to have been shot from behind by such a young man, too."

"You fool! If I didn't have to use your body, I would begin disposing of it now. It was just lucky that your son was able to sneak up on me. I am sure it was due to him being your son. When I leave your body, and I will soon enough, I will see to it that your death is a long and excruciating one at that! And then you can keep your presence with my father for all eternity."

"You and your powers are fading and you know it."

"The billions of ants under my control are just the tip of the iceberg to my powers."

"You can't even protect yourself from a small child. You are a fantasy of your own delusions. A small time heathen fraud."

"You're an insolent piece of prison trash. Did you like the way I had your ex-wife . . ."

He awoke in a sweating rage speaking aloud to Sven. The conversation had abruptly ended. He could feel it! Sven had cut communication with him as opposed to him trying to regain control of his mind. Sven had somehow learned how to sever communication between the two of them when he felt like it. He was outraged at the dream conversation with its innuendos to his lack of strength and wanted to hurt himself in order to get back at Sven. Was he going mad, he thought? He longed for his original body and its mind that lay in a thousand pieces, currently strewn about the front yard of the exterminator's house. He wanted that man dead as well as the woman with him.

Chapter Twenty-Three

Billy Finds God

Jesus, Sally, Old Man Johnson and Mick were sitting around the kitchen table when the phone rang. It was Leroy. He had called around to all of his sources and had gotten lucky. There was a massive shipment of South American scuttle flies, a million humpbacks, which had been due to be delivered to Alabama for fire ant containment purposes; but the governor, who had initially ordered them, was embroiled in a recall vote, and the funding was being held up by the legislature. Leroy let him know that he could have them rerouted and delivered in two days if he could get quick payment.

The lieutenant had the funds earmarked for dam maintenance sent by wire later that day. Within hours, one million flies were bound for Texas, packed on flat bed trailers along with two dozen attack boxes which had automatic temperature, humidity, lighting and mechanical controls that allowed the flies to emerge, mate and parasitize hosts without the need for constant human management. Even if the 'Pseudacteon' plan worked, it would be months, perhaps years, before the mutated ants were eventually eradicated, but it was a start. When the female fly injected her larva into the shoulder joint of the ant worker, the average incubation time was between fifteen and thirty days depending upon the size of the ant. With the size of these ants, they were hoping that the incubation time was cut in half. Essentially, when the larva was ready, it released a chemical like an enzyme that degraded the membranes that held the host's exoskeleton together. Once released, the larva then proceeds to consume the connective tissue that attaches the ant's head to its body until it drops from its shoulders.

"So, let me understand this and please correct me if I am wrong. If these ants are not going to be wiped out for years, just how are we supposed to defeat this devil man Sven?" Jesus asked.

"Well this is the tricky part of the plan. We need to confront him in an area that we have cleared out of his fire ants. An area that is beyond the range of his hum. Later, after we have vanquished him, we can methodically continue to clear the land of them. Initially I am going to have the flies delivered near the quarry as that seems to be his base of operations."

"Ok. But how are we going to get them to come out of their underground colonies on demand?"

"I have been listening to the different humming sounds that seemingly activate them and believe I can mimic it. Once we get them to emerge from the ground, we can release the flies."

Old Man Johnson sat back and laughed.

"You have gotten this all figured out pretty good, huh? Let me get this straight. You are going to activate the ants on command, release the flies, and then wait around for a half a week for them to die? And just how and where are we to release these ants and flies so we are not eaten alive? And who is going to account for Sven in the meantime while we are waiting for the ant's heads to drop off?"

Sally was glad that someone else had spoken about the gaping holes she had noticed in the plan. Mick, looking a bit perturbed at the easy unraveling of his plan, replied.

"Believe me when I say I don't have everything figured out yet. This is a fluid plan which is subject to change at any moment and has been put together without much sleep. I do know that we are able to use police helicopters after we get the ants out of their burrows and release the flies. In that way, we are off the ground and out of harm's way. As for Sven, we know he is injured and without a vehicle. We have some bloodhounds that are beginning to search for him as we speak. And we have a whole new supply of moonshine, compliments of our two friends Stan had released. Finally, we know we are going to eventually have to rid ourselves of these fire ants by way of flies, poison, fire. And we are hoping the scuttle fly's gestation period is much shorter based upon the size of the fire ants, which is based upon solid empirical evidence of humpback fly gestation periods being shorter in duration in larger ants, that is according to Leroy."

Jesus spoke next.

"I just know this. If you really want to make sure something is dead, you cut off its head. I would advise that once we see the ants coming out from their holes that we go after the source. The queen ants need to be identified and killed or you never really rid yourself of the problem. On my farm, we have used a combination of fire, dynamite, and gasoline to get rid of regular fire ants. It is kind of like killing ground bees. We wake up early in the morning after the holes have been identified the previous evening with flags, pour gasoline down the holes, stick a couple of sticks of dynamite in the different holes, then light one stick and stand back. I know I have never seen them ever come back to a place we have torched."

Everyone around the table were nodding their heads in agreement. He may not have been a classically trained entomologist, but he certainly knew what worked in protecting his farmland from invasive pests.

"That's an excellent idea," Sally said.

"I second that," Old man Johnson said.

Mick's head was bobbing up and down clearly happy at the addition to the plan.

"Jesus, that is a great idea. I was thinking we could use paint guns from up in the helicopters to mark the holes where the ants are coming from so that later we can destroy the colony nest with a concoction of my special poison and dynamite."

Over the next few hours the plan was hashed over, rehashed, and honed to the point where they each began to feel comfortable about their different specific duties and how they were going to handle different contingencies that were most likely going to arise.

Billy awoke to find himself lying in a hospital bed with his left foot sticking out from under a sheet in a white cast and his wrist shackled to the bed frame. He was nestled in amongst a dozen other men, men from the prison lined up in hospital beds within a long rectangular room. It was a hospital recovery room. He didn't know what to think because his mind was free to think for the first time in what seemed an eternity. It was like entering a clean white room and having a paint brush and not knowing how he should start to think. It felt unusual and a bit daunting to not be imprisoned within his own mind.

He knew what he had done. He remembered all of it. The images were racing through his mind. The bowling alley fight, being thrown by Sven, taping up the coyote, blowing up the guards, summoning the ants, and so much more. He knew exactly why he was the only one in the hospital room with a shackle upon his wrist. His life was over. But on the other hand, he was alive, gloriously alive, and free of that bastard demon that had tormented him. And although he really did not feel good about what he had done, he didn't regret settling some personal scores at the bowling alley. And then right afterward, he felt ashamed of himself for his thoughts. He was juggling so many different and varied emotions that he didn't even notice some of the other guys in the room looking at him. When he did notice them, he realized a half dozen sets of eyes filled with a mixture of hatred and revenge staring at him. It quickly dawned upon him that he was responsible for this whole room of men, with varying degrees of life-changing injuries, and that he had killed many of their friends. They wanted him dead.

Billy looked away from them. But just for a few moments. Billy had changed. The old Billy would not have looked back at them, would have avoided their eyes at all costs and not said a thing. But he could feel he was not the same person anymore. Nothing made a difference anymore but to tell the truth, be honest, and to ask for forgiveness even if he knew he may never get it. He was done hiding behind bedsheets, cowardice, or fear. He had no fear anymore. Billy had been changed forever.

When the night nurse walked in later that evening, she was amazed at what she discovered. The hospital ward was at rapt attention listening to the man that had tried to kill them all. She stood at the doorway and listened to the man speak. He had apologized profusely to everyone personally, was contrite, honest, and completely unafraid of the consequences that stood in front of him and in the future. All of the patients were listening in a sort of stunned disbelief at what he was telling them, the whole story from the very beginning to when he first went to investigate the explosion at his neighbor's house. The yarn that he spun was truly unbelievable, and yet it resonated with such force and was so detailed, that it would be impossible for someone to make it up on the spur of the moment. When he had finished, and apologized for the umpteenth time, the ward was so quiet the only sounds you could hear were medical machines beeping at different intervals. The nurse had forgotten her duties and just stood there at the door, transfixed with the skinny murderer who spoke of his failings and intimacies, with more honesty than anyone she had ever heard in her life. She turned around and got the officer in charge of the investigation. And for the next two hours, after his Miranda rights were read to him, in front of all of the other patients, Billy told the officer his story again, while answering questions from anyone who cared to ask. At the end of the questioning, they were all left scratching their head in wonderment with the most outrageous story they had ever heard. And yet, to a man, they all believed him. The revenge and hatred that many of them felt toward him earlier had turned to pity for the man that lay amongst them. Billy had asked for forgiveness and received it from most of the men he had hurt the most. There was a miraculous transformation within the hearts of those convalescing that day, and a turn to God that many of them had never expected, especially coming from the one that had been responsible for their physical injuries.

The officer had recorded the conversation. It wasn't often that a defendant in a mass murder investigation openly confessed to everything that he had done, helping to fill in all the details that were missing from the case. On the other hand, the case was certainly not a slam dunk. It could be fought with many different defenses including temporary insanity, schizophrenia, and possibly even on the grounds of demoniacal possession. What he did know was that he also believed the young man's version of things as he had told them. In his years on the force, he knew how to spot a man telling the truth and a bald-faced liar. He had witnessed the ants attacking people at the prison, the crazy weather, and had heard many strange things from the survivors of Bishop. Heck, he even knew that the police, were at this very moment, using bloodhounds in an attempt to catch the fugitive Sven. And Sven had been the first person to come into contact with Billy after he had blown up the guard tower. He had already viewed the surveillance video tapes earlier in the day, showing Billy driving up to the entrance, blowing up the guardhouse and then being unceremoniously thrown from the pickup truck.

The flatbed trucks were due to arrive later in the day. Mick, Sally, Jesus and Old Man Johnson were waiting for them. And while they were waiting, they had been investigating the inside of the quarry and the control room which was located at the very front of the quarry. Further inside the quarry entrance they had found it to be a labyrinth of tunnels which seemingly snaked endlessly around and forever, although occasionally they would find a room within the midst of the interconnecting shafts. For what purpose they could only guess, but Mick remembered the story that the lieutenant told him about being strapped down to a table of some sort and watching his hand being eaten away. He shuddered to think about it. Meanwhile, Old Man Johnson thought he had located a switch on the panel that was attached to some underground speakers, thereby activating the ants. It had four different settings, two to the right and two to the left, that could seemingly trigger or activate them into action or perhaps different states of agitation. They decided it would be better to not try activating the switch until they had the scuttle flies positioned surrounding the area, just in case they were wrong. Each of them realized much of what they were doing was guesswork, and they could not afford to be wrong hoping for second chances.

The flatbeds, all four of them, arrived with Leroy on board the lead truck. Hopping down from the cab of the big rig, he recognized Mick immediately. A big smile began spreading across his face. It had been a long time. It had been more than a dozen years since they had crammed for exams together and partied the night away when it wasn't time to study. Inseparable friends in college, they had gradually drifted apart, as their lives progressed beyond college and into adulthood.

"Mick-Mick-Mick-Mick Mickey, old boy, how you doing? I figured I would drive here personally after hearing about the current fix you got yourself messed up in."

Mick couldn't help but smile, hearing how his name was called out, almost like they were in college again.

"Aw fuck, 'pig porker', I feel downright honored. Didn't you end up marrying that girl?   And don't try and tell me no lies. I know exactly why you came down here in person. I got your stuff right here," as he patted the front pocket of his flannel shirt.

The two of them laughed and hugged as the rust from years gone by disintegrated.

"So just where do you want me to tell the drivers to set these hump-back flies up?"

Mick pointed out the quarry and described how he would need it surrounded.

"Ok, so as I see it, if we put one control box at each of the four directions, that should work, right?"

"Yeah, that's right, but afterward I want to make sure we cover our tracks so he doesn't get wise that we have been here."

Leroy nodded his head. He understood the need for secrecy.

It was time. Mick, completely covered in his protective gear, activated the switch in the quarry, and then watched as the ants began swarming out of a multitude of holes. The four flatbed drivers worked the control boxes. Upon seeing the ants, they released the flies. Like a horde of locusts, they descended down upon their unsuspecting victims. The ants fought them ferociously, as they did any of their other prey, but this time the roles were reversed. Their mandibles were of no use against the much smaller flies and their method of propagation. A million pregnant flies attached their larvae's on a million ants all within the time it took to drink a cup of coffee.

Mick turned off the switch, staring in disbelief as a red and black wave of frustrated killers receded back underground. He couldn't believe the plan worked. It was like clockwork. At the top of the quarry he could hear them whooping it up and celebrating the accomplishment.

Leroy and his crew were getting ready with spray paint cans to mark the entrances to the holes, and Jesus was preparing long fuses which would be used with the sticks of dynamite. Sally and old man Johnson were readying the cans of gasoline and Mick's special poison to pour down the holes once they were marked.

Methodically they poured copious amounts of gasoline down the ant holes first, inserted the dynamite, and then blew each hole hoping to kill the queen that rested comfortably down below. And with that, the crew felt confident that multiple queens had been killed and that any surviving males would lose their heads, literally, within the following week. Coupled with a recording Mick made of the humming sound coming from the quarry, it was time to move on to the next patch of land.

Sven's breakfast was finished and it was time to cover his tracks and move on. The smoldering logs from his campfire shot out from his boot as he kicked them skyward into the dense dry bush surrounding him. It was late summer, when temperatures reached a hundred degrees every day, and the ground was bone dry. The grey underbrush, interspersed with parched partially dead brown thorn bushes and dry pines, were a spark away from conflagration. Before he could even blink, a fire had begun burning at the base of a large dead pine tree. Hoping that the ensuing fire would keep the dog's noses busy or burn away his tracks, he watched with pleasure as the surrounding brush easily caught fire. With the wind blowing eastward, the fire spread back toward the river, whence he had come.

He hadn't heard from Sven since the early morning, and was not even sure if it was a dream he had, or if he really had been communicating with him. He just knew for sure that the physical pain was taxing his mind and that in turn made him vulnerable to possible hallucinations. He also knew that he needed to get back to the quarry and regroup while healing Sven's body, either that or find a new host. He thought about that Mormon he had thrown to the side of the road. Enviously he thought of him. He could have used that body in his present state.

Momentarily gazing back at the fire, as it curled amongst the dead underbrush, he thought of how they were going to try and defeat him. He was prepared for them. He had been preparing his whole life. But he hadn't been ready for Mick, nor Sally. It occurred to him, although he did not want to believe it, that divine intervention had played a role in the two of them meeting up with him just as he had begun to execute his plan. The odds against it were astronomically high, and yet how could they manage to be in the same small town, and with a poison almost specifically designed to kill his ants. Sven shook his head. He was cracking up. How could he even believe that this man was an adversary. He was the almighty spawn of the devil. But the problem was, he thought, that this man and his girlfriend had tried to assassinate him two times already and on one of those times they had succeeded! He knew they would be waiting for him at the quarry if they were still alive. He relished the thought.

The fire quickly spread its liquid orange tentacles, feeding like a voracious plague on the dried-up leaf of the land. The eastward blowing breeze fed its momentum back toward the river. Feeling confident the fire would throw any pursuers off his trail, he turned west without looking back. He had a hunch that if Mick was alive, he would be waiting for him at the quarry. Walking away from the fire with a single-minded determination and purpose, he listened to the crackling fire provide sweet music to his ears. He knew he had a long journey in front of him. A few days later he reached the quarry.

He could sense nobody was around. Yet, he could also sense that they had been. Sven walked toward the road that connected the quarry to civilization and noticed the destruction of the land. It had been disturbed. The soil had painstakingly been raked and made to look like it had never been disturbed, but it had. His heightened senses told him that they had waged war on his fire ants while he was away. Going down on one knee, he picked up a handful of the dirt and smelled it. The smell was a mixture of burnt sandpaper, crispy ant, and gasoline. Mulling it over in his mind, he smiled. They had poured gasoline down the ant holes and then dynamited the holes. He wondered how many of them they had killed.

Walking around the land that surrounded the quarry was tiring but necessary. Wary of walking into a trap, he continued to reconnoiter the area until he came upon a large depression in the ground. It was a tire track, and there were more of them centered behind the initial one he found. They had obviously brought along some large trucks, but for what? He was puzzled by the development, curious, and bit concerned. His brain whirred as he tried to think of what they could be planning. Cautiously he made his way down the slope and to the entrance embedded within the stone pit. Once again, his senses told him that nobody was around. Nevertheless, he approached the entrance with care, looking for booby traps. He didn't find any.

He could sense that they had also been inside his control room fiddling with the controls. His chair had been moved and where there should have been dust there wasn't. Walking to the left of the main panel he stared at the wall. He examined it closely. Carefully he pushed inward upon a certain spot in the stone wall which was hidden to the naked eye. A panel moved outward toward him with a string attached to it. Without pushing it completely out, he proceeded to cut a string connected to a lever, thereby bypassing the activation of some ants he controlled in a lower chamber. After looking at it for a while, he was satisfied. He put a new string in its place and closed off the panel. He smiled inwardly. They had not discovered his secret underground lair of his special experimental fire ants. He would be ready for them.

"Hey guys, we have movement." Sally announced.

Sally was on duty monitoring the hidden camera they had placed within the control room and was the first one to glimpse Sven. He was enormous. He was checking some sort of opening within the wall of the carved-out cavern. Crowding around the camera, they watched as he made his way around the room. He was in obvious discomfort, but not as much as they would have expected for someone who had recently been shot.

"I wonder what he was looking at?" Mick said.

"Yeah, me too. That worries me. I think we might have missed something." Old man Johnson said.

"And he checked on it immediately. It must be important." Jesus chimed in.

Comfortably shacked up within Mick's house, they tracked the movements of their nemesis while sipping coffee and munching on cream cheese covered toast.

"Uh oh. I think he found our camera." Sally said.

He had been sweeping the room with some sort of electronic surveillance device and had honed in on the camera. Picking it up he stared directly at the screen and smiled, a smile that was pure evil. The transmission ended. And with that they looked at each other. It was go-time. The call to the lieutenant had already been made once they confirmed he was at the quarry. The helicopters were on stand-by, and the flies were being transported just in case they needed them. Everyone was aware of their role.

Chapter Twenty-Four

Spiritual Epiphany

The flatbed trucks were idling along the side of the road, with Leroy at point in the first truck, just waiting for Mick. Driving up alongside of them, Mick gave each of them the thumbs up signal, and they slowly moved along in convoy fashion toward the rendezvous location. Peering up through the car's windshield, against a clear blue sky, Sally spotted two helicopters circling just to the south of the meeting point. The lieutenant and the medical examiner should be in one of them, she thought.

Everyone was anxious. They had really no conception of how Sven would react to them or for that matter what he could do to them. Mick wondered what powers they hadn't witnessed yet, while Sally had this awful feeling that they were walking blindly into a trap. Jesus was bothered by the smile he had just seen on the camera. He had seen that smile before and things had not gone well for him after seeing it. Then again, he thought, he had messed with the wrong 'Vacquero', and he had a little surprise for him just in case the plan went awry. Old Man Johnson was silently rubbing the barrel of his rifle, thought the plan was much too confusing and with too many moving parts to succeed. He was just hoping to get a shot off at the man and split his head with a bullet.

In each of the two helicopter's there were three men aboard. Both pilots had been trained by the Air National Guard and were also part of the Lubbock police department. Flying directly south of the quarry so as to not alert their intended target by the sound of the rotors, the lieutenant and the doctor were looking with binoculars for the trucks carrying the flies.

"I see him," yelled the doctor over the noise of the whirring blades.

The lieutenant nodded back at him and double checked the harness that was holding him in his seat. He was flying in the back of the copter with a dozen smoke producing canisters surrounding him. It was payback time, and even if he couldn't be the one to kill him, he certainly was going to enjoy being part of it. He was looking for revenge. On the other helicopter were two of the best marksmen in the state of Texas. The doctor rechecked the flare gun he held, took it off safety and told the pilot to radio the other helicopter just in case they weren't aware of the approaching trucks. His job was to shoot flares at any sign of trouble so as to alert the others. He felt comfortable with his assignment.

The four trucks positioned themselves around the quarry and the men working the control boxes released the flies. In great swarms, the flies rose up and spread out across the land. Mick and Sally positioned themselves in a rock blind, constructed especially for this, while Jesus and old man Johnson did the same. Each of them wore a pair of noise cancelling headphones and were armed. They were not going to try to keep Sven alive, nor try and do any type of transference. With the helicopters circling above and the four of them hidden behind the rock blinds, Mick turned on the recording of the hum.

Turning up the volume, he and the others strained their eyes to see if there were any signs of crawling ants emerging from the ground, or if the satanic one dared to show himself. There was no sign of any ants or him. With sweaty palms, a half dozen fingers were itching to pull a trigger at any sign of movement. What they didn't expect was for him to be watching them as they were preparing for the assault.

Tucked up in a crotch amidst a few pine trees and some large boulders along the western ridge of the quarry, opposite to the control room entrance, Sven had been watching them ever since they arrived. He saw them position themselves, the helicopters with the men inside of them with their guns drawn, and the release of the flies. He realized that they had used these same flies to try and kill the ants that surrounded his base of operations. What they didn't realize was that he was going to use them also.

Sven, with a loudspeaker in his hand, began transmitting a low frequency hum almost indiscernible to the human ear, but one that instantly caught the attention of the flies. Scattered across the area were one million humpback flies. The humming increased in intensity with intermittent staccato bursts, causing the flies to become agitated and form in larger and larger groups. Soon the flies were split between a half-dozen different groups and were swooping and diving as though they were a flock of birds.

Utterly amazed, the onlookers on the ground watched as the flies congregated in groups and began flying together in packs, like locust's ready to pounce upon some unsuspecting prey. Swooping and diving, twisting and turning in the air, the flies were sweeping across the sky at incredible speeds, moving in unison like a crazed whirling dervish.

Old Man Johnson and Jesus watched stupefied at the spectacular show that played out above their heads. The four control box operators standing outside of their trucks, were lulled into a state of false security as well, not ever having witnessed their cargo ever display such skill and flying precision in the past. Meanwhile, the men flying the helicopters were struggling to control their movements in the sky, while the flies swirled and twirled and danced amongst them. Unbeknownst to them, hypnotized by the spectacle that played out around them, they were oblivious to the dangers that the flies presented.

Mick ripped off his headphones and listened. He thought he could hear some sort of sound below the surface of his mind; but where it was emanating from, he couldn't tell. It was maddening. Putting his rifle down, he grabbed the binoculars and began searching for the source of the sound. He wasn't sure why, but he seemed to keep focusing on a grove of trees out on the western edge of the quarry. That was when he saw a slight bit of movement. Sven was there and had seen them all. At that moment, he realized that all of their lives were in grave danger. Grabbing Sally's hand, he yanked her out of her transfixed state. With him leading, pulling her onward as fast as he could, they made a mad dash for the car. Mick had a reasonable idea of what was about to happen, and it was not good for any of them.

Swarming faster and faster, erratically moving across the sky, the flies seemed to hesitate for just a slight moment before the two largest swarms attacked the helicopters. The men of both machines, instantly engulfed in a black cloud of flies with tornado like movements, were blind to anything but them. The flies coated the inside of each helicopter as well as the men inside, flinging themselves at the intruders, crawling inside any open orifice they could find. They filled every conceivable space within the helicopter. The coughing and choking began as they made their way inside of ears, mouths and noses. Gagging and reflexively screaming, and then not screaming after finding out its consequences; with a mouth full of flies, the men struggled helplessly against the onslaught. They all could feel the light feet of the crawling flies, grasping for fluid where ever they could find it, searching desperately for the open membranes of the human body, and finding them.

Safe inside the car, Mick focused on Sven as he watched him conducting the flies with his hands and arms, violently thrusting them upward and downward, much like an orchestra conductor directing a Brahms dramatic symphony. The two copters swung violently in the air. Desperately out of control, spinning in circles and losing altitude, both of the pilots battled furiously to keep their crafts in the air.

Mick grabbed the duct tape that was in the glove compartment and began furiously closing off the interior vents in the car while his mind raced. He hadn't expected Sven to be able to control the flies, but he should have anticipated the possibility. Sally was watching Mick out of the corner of her eye while also looking at Sven, whom Mick had pointed out guiding the flies attack on the helicopters. The other swarms of flies were still dancing about presumably getting ready to attack.

"What are you doing?" Sally said.

"I'm trying to close off the vents where the flies could enter the car. I can get the openings on the dash and where the defroster hits the windshield, but the openings at our feet is a little tight for me."

He looked over at Sally who looked like she was about to get sick. She nodded and grabbed the tape roll from his hand, pulling off a long piece, and immediately went to work on her side of the car. It was while she was taping closed the floor vents that he began talking.

"I didn't see this coming. His powers are more immense than I imagined. Not only has he been able to control the ants, but obviously he is able to control the flies as well!"

"Yeah, but we already knew his powers. He controlled those two pussy cats, inciting them to kill their sweet owner. And he didn't seem to have any problems handling that coyote. He's obviously good with the mind control stuff whether it be on humans, animals or insects."

"I should've foreseen the possible consequences if only I had thought it through. I mean, if he truly is the spawn of the devil, then he is directly related to Beelzebub or Satan, otherwise known as the 'Lord of the Flies'. And if he can control these flies, than we are in for a whole lot worse."

Sally sat back in the car seat for a second and looked at him with a dumbfounded expression.

"What are you talking about?"

"What I mean is, that since he can obviously control the flies, then we are going to have a serious health problem on our hands. These flies, scuttle or humpback, or whatever you want to call them, are very unsanitary and are predominantly found around leaking sewer lines, rotting produce or dead animals. They love decaying organic matter and can be a real problem with the spread of disease, especially around restaurants and hospitals and the such. Naturally the devil, the grim reaper, Satan or the likes . . ."

He probably should have seen the left cross coming toward his jaw, which clicked his jaw shut, but he was too busy thinking and talking about how to remedy the situation. Sally had just punched him, purple with rage and screaming at the top of her lungs.

"You, stupid ass! Are you telling me that you just hatched a plan that required a million shit licking flies to be bought and used against our arch-nemesis, only to hand them over to him on a silver platter for his own personal use, as the 'Lord of the Flies!' Not only did you not tell us about the possible repercussions when the plan was created, but now, after the facts are known, he is subsequently going to use them to kill us. What were you thinking. Are you that goddamned stupid? If I get out of this alive, I am going to strangle you. I swear I will."

Mick caught by the surprise of the sucker punch just looked at her in amazement. It hadn't hurt, but it sure did shut him up for a second, and made him momentarily think. Here he was driving this poor woman insane, he thought. They had been co-workers at best just a little over a week ago, then had become lovers after being shoved together by necessity, and now she was ready to kill him. Well, that about summed up his relationships over the past few years, he thought. Only this time, it had been speeded up by the quickly moving events ever since the call from Edith Baxter's house.

He needed some time to think. With everything he had been doing, he seemed to always be one step behind the devil. He was playing on his terms and losing, while his plans were going badly awry. Sally was angry with him, and understandably so, given the current screw up with the flies that he now controlled. He was somehow missing the big picture on just how to defeat him, and his head was aching from trying to figure what the missing puzzle pieces were. In the back of his mind, he had been thinking about it for days, but the lack of sleep and sense of urgency was causing him to create reactive plans, rather than be proactive, he thought.

With Sally watching him, knowing that he was thinking hard, she noticed he gasped out loud. The hit to his jaw had caused him to have an epiphany. He had to use God, goddamn it, he thought. How stupid he had been. If the devil was controlling the insects by manipulating them to do his bidding, then he could do the same. Since Sven was altering their brain waves with sound he should be able to appeal to their other senses with what God preordained for them as the natural creatures that were his creations. If Sven could get the flies to swarm and dive for him toward people and objects by using sound, then maybe he could use their sense of smell innately given to them by the Almighty to find sewers and feces and rotting garbage, and control them as well. And conversely, just like ants are innately attracted to super sweet foods and sugars and repelled by smells such as peppermint and cinnamon, then he could use that innate desire to counter and control them against the humming sounds. He needed to utilize his training and bring forth to bear God's natural animal instincts and tendencies in order to combat the devil.

"Sally, old girl, I believe you just knocked some sense into me. I know how to fight this guy now and beat him at his own game!"

The banging on the car, coupled with Jesus screaming at the top of his lungs to let them in, brought him out of his thoughts. Jesus and Old

Man Johnson were desperately trying to get into the locked car. A cloud of flies was diving directly at them. Without a second to spare, they made it into the relative safety of the car. Instantly the vehicle was surrounded and engulfed by a swarming mass of black flies. The car almost appeared to hover in the air as the vortex of flies spun around, above and under them. Soon enough they could see the duct tape starting to pulsate and ripple, as a multitude of flies pushed against it trying to make their way inside the car. Clamping their hands down on the tape, Mick and Sally fought against the onslaught, trying in vain to hold them back. It was like trying to keep water from entering a leaky boat. There were just too many openings and the flies were infinitely small. Slowly the car began filling up with hundreds, and then thousands, of the miniscule flies with Jesus and Old man Johnson in the back seat trying to fend them off and kill them by swatting them with their hands. And then the swarm moved away from the car as suddenly as it had moved upon them, heading off in the direction of the flatbed trucks. They looked out of the windows with a sense of relief and astonishment.

Off in the distance to the south, black smoke billowed up into the sky from a flaming wreck that used to be a helicopter. In between the smoke and the flames, they could just make out a few figures struggling to move away from the wreckage. At the bottom of the quarry, they spotted the other helicopter which lay limp upon the ground like a broken tin toy, with its tin toy soldiers spread across the ground, permanently knocked out of action. Glancing to the west, they surmised that one of the truckers had tried to make a break for it. The truck lay on its side overturned in a ditch on the side of the road. There was no sign of the other truck drivers, although individual swarms of flies were hovering at different spots along the horizon. They assumed the worst. The plan had ended before it had even begun. It was a disaster.

Striding along the far edge of the quarry, Sven was making his away to the entrance, while still guiding the flies with orchestrated hand movements. Jabbing and thrusting his arms and hands in circular motions, he controlled their movements as they dove and attacked and did his bidding. Occasionally, he had to stop in his tracks while he kept them hovering. All the while he was having to keep up the hum that ultimately drove them onward. It was exhausting for him. Coupled with being injured, he felt like he was at his breaking point. He felt that if he could just reach the quarry and activate the lower chamber of ants, he could finish them off once and for all. The ants were so deep below ground, they would need to be activated by a speaker system connected to the control panel.

"Feeling tired?"

"What?"

"I don't think this is going to work. You are overexerting yourself."

"I most certainly will get there."

"No, I think your time is up."

"Humph. What do you know? You are a prisoner in your own mind."

"I know that you are weak and losing control of the body you inhabit."

"Shut up you piece of trash. When I'm done with you I am going to burn your body eternally in the fires of hell."

Mick had been intently watching Sven with his window rolled down so he could hear him. He appeared disturbed. He was yelling, in some sort of conversation with himself, while moving his arms about in ever more erratic movements. Something or someone was causing him to lose control. The flies which had been grouped in multiple swarms were disbanding. This just might be the break they needed. Mick turned to Jesus.

"How many sticks of dynamite do we have planted above the entrance?"

"I stuck enough dynamite up there, about thirty sticks, to take down the whole face. If we blow it, nobody is getting out of there."

"And the control panel?"

"I set it on a timer, so that if anyone uses it now, it should have a delayed short circuit and throw a thousand volts into the person at the controls after a few minutes time."

"Excellent. Let's execute the first steps of plan B, demonic oppression and satanic agitation. He seems a bit preoccupied at the moment. Let's see if we can maneuver him to go use the control panel."

"Yeah and how are we going to do that?"

With a glint in his eye, Mick jumped out of the car and made his way to the trunk, popping it open. The rest of them followed. Rummaging his hands through the trunk he pulled from far in the back a large five-gallon plastic container filled with maraschino cherries. Then, from underneath the floor of the trunk, where the spare tire should have been, he pulled out a plastic container about the size of a shoe box. It was black, oily looking, almost like tar but it clearly wasn't. He knew the sticky syrup would be nirvana for the ant's olfactory senses and the other container was to attract the flies. Turning to the others he let them know his impromptu plan.

"If I can get these down to the control room before he gets there, then I can set both of these up to drop on him. Then just maybe we can get his minions to turn on him. Their senses will be divided between their instincts and him. If I can get you two, as he motioned to Sally and Old Man Johnson, to make sure he is distracted long enough so that I can set the trap with Jesus, we might just be able to flip the script on this guy. Jesus, can you help me bring down the container of cherries while I carry down Patches?"

With an unspoken anticipation, they stood staring at him waiting for an explanation.

"Patches was my puppy and I promised myself I would bury him next to his mother, but haven't gotten around to it just yet. Anyways we need him now."

Each of them stole a look at the container that Mick was holding with a newfound horror that was hard to describe. The word puppy and the black gel like substance that was inside of the container were incongruous. Sally began retching as Old Man Johnson involuntarily found himself saying the Lord's prayer. Jesus just looked at Mick with an incredulous expression.

"I know, I know, it isn't right, but I haven't had the chance to make it to Corpus Christi these past few months and the Texas heat this summer has been . . . anyway this should bring the flies."

Jesus interrupted the explanation by hoisting the plastic container of cherries and starting off down the side of the quarry as fast as he could. Mick was glad for it. He hadn't liked the sideways look he had seen Sally give him. He followed with the container carrying Patches and a nylon rope he dug out from the other corner of the trunk. There was no time to waste on explanations about his idiosyncrasies and failings.

Securing the glass container of maraschino cherries and the container carrying "Patches" so that they both would fall when the nylon cord was triggered, they hurried to get away from the control room. With a silent prayer to God for having to utilize the remains of his late puppy in such a diabolical fashion, Mick made sure that the cordage would effectively twist open the container, thereby releasing the foul remains of the carcass that lay inside. Rushing up over the rocks, they were out of breath by the time they had made it back to the car.

Sally and Old Man Johnson had provided the diversion. They had been firing their rifles at Sven on the other side of the quarry. They knew they were well out of range to have a chance of actually shooting him, but it was part of the plan to redirect his energy and attention toward the car and act as a diversion of sorts. It worked. The flies had enveloped the car, from where they were now trapped, to the point that it was not visible to the naked eye. It had given Jesus and Mick just enough time to lay the trap and skedaddle.

Beneath their feet, atop the ridge, the very slightest of vibration could be felt coming from underground. Sven had reached the control room and switched on the speakers which activated his special experimental ants housed in colonies far below ground. A second later the glass container smashed on the rock floor splattering the sticky cherries across the room as well as the putrid, overpoweringly rancid remains of Patches the puppy. The reaction to the release of the evil smelling corpse coupled with the sickening sweet smell of the cherries was instantaneous. Wafting across the land, the powerful smell had everyone gagging and coughing, spitting and fighting for a breath of fresh air when none was to be had.

Taken aback by the crash of the glass container at his feet, Sven slowly began to realize the implications of the trap which covered the floor, control panel, walls, his legs and torso. The sweet red cherry sauce, mixed with the black decaying matter, was spread across everything.

One million flies, disbanded and distracted, suddenly swarmed toward the putrescence of death, like a pack of piranhas rushing in for the kill. And one million ants, summoned by a driving hum that itched at the back of their exoskeleton head, were redirected by the most obnoxious, tart, putrid sugary smell their olfactory senses had ever encountered.

They watched as the humpback flies flew in swarms, by the hundreds of thousands, toward the opening of the quarry, darting inside, with its tantalizing smells of sugar and death. And by land, the fire ants glistening red and black, an army unto itself, converged like one tidal wave of motion toward the control room. Viewing the entrance to the control room, they could see the hulking erratic movements of Sven struggling against a tornado of black flies. The desperate movements were those of a man inundated and covered in scuttle flies. It was only when the ants surged in for their rightful share of the prize that they began to hear the wails of the demon being stung by his own minions. The rage in the voice was countered with sputtered coughing. Having just experienced the nightmare of having flies enter every open orifice on their own personal bodies, they could imagine what he was experiencing. The time had finally come to send him back to hell.

Jesus pushed down on the plunger which triggered the dynamite. The explosion was so loud, and the ensuing cloud of dust and ash so great, that they could not view their handiwork for some time. It didn't much matter. To a person they had each been doubled over coughing from the wretched smell that emanated from Mick's concoction. The whole face of the mountain, directly above the quarry entrance, cascaded downward in a deafening crash of rock against rock. And against that backdrop, a piercing scream could momentarily be heard, that sounded like a man being electrocuted. Peering between the shifting dust particles still hung up in the air, they could see that there was no longer any opening at the base of the quarry. And the air they were breathing had been cleansed of its wretched smells only to be replaced by the smell of sulfur. The entrance to the lair of the devil was closed off by thousands of tons of rock.

Mick looked around him. Jesus had a wide grin on his face. It was the first time he had ever seen him smile, he thought. Glancing over at Sally and Old Man Johnson, they still had rifles in their hands pointed toward the opening, but smiles were beginning to break out on their faces. Gradually the guns came down from their shoulders, as everyone began to celebrate the fact that they had trapped him inside the mountain to die. They would never know if he had died in the blast or if he was still there fighting off the ants and the flies. All they knew and cared about was that he would no longer be around.

Old Man Johnson pointed over to the rim of the south side of the quarry. The lieutenant, medical examiner and pilot of the one helicopters were all waving their arms at them, shouting and whooping it up in general. They had been witnesses to the last moments of Sven.

Chapter Twenty-Five

Vacation

Hawaii

"Have you ever read *'From Here to Eternity'* by James Jones? It is one of the best, most raw, in depth looks at being in the military right before the Japanese attacked Pearl Harbor. That story was based around here at the military base. I would like to go see it. What do you think?"

Mick was talking to Sally. In her flower covered bikini, she lay flat on her back gazing up at the white clouds, that slowly moved across the majestic blue sky that was endemic to Hawaii. She was gathering in the sun's rays and for the most part trying to ignore him, while she breathed in the salty air that cascaded off the gigantic waves, which rhythmically crashed along the shoreline. With each different wave that crashed, she was timing her deep breaths, greedily sucking in the fresh salty air. Combined with the delicious sun, the pounding in her ears from the crashing waves, and the refreshing smell of the ocean, she had been clearing her mind of all of her past troubles and worries. They had been vacationing for the better part of a week since leaving Texas, and she had decided that it was better to be with Mick when you sometimes just didn't answer him. He didn't seem to mind.

"I wonder how the lieutenant and doc are making out? At least they are at the same hospital getting treatment for their burns and the doc's broken leg. They were actually pretty lucky to survive that crash with such minor injuries. I told them I would send them a few postcards on our travels. Do you remember where we put their addresses? You know what, never mind, I can just look up the hospital address and send them there."

Sally heard it all but didn't move a muscle. If she didn't like hearing the sucking of the water so much, as the waves ripped the water from the shore only to curl it back around and pound it downward onto the beach, she would have probably put in her ear buds and blocked out Mick's incessant talking. Again, she didn't answer him. They had grown to know each other, and each other's ways.

"Tomorrow we are scheduled to fly to O'ahu in the morning. That should be incredible. We have to make sure we wear hiking boots and breathable clothing. I have heard the hike is about seven miles roundtrip from the beach to the waterfall. Also remind me to put repellant on the both of us. I have been studying the types of ants they have out here and some of them are nasty. They have tropical fire ants, Argentine ants, white footed ants, carpenter, pavement, Pharaoh and even big-headed ants. None of them are native to the island, but over the centuries have been inadvertently left here when ships came to port. Are you interested in going to the university of Hawaii's insect museum?"

Mick hadn't been expecting an answer, but he got one. A handful of sand hit him in the face. Well, at least he got an answer from her. He smiled broadly, while wiping away the sand from his face, knowing she was madly in love with him despite his plethora of faults, as Exterminator 69.

About the Author

John Tanner is a UCLA graduate with a degree in history, is happily married, and is the father of three amazing children. He currently resides in New Mexico and is a firm believer in the Golden Rule: do unto others as you would have do unto thee. He considers himself a lucky man to have the opportunity to share his collection of short stories with the public.

Now Available!

JOHNATHAN HERBERT'S
BUTCH SANDS SERIES
BOOKS 1 – 2

**For more information
visit: www.SpeakingVolumes.us**

Now Available!

RAY DAN PARKER'S
THE TOM WILLIAMS SAGA
BOOK 1

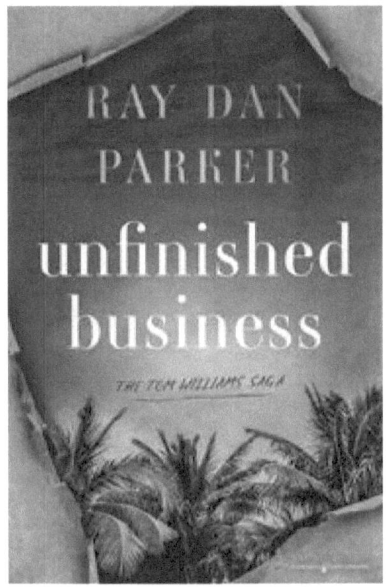

**For more information
visit:** www.SpeakingVolumes.us